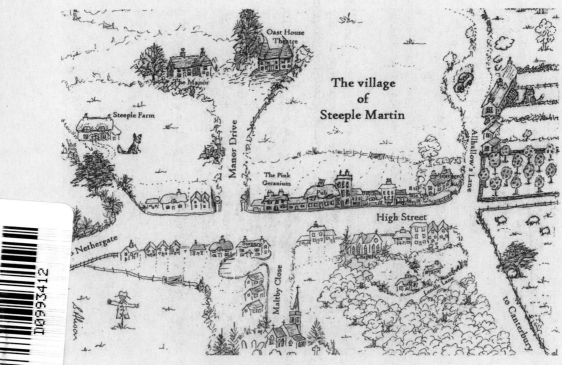

The village
of
Steeple Martin

Oast House
Theatre

The Manor

Steeple Farm

Manor Drive

Allhallow's Lane

The Pink
Geranium
Pub

High Street

Nethergate

Surgery

Chapel

Maltby Close

Lendle Lane

to Canterbury

WHO'S WHO IN THE LIBBY SARJEANT SERIES

Libby Sarjeant
Former actor, sometime artist, resident of 17, Allhallow's Lane, Steeple Martin. Owner of Sidney the cat.

Fran Wolfe
Formerly Fran Castle. Also former actor, occasional psychic, resident of Coastguard Cottage, Nethergate. Owner of Balzac the cat.

Ben Wilde
Libby's significant other. Owner of The Manor Farm and the Oast House Theatre.

Guy Wolfe
Fran's husband, artist and owner of a shop and gallery in Harbour Street, Nethergate.

Peter Parker
Ben's cousin. Free-lance journalist, part owner of The Pink Geranium restaurant and life partner of Harry Price.

Harry Price
Chef and co-owner of The Pink Geranium and Peter Parker's life partner.

Hetty Wilde
Ben's mother. Lives at The Manor.

Greg Wilde
Hetty's husband and Ben's father.

DCI Ian Connell
Local policeman and friend. Former suitor of Fran's.

Adam Sarjeant
Libby's youngest son. Lives above The Pink Geranium, works with garden designer Mog, mainly at Creekmarsh.

Lewis Osbourne-Walker
TV gardener and handy-man who owns Creekmarsh.

Sophie Wolfe
Guy's daughter. Lives above the gallery.

Flo Carpenter
Hetty's oldest friend.

Lenny Fisher
Hetty's brother. Lives with Flo Carpenter.

Ali and Ahmed
Owners of the Eight-til-late in the village.

Jane Baker
Chief Reporter for the *Nethergate Mercury*. Mother to Imogen.

Terry Baker
Jane's husband and father of Imogen.

Joe, Nella and Owen
Of Cattlegreen Nurseries.

DCI Don Murray
Of Canterbury Police.

Amanda George
Novelist, known as Rosie

Chapter One

'HEY, MA, GUESS WHAT?' Adam's voice was jubilant.

'Hello, darling,' said Libby Sarjeant. 'What's happened?'

'I found a body!'

Libby's stomach seemed to roll over and her legs felt suddenly icy. She sat down abruptly.

'A body?' she said.

'I knew you'd be interested,' said Adam. 'I told Mog you would be.'

'Mog?'

'The bloke I'm working with. I told you. Don't you remember?'

Libby racked her brain. 'Vaguely,' she admitted. 'What body?'

'A skeleton,' said Adam, his excitement clearly audible. 'Or part of one, anyway. A skull and a few bones, although I think they've found a bit more now.'

'They? The police?'

'Yeah. They've been here all day.'

'So where are you?'

Adam sighed in obvious exasperation. 'Oh, Ma, don't you ever listen? Creekmarsh Place.'

'Oh, yes!' Libby got up from the stair she was sitting on and carried the phone into the sitting room, where she turfed Sidney the silver tabby off the cane sofa. 'Gardening for some famous person.'

'Not gardening exactly, more redesigning,' corrected Adam. 'Mog's a designer.'

'Oh, right.'

'This is his first big commission, and I'm helping him.'

Adam sounded proud.

'But you're not a gardener,' said Libby. 'I've never even persuaded you to mow the lawn.'

'Thanks, Ma. I thought you'd be pleased.'

'Sorry, darling, of course I am, but you've just graduated with a sociology degree.'

'Not just, Ma. Last bloody year, and I still haven't got a job. I told you, Mog asked if I'd like to give him a hand with this, as it's big and there's a whole load of clearing to be done.'

'And Mog is …?'

'That mate of Dom's who used to be an accountant. Lives in Canterbury.'

'Oh, right, I remember.' Libby felt she was shaking off the onset of senile dementia. 'He married that nice girl Fiona, didn't he?'

'Now you've got it,' said Adam. 'And he went back to college to learn how to be a garden designer and now that's what he does. When he can.'

'When he can?'

'There isn't so much work around now, despite the fact that people still love the gardening programmes on TV.'

'No, I suppose not,' said Libby. 'More people are digging up the flowers and planting vegetables, aren't they?'

'Exactly,' said Adam. 'But this job is fantastic and could put Mog on the map.'

'Creekmarsh Place? Where is it?'

'Aha! Bit of a secret destination,' said Adam. 'Never heard of Creekmarsh?'

'No,' said Libby.

'It's just along the coast from Nethergate before the marshes begin.'

'Where the Wytch comes out?'

'That's it. It's actually on the banks of the Wytch. Tiny place, just a few houses, a pub and the Place.'

'Stately home?'

'Sort of. Half of it's derelict, or almost. It's Tudor – fantastic place.'

'And who's the famous person?'

'Lewis Osbourne-Walker.'

Libby sat up straight. 'You're not serious?'

Adam chuckled with glee. 'Absolutely. Fantastic, eh?'

'Well, yes,' said Libby, 'but you're not a fan of his, surely?'

''Course not, but the rest of the world is.'

'But he does gardening programmes.'

'He does home programmes,' corrected Adam, 'with gardens thrown in.'

'So why isn't he using one of his TV garden personalities to design his garden?'

'Because they're too famous to do that any more, and he wanted someone who could carry on looking after the garden. He met Mog at some band's gig and asked him to show him some drawings.'

'Wow.' Libby stared thoughtfully into the fireplace. 'So what's he like? I've always thought he might be – er –'

'Gay?' suggested Adam. 'Yes, he is, as a nine bob note, but what's that got to do with anything? Two of your best friends are gay.'

'I know that, but Lewis is the housewife's favourite, isn't he? Wasn't he voted some magazine's sexiest man?'

'So what? Come on, Ma. That's a bit of an old-fashioned attitude, isn't it?'

'It was a bit of an old-fashioned magazine, as I remember,' said Libby.

'Whatever. He's a great bloke. I get on really well with him.'

'Oh?'

'Oh, Mum,' said Adam, making two syllables of her name and reminding her how young he still was.

'Well, I'm really pleased,' said Libby, 'but what about this body?'

'There's this part of the estate that was really overgrown, bordering on the main lawn, which we've already been working on, and Lewis wants to turn it into a wildlife area, but with paths so people can walk through it.'

'Is he going to open it to the public, then?'

'He's thinking about turning it into a venue,' said Adam, sounding as though he knew what he was talking about.

'Like Anderson Place?'

'Where? Oh, yes, where Harry and Peter got married.'

'Civil partnered, dear,' said Libby. 'Harry always corrects me.'

'Whatever,' said Adam, 'but yes, sort of like that.'

'OK, but what about the body?'

'Oh, yes. Well, I was using the mini digger to clear some of the undergrowth and Mog suddenly shouted at me. And there it was.'

'The skull?'

'And an arm bone. Turned me up a bit, I can tell you.'

'I bet,' said Libby. 'So what happened next?'

'Mog called Lewis, who's in London – well, he was, but he's come back now – and then the police. They're finding out how old it is now.'

'Is it very old, then?' asked Libby.

'They think so. Well, not recent, anyway. There's been a news blackout for the moment, so don't go telling your friends Jane and what's-'is-name, McLean.'

'McLean's hardly a friend,' said Libby, amused. 'And I don't even know if he's still with Kent and Coast Television.'

'Well young Jane's still with the Mercury, isn't she?' said Adam.

'Young Jane's nearly ten years older than you,' said his mother, 'but yes, she's still there.'

'Anyway, I expect it'll be on TV tomorrow when they've found out how old it is,' said Adam.

'And what sex it is,' said Libby.

'Oh – yes, I suppose so,' said Adam. 'Well, I'd better get off. I'll keep you posted.'

'Where are you staying?' asked Libby. 'I thought you were still in London.'

'Hardly, if I'm working down here. I'm staying with Mog in Canterbury.'

'I'll bet Fiona's pleased,' muttered Libby.

'What's that?'

'Nothing,' said Libby hastily. 'Don't forget you can come here if you want.'

'Sunday lunch?' asked Adam, hopefully.

Libby laughed. 'Of course.'

'Otherwise it's easier if I'm here. I can go to work with Mog as I haven't got transport.'

'I can always come and pick you up if you want to come here for a night.'

'Keen to see the scene of the crime, eh, Ma?' Adam laughed. 'I'll see what I can do.'

'Don't be daft,' said Libby, feeling a blush creep up her neck. 'Ring me tomorrow.'

'Will do,' said Adam. 'Night night, Ma. Love you.'

The sound of the kitchen door opening heralded the entrance of Ben Wilde, Libby's significant other, who spent most of his time at Number 17, Allhallow's Lane, with Libby and Sidney, and the remainder with his parents, Hetty and Greg, at The Manor as estate manager. A former architect, Ben had sold his flat and partnership after meeting Libby and was trying to persuade her to move in with him permanently, or better still, marry him. Libby was having none of it. She insisted they were Living Apart Together, a fairly new phenomenon known as LAT and particularly popular with the thirty-nine to sixty age group, into which they both fell.

'Drink?' he asked after kissing her on the cheek.

'Not yet.' Libby stroked Sidney absently.

'What's the matter?' asked Ben, coming to sit opposite her by the empty fireplace.

'Adam phoned.'

'What's up?'

'Nothing. He found a body.'

Ben closed his eyes. 'Oh, no,' he groaned.

Libby eyed him thoughtfully. 'That's exactly what I said, but from a totally different perspective.'

Ben opened his eyes. 'What do you mean?' he asked cautiously.

'I was worried for Adam. Finding a body isn't something you would wish on anyone, let alone your youngest son.' She looked away into the empty fireplace.

'Sorry.' Ben was contrite. 'Can you tell me about it?'

Libby told him everything Adam had told her.

'It's nothing to do with Adam, then, is it? Or even the owner?'

Libby shook her head. 'It doesn't look like it. Lewis Osbourne-Walker's only just bought it.'

'Who is he exactly?' Ben got up to refill his glass. 'Want one yet?'

'Go on, then.' Libby tucked her feet under her. 'Lewis Osbourne-Walker is a television personality.'

'I gathered that. But is he just a personality, or is he a real person?'

Libby grinned and accepted her glass. 'Just a personality, I suppose, but quite a nice one.'

Ben snorted. 'Don't tell me – a reality show discovery.'

'Not quite. He was a builder and general handyman on one of the home improvement shows and started getting so much fan mail they gave him his own show.'

'What sort of show?'

'Daytime magazine programme,' said Libby. 'Very popular, I'm told. Has a very good film critique panel.'

'And he's bought Creekmarsh Place?'

'Yes.' Libby looked across at him. 'Do you know it?'

Ben nodded. 'We used to go sailing there when I was a boy. There used to be a very small sailing club at the mouth of the Wytch, and the grounds of the Place come right down to the river. But we always thought it was a bit spooky. There's a lane that leads up beside it from the club, which disappears into the trees. Goes past the church, and the pub's a bit further up on the main road.'

'Did you ever explore?' asked Libby.

'Only up the lane. That's the only way to get to the sailing club except by sea or river. We used to cycle there.'

'Who's we? And whose boat did you sail?'

'Do you remember Basil?'

'Basil?' Libby giggled.

'Obviously not.' Ben frowned at her. 'I went to school with him.'

'Well, I didn't know you then, did I?'

6

'No, but he was still around when we first met.'

Libby shook her head. 'Don't remember, sorry.'

'Bas's dad had a little Mirror dinghy and we used to go down and crew for him. Crewed for some of the other members, too. I got quite good at it.'

'But you gave it up?'

'When I went to university. Never thought about doing it again, although I sailed on holiday in Corfu a couple of times.'

'When was that?'

Ben sighed. 'When I was married, of course. We went to Corfu several years running.'

'Oh.' Libby inspected her glass. Both of them had been married before, and both of them had children from these marriages, but she still hated being reminded.

'So.' She looked up. 'Is the sailing club still there?'

'No idea.' Ben looked surprised. 'Why? Do you fancy taking it up?'

'No fear. Just wondered. If it was there, I thought Adam might be interested.'

'Not as a novice without a boat,' said Ben. 'They didn't have a training programme or anything. Too small.'

'Oh, well. Just a thought.' Libby stood up. 'I'd better get dinner started.'

'We can go out if you'd prefer,' said Ben. 'I don't suppose Harry's full tonight.'

'I fancy meat,' said Libby, who nevertheless loved The Pink Geranium, Harry's vegetarian restaurant.

'Pub, then,' suggested Ben. 'Especially if their steak and ale pie's on.'

Libby patted his cheek and then his stomach. 'OK, tubby,' she said. 'You give them a ring and I'll put a bit of face on.'

'I'll give you tubby,' said Ben, catching her as she tried to pass him and pulling her close.

'Really?' Libby raised an eyebrow. 'Now?'

'In front of Sidney?' he whispered, running a hand down her back. Libby shivered and wondered how a greying, middle-aged man could still send her hormones spiralling out of control after nearly two years together. Then she stopped wondering.

Chapter Two

It WAS ON THE national news the following morning. Libby turned up the volume on the kitchen radio and stood sipping tea. Ben had already left for The Manor and Sidney had sniffed dismissively at his breakfast and gone about the business of the day.

'The skeletal remains of a body discovered in a garden in Kent have been identified as that of a male aged between thirty and fifty,' read the announcer. 'Police expect to know later today how long the bones have been in the ground. Meanwhile, the location of the find is not being made known to the public.'

'Because it belongs to Lewis Osbourne-Walker,' Libby told the kettle. 'If it was on a council estate the world and his dog would know the actual address.'

She went to turn on the television to see if there was any more information on the local news programmes, but the phone interrupted her.

'Fran, hello.' Libby sat down on the sofa. 'It's a bit early. Is anything wrong?'

'N-no.' Fran hesitated. 'I just wondered if you'd like to come down to lunch today.'

Libby frowned. 'Sure. Any special reason?'

'Um,' said Fran. 'I'd like your advice.'

'*My* advice?' squealed Libby. 'That'll be a first.'

'Don't get above yourself. Do you want to come down by train so you can have a drink?'

'Too far,' said Libby. 'Remember when Campbell McLean took us to lunch? It took me an hour and a half to get there. I'll drive and be good.'

'OK. One o'clock?'

'I'll be there,' said Libby, and she switched off the phone with another frown. Fran had become her best friend over the past couple of years, apart, of course, from Ben and his cousin Peter and Peter's partner Harry, but it was most unlike Fran to ask advice, or even give much of herself away.

When Fran was introduced to Libby's friend Guy Wolfe, who lived a few doors along from Fran in the seaside town of Nethergate, a relationship had developed between them, and Libby saw less of Fran now than she had when they first knew one another.

Later in the morning, the phone rang again.

'Ma, it's me again,' said Adam. 'I suppose you couldn't pick me up from work this evening, could you? You did say you wouldn't mind.'

'Of course, darling,' said Libby, her interest quickening. 'Can't you go home with Mog for some reason?'

'Oh, it's part of this bloody body thing,' said Adam. 'They've stopped us working in the wood – obvious, I suppose – and we've started on another part of the garden, but Mog hadn't got all the plans with him, so he's going home to work on them while I dig up some paving. He'd have to come back and get me unless you pick me up.'

'So it's no great desire to see me, then?' Libby was amused.

'Hey, Ma, I'm sorry.' Adam sounded embarrassed.

'Don't be daft. I'll be there at – what? Five?'

'Bit earlier? Four thirty? I've been here since eight.'

'OK. Will the police let me through? And do I come down the lane from the main road?'

'Do you know it?' Adam sounded surprised.

'Ben does. Anyway, do I?'

'Yeah. There's a drive round the side of the house. I'll tell the police you're coming.'

'Good-oh,' said Libby. 'I'll see you then.'

At one o'clock, she parked Romeo the Renault on Harbour Street, a little way from Fran's Coastguard Cottage. As it was still only early summer, the beach was not yet crowded, and the little boats that took out day trippers, the *Dolphin* and the *Sparkler*, rocked gently at anchor outside The Sloop at the end of the hard. Their captains, George and Bert, sat outside Mavis's Blue Anchor café drinking huge mugs of tea. Libby waved and Bert waved his pipe back at her.

Fran was waiting with her door open, looking nervous. Libby kissed her cheek and stood back to stare at her.

'Come on,' she said. 'What's up?'

Fran closed the door and indicated an armchair.

'It's Guy,' she said, taking the chair opposite.

'Guy?' Libby was surprised. 'What's the matter with him?'

Fran took a deep breath. 'He wants to get married,' she said.

Libby let out a whoop. 'Fantastic, Fran! Congratulations!'

'Hey!' Fran looked startled. 'I didn't say I'd said yes. You won't marry Ben, after all.'

'But that's me,' said Libby. 'I'm a stubborn old cow –'

'Old trout,' corrected Fran with a grin.

'All right, old trout,' agreed Libby, 'but you aren't. You're much more sensible than I am, and more conventional.'

'Thanks,' said Fran. 'That makes me sound like a right old bore.'

'Oh, you know what I mean,' said Libby. 'And you said after you'd moved in here that you wanted to be on your own to savour it for a bit. Well, you've done that. You've had the cottage for well over a year and your relationship with Guy has got much closer, hasn't it?'

'Yes.' Fran twisted her hands together. 'I don't think I could live without him, now.'

'What's the problem, then?'

'The children,' said Fran, looking anguished.

'The *children*?' gasped Libby. '*Your* children?'

Fran nodded.

'What the hell have they got to do with anything?'

'They don't approve.'

Libby sat back in her chair and shook her head. 'And just what don't they approve of? You getting married again?'

'Oh, I haven't told them that,' said Fran. 'It's just the girls, of course. They think I'm too old to have a new relationship with anyone, and they're also worried about money.'

'Money?' repeated Libby stupidly.

'Oh, you ought to hear Chrissie on the subject.' Fran smiled wryly. 'She's convinced that my inheritance should have been divided between the children. She can't understand why I couldn't just sign over most of it to them. Lucy feels the same. They're both convinced that Guy will deprive them of their own inheritance.'

'I've never heard anything like it!' Libby shook her head in disbelief. 'I'd marry him quick and then change your will!'

'That's what you'd do,' laughed Fran, 'but then your lot would never behave like this.'

'With a lovely mum like you, I can't understand why yours do,' said Libby.

'I've told you,' said Fran with a sigh. 'I wasn't there for them enough when they were growing up. Too intent on pursuing my career.' She shrugged. 'All to no avail.'

'Well, I say go for it,' said Libby. 'And don't invite them to the wedding.'

'I can't do that, it wouldn't be right,' said Fran.

'And what happens if they go all sniffy and horrid on the day and spoil it for you?'

'Do you think they would?'

'From what I've heard about them – and don't forget I *have* met them – I bet they would. We'll just have to station bouncers all round the place to keep them in order.'

Fran laughed again. 'So you say go for it?'

'Of course.' Libby bounced up and gave her friend a hug. 'With bells on.'

'Then I'll get out the champagne,' said Fran. 'You can have just one glass before lunch, can't you?'

Libby rubbed her hands together. 'You bet!' she said.

Guy joined them for lunch, obviously delighted at Libby's reception of their news. Watching them together, she realised that Fran's mind had been made up before she asked Libby's advice, even if she wouldn't acknowledge it to herself. Fran's lack of self-confidence was still very much in evidence, even though she now owned a beautiful cottage in a highly desirable location, in the past two years had not one but two men interested in her romantically and had been successful in helping the police in four previous murder cases.

But now there was a glow about her. Seeing Fran throw back her head, dark hair swinging, when she laughed at one of Guy's wicked sallies, Libby was proud of having introduced her to him, a middle-aged puckish figure with a dark goatee and snapping brown eyes.

At four o'clock she got up to go, having helped clear away the champagne glasses and the remaining crumbs of the lunch.

'You don't have to go,' said Fran, freeing herself from Guy's arm about her shoulders.

'I do,' said Libby. 'I promised to pick Ad up from his job.'

'What job?' Guy stood up.

Surprised at herself, Libby realised she hadn't told either of them about Adam's discovery, let alone his illustrious employer. She explained.

'You're not going to interfere, are you?' Guy looked suspicious and Libby sighed.

'Why does everybody think I will?' she said. 'Ad hasn't got transport back to Mog's, so he asked me. That's all.'

'I didn't see anything about it on the news,' said Fran.

'It was on the national news this morning, but it didn't say where, exactly, or who owns the garden. Ad says they're keeping it under wraps, and as it's an old body it isn't a big thing.'

Fran looked dubious. 'But old bodies are often very big news,' she said. 'Remember those girls who were buried? They were old, but that was a huge investigation.'

'Yes, well,' said Libby, feeling uncomfortable, 'that may be so, but Ad says it's all very low-key so far.'

'Perhaps for once the media are being respectful to one of their darlings,' said Guy. 'Lewis Osbourne-Walker's a celebrity, isn't he?'

'With nothing known about him,' said Fran.

'Except he's gay,' said Guy.

'Guy!' Libby and Fran turned on him.

'I only meant it's the sort of thing they make a big thing of, isn't it?' Guy looked defensive.

'Hardly.' Fran was scornful. 'Half the celebrities on TV are gay these days. It makes no difference.'

'I did mention that to Ad yesterday,' said Libby. 'He told me off, but I said Lewis was a bit of a housewives' favourite and wouldn't that make a difference.'

'Of course not,' said Fran. 'Only the very oldest housewives would be put off.'

'Really?' Libby looked doubtful. 'What about those people who disapprove of Peter and Harry?'

'Particularly Harry!' grinned Guy.

'So who are they?' asked Fran. 'I've never met any, and you said yourself how lovely it was in the village with everyone cheering them on when they got married.'

'Partnershipped,' corrected Libby automatically. 'But there was that letter, wasn't there?'

'What letter?' asked Guy, sitting down again.

'Oh, it was from an old lady in a home, saying that it was an abomination against the Lord, or something,' said Libby.

'Don't be dismissive, Lib,' said Fran. 'She was expressing the view that the Bible says it's illegal and marriage was for the procreation of children.'

'Oh, I hope not,' said Guy, making a face at her.

'I know, bless her, and unfortunately, you can't argue with someone like that, who's so entrenched in her own views that she can't appreciate any other, and certainly wouldn't want to discuss the truth or authority of the Bible.' Libby smiled. 'I can just see her sticking her fingers in her ears and going "La-la-la-la!", can't you?'

Fran sighed. 'I know what you mean. It's such a shame that devotion to religion like that is so blinkered and nothing to do with reasoned argument.'

'That's why it's called "blind faith",' said Guy.

'Anyway,' said Libby, gathering up her basket, 'I meant to leave ten minutes ago. I shall be late for Ad, especially as I don't know exactly where I'm going.'

'Coast road out and turn left after Canongate Drive instead of straight on to Steeple Martin,' said Guy. 'Takes you right along the coast to Creekmarsh.'

'Oh, you know it, too?' said Libby, stopping at the door.

'Of course. Creekmarsh Place was used as a military base or something during the war, like Anderson Place was.'

'That's what Lewis wants to do with it,' said Libby. 'Turn it into a venue.'

Guy looked at Fran. Fran looked back at Guy. Libby looked at both of them.

'But not yet,' she said, 'it won't be restored for ages.'

'Oh,' said Guy and Fran together.

'And they've got to sort out this body first, anyway.' Libby opened the door and grinned over her shoulder. 'Bit gruesome for a wedding, wouldn't you say?'

Chapter Three

THE ROAD ALONG THE coast twisted and turned, alternately hiding and revealing glimpses of the sea. Banks clothed thickly in cow parsley, campion, bent and windblown hawthorn and elder crowded in on either side, until the road widened and turned sharply to the right. A pub stood on the right-hand side, and a heavily wooded lane led off to the left, with an old signpost pointing to 'The Church' and a small wooden finger post announced 'Creekmarsh Place'. Libby braked suddenly and with a hasty look in her mirrors swung into the lane.

The trees overhung the lane, blocking out the sunlight, before opening out to show the little church on the left. To the right, all Libby could see was thick woodland, part of which, no doubt, Adam had been clearing. Finally the lane began to slope down and she could see the sea. Now there was a lawn to her right, an old wall and what appeared to be gateposts. Adam stood beside them in very grubby jeans and a shirt, looking forlorn.

'Hello, darling,' said Libby. 'Hop in.'

'Thanks, Ma.' Adam stopped looking forlorn and came round the other side of the car. 'You can turn round on the drive there.'

'Through the gateposts?'

'Yeah. Lewis is having new iron gates made by some blacksmith who's won awards. We park on the drive.'

Libby drove carefully between the gateposts and began to manoeuvre the car. A figure appeared in the mirror and she stood on her brakes.

'Shit,' she muttered.

Adam swivelled round.

'Oh, that's all right, Ma,' he said. 'That's just Lewis.' He wound down the window and waved. The figure came round and leant in.

'Whatcher, Ad,' said Lewis Osbourne-Walker. 'This your mum?'

'Yes. Ma, this is Lewis, Lewis, my mum, Libby Sarjeant.'

'Howjer do?' Lewis stuck his hand across Adam. 'Bit of a detective, Ad says.'

'Hello,' said Libby, awkwardly shaking his hand.

'Just off home, then?' Lewis withdrew his hand.

'To Ma's,' said Adam. 'Give Mog's pregnant missus a bit of a rest.'

'Your mum looks as though she didn't know about that,' said Lewis.

Libby laughed. 'I didn't, but he's welcome.'

'Can always stay here, y'know, Ad. Plenty of bedrooms done up already.'

''S OK, thanks, Lewis,' said Adam. 'Don't see enough of Ma, anyway.'

'Right.' Lewis stood away from the car, his spiked blond hair glinting in the sun. 'Don't forget to tell her all about our body.'

'He seems nice,' said Libby, as she drove back down the lane.

'He's a great bloke,' said Adam. 'I never thought a celeb would be an OK person, but he is.'

'What did he mean, tell me all about your body?'

'Oh, the police were back again today, doing more searching, and some woman came to talk to us all.'

'Woman?'

'Policeman. Well, police person, I suppose. Higher up than your mate.'

'Chief Inspector?'

'No – Superintendent. That was it.'

'Really?' Libby turned back on to the coast road. 'So it's become a big thing, then? Have they released details to the press?'

Adam shrugged. 'There haven't been any of the vultures around, so no, I don't think so. We've been told to keep quiet.'

'So why did Lewis say tell me?'

''Cos I told him all about your cases.'

'They aren't my cases!' Libby was exasperated. 'I was just a bit involved.'

'Oh, yeah?' Adam turned and grinned at her.

'I couldn't help it,' said Libby grumpily.

'Anyway, when we get home I'll tell you what Big Bertha said.'

'Big Bertha?'

'The super Super.' Adam grinned again. 'She's scary.'

However, Libby had to wait for her explanation, as Adam demanded a shower before he did anything else, so she made tea and phoned Ben to tell him Fran's news.

'Hmm.' He was non-committal.

'What's the matter? Aren't you pleased?' Libby frowned.

'Of course. Good luck to them.'

'Well, you don't sound pleased,' said Libby.

'I said, I *am.*'

'Oh, well,' said Libby with a sigh. 'Just thought I'd tell you, and that Ad's here for supper. I had to pick him up today.'

'Had to?'

'He had no transport.' Libby frowned again. 'Ask him if you don't believe me. What's up with you?'

'Nothing.' There was a pause. 'I'll see you later – if you're still expecting me?'

'Of course,' Libby's voice rose in surprise. 'Come when you like.'

Ben's voice softened. 'About six, then,' he said.

Libby was still frowning when Adam came downstairs in a clean T-shirt and jeans.

'What's up, Ma?' he took his mug of tea and sat down at the kitchen table.

Libby sat opposite him. 'I think you'd better tell me about your body now, and then not mention it when Ben comes round.'

'Aha!' Adam laughed. 'Getting shirty about the detective business, is he?'

'Suspicious, anyway,' said Libby, with an unwilling smile, 'so please tell him it was your idea that I picked you up.'

''Course I will.' Adam took a mouthful of tea and reached

round for the biscuit tin on the dresser. 'And now I'll tell you all about our body.'

'Go on, then,' said Libby, and settled back in her chair.

'Well, apparently, they found about seventy per cent of the skeleton, and the scientist bloke –'

'Pathologist?'

'That'll be the one. He thought the body was only a few years old, not ancient, like we thought at first. So they did some tests, and he's right. They're doing more, but it looks like murder.'

'And not very old?'

'Well, not brand new, but only perhaps three or four years old. They've found some bits of stuff that might help identify him –'

'It's definitely a him, then?'

'Oh, yeah, didn't I say? Yes, a him. So Big Bertha comes along and interviews us all about how long we've known the place, and how long Lewis has been here. Daft, isn't it? As if we'd dig up someone we buried, or Lewis would ask us to do it.'

'Yes, but she's got to ask,' said Libby. 'She's the SIO is she, then?'

'SIO?'

'Senior Investigating Officer.'

'Like that Inspector who fancies Fran?'

'No, Ian Connell is only an Inspector, and he works under an SIO who directs operations from the office. Chief Inspector Murray is often SIO.'

'That's the bloke who did Paula's murder, isn't it?'

'Nicely put,' said Libby. 'He was in charge of the investigation, yes. But a superintendent – that means it's a bit higher profile. Because of Lewis, do you think?'

'Don't know,' said Adam with a shrug. 'Maybe.'

'I'd wondered if it was really old, from when it was occupied during the war.'

'Didn't know it was.'

'Guy told me. Oh – and I meant to tell you – Guy and Fran are getting married.'

'Wicked!' Adam laughed. 'That's one in the eye for old Ben,

18

then, isn't it?'

Libby went cold. 'What do you mean?'

'You've been refusing him all this time. He's not going to take kindly to this, is he? You've been together longer than Fran and Guy.'

'Ah.' Libby understood. So that was why Ben hadn't sounded like himself. This was going to take careful handling.

It wasn't until after supper that either the body or Fran and Guy were mentioned. Ben and Adam discussed ground management, to Libby's amusement, followed by the difficulty of getting a job and, finally, sailing.

'Who was this Basil, then?' asked Adam.

'I went to school with him back in the dark ages,' said Ben, leaning back in his chair and twirling his wine glass.

'Where is he now?'

Ben raised his eyebrows. 'Why? Fancy a sail?'

'Well, yeah,' said Adam, with a grin, 'but I just wondered if he might know anything about Creekmarsh before Lewis bought it.'

'I expect the police will have done all that,' said Libby.

'Just wondered,' said Adam. 'Like you do.'

Libby shifted in her chair. 'Not this time,' she said, deliberately not looking at Ben.

'Bas is still around, actually,' said Ben, ignoring this exchange, 'but I haven't seen him for ages. Not since he came back to the area, in fact.'

'What about his dad? He still alive?'

'No idea. I would have said no, but both my parents are still alive, so perhaps he is.'

'Why, anyway, Ad?' asked Libby. 'He wouldn't know anything about this body.'

A small silence descended as all three realised that they were actually discussing the murder despite Ben's reluctance. He sighed.

'Sorry, Ben,' said Adam. 'But honestly, Ma hasn't tried to find out anything. I'm interested – perhaps it's in the genes – but it was Lewis who told me to tell her all about it.'

'Why?'

'Because when we found the skeleton I told him about her murders.'

Libby winced.

'And did you also tell him how much trouble she got into?'

Adam looked at Libby in apology. 'No,' he said.

'That's why I don't want to know about this one,' said Libby firmly, 'unless it affects Lewis's ambition to turn Creekmarsh into a venue.'

'It might put a damper on a wedding,' said Ben, with a degree of relief at the change of subject.

'That's what I told Fran and Guy,' said Libby, and could have bitten her tongue out.

'That'd be cool, wouldn't it?' Adam rushed in to cover the awkward moment. 'D'you reckon Lewis would let Harry do the catering?'

'I'm sure he'd *love* Harry,' laughed Libby, 'but I doubt that Fran and Guy want veggie food.'

'What *do* they want?' asked Ben.

'No idea.' Libby shrugged. 'I didn't discuss it with them.'

'I bet,' said Ben, and stood up. 'Shall we clear away?'

Adam and Libby exchanged a complicit glance. 'OK,' said Libby.

Ben left an hour later, saying he knew how much Libby wanted to have time with Adam.

'Honestly, Ad,' she said, coming back into the sitting room and removing Sidney from the sofa. 'Whatever is the matter with him? He practically lives here, and now he's behaving like a mere acquaintance.'

'You know what's the matter with him. I said earlier. He wants to marry you, or at least put your relationship on a firmer footing so he has the right to protect you and share in your life properly.'

Libby looked at him admiringly. 'Gosh, Ad, you are grown up,' she said. 'But what you don't realise is that the tax position would change radically if we moved in together. And if we got married. And not to our advantage.'

'So why do people ever get married, then?' asked Adam, slinging long legs over the arm of the armchair. 'I thought the older generation were supposed to be in favour of it and encourage us lot to stop living in sin.'

'I don't think it means very much any more,' said Libby, leaning over to top up his wine glass. 'It didn't stop your father or Ben's wife from going off with someone else, did it? What price marriage vows, then?'

Adam frowned. 'Protection?'

'From what? People can be left destitute after the breakdown of any relationship, including marriage.'

'Children?'

'How many children did you know at school who came from a traditional family? How many of your friends had double-barrelled surnames because the school included both parents' names?'

'That's true.' Adam held his glass up to the light and squinted through it. 'I can't think of anything, then. But surely, the whole commitment thing is living together? Ben wants commitment and you don't.'

Libby was feeling more and more uncomfortable. It just wasn't right discussing this sort of thing with her son.

'I do want commitment,' she said slowly, 'but I want my independence, too.'

'That's a man's argument,' said Adam with a knowing grin. 'And a woman would say it meant he didn't love her enough.'

'But it's an acknowledged thing nowadays,' Libby persisted. 'LATs are more and more popular. Even with married couples. I know several.'

'Several?'

'Well, one or two,' admitted Libby. 'Do you remember Marsha? When you were little?'

'Your mate at the theatre? With all that black hair?'

'That's the one. Well, she met this man a few years ago and they got married. Went to live in London. But they bought separate homes. He's got a flat and she's got a little mews house with a huge studio space.'

Adam frowned. 'How far apart? And when do they get together? Does she invite him over for dinner? Or does he ask her back for coffee?'

Libby sighed. 'Only round the corner from each other, and I suppose they handle it like Ben and I do. He spends most of his time here, but goes back to The Manor when he's finished work for the day to have a shower, and back there in the morning to change into his work clothes.'

'But that's because he lives with his mum and dad and works for them, in a way.' He held out his glass for a refill. 'Mind you, I think it's weird that someone in his fifties is still living with his mum and dad.'

'It's not quite like that, is it?' said Libby, feeling that this conversation was becoming positively mired in the unexplainable. 'He only went back to live there the year before last.'

'He could have moved in with you then,' said Adam.

'We'd only just got together,' said Libby. 'Anyway, Ad, I think this conversation's gone far enough. I'll have a chat with Ben and see if we can't smooth things over.'

Adam looked doubtful. 'Have a chat with Pete and Harry first,' he suggested. 'Pete knows Ben better than nearly anybody else, doesn't he?'

'OK,' said Libby, more because she wanted to end the conversation rather than in a spirit of agreement. 'So tell me more about your Superintendent.'

Chapter Four

LEWIS OSBOURNE-WALKER SAT in the solar at Creekmarsh Place. His laptop sat open but ignored beside him as he watched darkness falling over the inlet that led to the Creekmarsh Sailing Club and the sea beyond. The sky, streaked with orange and greyish purple, looked like an improbable picture painted by a four-year-old.

Lewis sighed, and looked back at the email he had just opened.

'Just remember who helped you buy that sodding awful house,' it said, 'and remember where you came from.'

It was unsigned, but Lewis knew where it came from, and what it meant. He sighed again, and returned to the sunset.

Libby went up to The Manor the following morning after driving Adam back to Creekmarsh Place, and asked Hetty where Ben was on the estate.

'In the office, gal.' Hetty looked at her oddly. 'You can go on in.'

'Thanks, Hetty,' said Libby, her solar plexus fluttering like a teenager's. She walked along the dark passage and knocked on the green painted door.

'Lib?' Ben looked up in surprise. 'What are you doing here?'

'I – um – well, I've come to –' Libby paused and took a deep breath. 'I've come to apologise.'

Ben stood up. 'What for?' He came round the old partners desk and pulled up a chair. 'Sit down, for goodness' sake. Do you want coffee? I'll ask Hetty–'

'No, of course not.' Libby sat down feeling distinctly uncomfortable.

Ben went back behind the desk, which made her feel like a

naughty schoolgirl in the headmaster's office.

'What's up, then?' he said, after a long silence.

'You weren't happy last night.' She swallowed. 'Adam says I haven't been fair to you, and I quite see what he means.'

Ben smiled slightly. 'Well, I would have preferred you to have realised without your son's intervention, but you can't have everything.'

'Oh, Ben.' Libby looked up. 'This isn't like us. Can't we go back to being normal?'

'Normal? On your terms?' Ben sighed. 'I suppose if I want to continue seeing you, that's the way it'll have to be.'

'I thought you were happy with the way things were,' said Libby, the little worm of doubt and fear growing bigger inside her.

'In a way,' said Ben, 'but both I and my Mother have tried to persuade you to come and live here, haven't we? Didn't that give you a clue? And I have, I'm sure, mentioned it several times.'

'Well, yes, but not seriously,' said Libby, 'and I remember you telling me all about the LAT relationships and saying you were happy with it. That was just after your mother asked if I wouldn't be happier moving into The Manor.'

'I was trying to put our relationship on some kind of formal footing,' he said, leaning back in his chair. 'But that was nearly eighteen months ago. We'd only been together six months – less, actually.'

Libby nodded and looked down at her hands. 'So what do you want to do?'

'Nothing right now,' said Ben. 'I want you to go home and see if there's any chance of our relationship lasting without either of us having any rights in each other's lives. Think about what you want from it.' He stood up. 'Go on, off you go. I'll do the same and perhaps we could meet up in the pub this evening?'

'This evening?' Libby frowned. 'Not lunch-time?'

'I'm working, Lib,' Ben said gently. 'Come on. I'll see you about seven, unless you've got something else on?'

Libby stood up and turned to the door. 'You know I haven't,' she said.

Hetty was in the hall as she went out.

'All right, gal?' she asked, flicking a duster over the carved door-frame.

'Yes, thanks, Het,' said Libby. She turned and frowned at her. 'Did Ben tell you Fran and Guy are getting married?'

'Yeah. Makes yer think, don't it?' She gave Libby a penetrating look and stuffed the duster in her apron pocket.

'Mmm.' Libby smiled and nodded and started down The Manor drive feeling like the victim of a natural disaster. When her mobile rang in her pocket, she answered it thankfully, glad to take her mind off her unexpected romantic problems.

'Hey, Ma, it's me again.'

'Ad? What's up?' Libby slowed to a stop.

'I don't suppose you could pop over here again, could you? Lewis wants to talk to you.'

'*Lewis* does? What on earth for?'

'He's being very secretive about it, but I think it's something to do with the body.'

'Then he should tell your friend Big Bertha, shouldn't he,' said Libby, wondering what Ben would say about this new development. She straightened her shoulders and decided he couldn't tell her what to do. He had no right. She bit her lip. 'Yes, definitely,' she went on. 'He should tell the police.'

'I don't think it's quite like that, Ma,' said Adam. 'Just come over and have a word with him. Please. Unless you've got something else to do?'

Libby thought. 'Not really,' she said. 'I suppose I could, but Ben won't like it.'

'Come on, Ma, what's it got to do with Ben? I'll square it with him, if it's that important.'

'Remember our conversation about him last night?' said Libby. 'I've just spoken to him.'

'And?'

'He wants me to think about our relationship.'

'Ah.' Adam was quiet for a moment. 'Well, I think you ought to, as well, but meanwhile, pop over here and let Lewis give you some lunch. Just see what he wants.'

25

Libby sighed. 'OK,' she said. 'I've got to go home and clear up first – don't forget I drove you over at the crack of sparrow's fart – then I'll make myself presentable. I'll ring you when I'm on my way.'

'Great.' Libby could hear the bounce in Adam's voice. 'See you later.'

It was half past eleven when Libby drove down the lane towards Creekmarsh Place. Wondering whether to drive right up to the house, she was glad to see Lewis coming towards her down the drive.

'Leave it here, Mrs S,' he said. 'It's a bit boggy up near the front door.' He held the door open for her and waited while she locked it.

'Thanks for coming.' He stared down at his boots as they walked towards the house. 'After what Ad said I thought you'd be the one to talk to.'

'But I'm not police,' said Libby, casting him a worried glance, 'or a private investigator or anything.'

'No, I know. Ad told me all about the other stuff, like that woman at your theatre and your mate's auntie.'

'Yes, well, they were things that involved me personally,' said Libby.

'But that other theatre business – where was it?'

'The Alexandria in Nethergate.'

'Yeah, that one. And that body on the island. They weren't nothing to do with you, were they?'

'Well, no. And strictly speaking, I shouldn't have been involved. My friend Fran was asked to look into them, really.'

'She the Mystic Meg?'

Libby looked amused. 'You could say that.'

'Don't think I need that,' said Lewis, pushing open the heavy oak door. 'Come up to me sun room.'

He led her up a beautiful staircase, already restored, she noted, and through another oak door.

'It's a solar!' she said delightedly. 'I didn't notice it from outside.'

'It's not right over the front door like some of 'em,' said Lewis. 'Least, that's what I've been told. My favourite place.'

He went to the window and Libby followed him.

'I can see why,' she said. 'That's the river Wytch down there, isn't it?'

'A little bit of it,' said Lewis. 'That's just a what-d'yer-call-it from it.'

'A tributary? No, that wouldn't be it. An inlet.'

'Inlet, that's it. Goes just to the sailing club. I'll take you down there, if you like.'

'Lovely,' said Libby.

'Come and sit down, then.' He seemed suddenly nervous as he turned sharply and made for a chair beside a desk, where a slim silver laptop sat, open. Libby took the chair opposite.

'Wanna drink? Ad's coming up about one fer some lunch if you want to stay.'

'If I'm still here,' said Libby, 'and yes, a cup of tea would be nice.'

'Nothin' stronger?' Lewis got up and went to the door. Libby shook her head. He opened the door and stuck his head out. 'Can you stick the kettle on, Katie?' A muffled shout answered him.

'I'll pop down in a minute and get it,' he said, returning to his chair. 'They all say I should get used to Katie looking after me, but I can't be doing with it.'

'Who's Katie?'

'My – well, housekeeper, I suppose. Katie North.' He grinned. 'Minder, more like. She organises everything. Great girl. I met her when we was doing the telly.'

'Aren't you still doing the telly?' asked Libby.

'Oh, yeah. I meant when I was doing that *Housey Housey* one.'

'Oh, where you were discovered,' Libby nodded.

'Yeah. Right laugh, that was. I mean, who would of believed it?'

'That you were discovered?'

'Yeah.' Lewis looked uncomfortable and shifted in his seat. 'Hang on, I'll go and see about that tea.'

'No need,' said a voice, and a tray came into the room followed, Libby presumed, by Katie North. Who was a shock. Somehow, the name had suggested someone young and slim in a cropped top and a mini-skirt. And Lewis had said 'girl'. Katie, however, was a stout middle-aged matron, who would have been right at home in the sort of book Libby had read as a child.

'I put coffee and tea bags there, lovey,' she said, for all the world as though Libby still *was* a child. 'And that there's boiling water in the flask. Staying for lunch?'

'Oh – yes, please,' said Libby.

'You said you didn't know,' said Lewis, looking put out.

'I do now,' she said, turning to him with a bright smile.

'I'll yell when it's ready,' Katie said and disappeared.

'I like her,' said Libby, helping herself to a tea-bag and boiling water.

'Everyone does,' said Lewis. 'She's like everyone's mum.'

Libby nodded and leant back in the carved wooden chair. 'Go on, then,' she said.

'It's a bit difficult,' said Lewis, after a long pause. 'See, I wasn't actually "discovered" on *Housey Housey*.'

'No?'

'No. It was a bit of a set-up.' He sighed and poured himself coffee. 'I'd been doing this house up in Hampstead for this bloke, see. Not on me own, with a team. Worked for a subcontractor, didn't we, specialising in posh houses, and we'd been there weeks.' He took a breath. 'Well, I got on well with this bloke and once or twice he asked me to stay behind for a drink.'

'Weren't you driving?'

'Didn't matter. I don't drink.' Lewis grinned at Libby's surprise. 'And anyway, I didn't just stay for a drink.' He looked down, then up under his eyebrows. 'You shocked?'

'Should I be?'

'Ad says you've got best mates who got hitched.'

'Civil partnership, yes. I was their best woman.'

'So you're not shocked.' He nodded. 'Good. Well, see, this bloke is married and no one knows he's gay. Mind you, I bet there's a bloody regiment out there who really *do* know. You can't keep it that quiet. But on the surface, let's say, the great British public don't know. So it's all very hush-hush. I only stayed when the wife wasn't there.' He took another mouthful of coffee.

'Anyway, he reckons I'm a bit of a jack-the-lad, and he's got contacts with this telly company, so he gets me this interview with 'em, and next thing you know, I'm on *Housey Housey* playing the cockney cheeky chappie with an 'ammer in me 'and.'

He smiled ruefully and looked out of the window. 'Shouldn't mock. It's got me all this, ain't it?'

'Has it?' said Libby. He looked at her quickly.

'Yeah, that's the problem, see. Somewhere along the line, I realise that I'm being set up for this other show. It was all a bit too – too – what's the word I want?'

'Pat?'

'Maybe. Anyway. It felt like someone had it all mapped out. But as if they didn't want to, if you know what I mean.'

'As if they were under pressure. As if someone was blackmailing them?'

Lewis looked up in surprise. 'That's it exactly,' he said. 'As though someone wanted me doin' this programme, and they was forcing someone to do it – make it work, like.'

'Who? Do you know?'

'I thought I did, but I don't really. I reckon my Hampstead mate's behind it all, but I don't know who it was at the telly company he was leanin' on. And what I don't get is why? Why did he want me doin' that show? He wasn't that fond of me.'

'So why did you want to talk to me?' prompted Libby, after a pause.

'After that body was found, I got this email.' He pulled the laptop towards him and turned it to face Libby. 'See?'

'"Just remember who helped you buy that sodding awful house and remember where you came from."' Libby looked up. 'Is it from your Hampstead friend?'

'It don't say. Don't recognise the address, but I reckon so.'

'And why is it worrying you?'

'Because it sounds like a threat to me. A warning. So it looks like my Hampstead friend might have something to do with this 'ere skeleton.'

Libby watched him. Lewis Osbourne-Walker was frightened.

'So you're being warned to say nothing about him? But what's he got to do with this house?'

'He put me on to it. All a bit – y'know – under the counter. Cos 'e knew the bloke what was 'ere before. And 'e's been gone years.'

'Moved out?'

Lewis shook his head.

'Disappeared,' he said.

Chapter Five

'WELL,' SAID LIBBY AFTER a moment, 'the police will probably know that by now. Know who the previous owner was and that he's disappeared, I mean. I expect they're trying to match these bones up to his DNA or something right now, so what's the problem?'

Lewis looked exasperated. 'Because I told you, I got this place through – you know – and he doesn't want the police to know he's got anything to do with it.'

'So he's telling you – what, exactly?' Libby looked again at the email. 'Remember how you got this house – well, yes, but he's not going to tell anyone how you got it, is he? And what else is he going to expose? That you've become a household name through his machinations?'

'His what?' Lewis stared.

'That he got you the job by leaning on someone. He'd be exposed then, too.'

'So what's he mean, then?' Lewis frowned.

'I don't know, but I honestly think you should tell the police.' Libby leant forward. 'Lewis, listen. I'm not a detective, but I have been involved in four different murder cases, and believe me, the police find out everything. People only make things worse for themselves if they try and hide stuff. And what's the worst that can happen?'

'I'd lose me job and this place.' Lewis scowled at her.

Libby shrugged. 'You asked for my opinion. Keep quiet if you like, but that'll look bad when the police find out, won't it? And if, as you say, there was something odd about the way you bought this place, they'll definitely find that out.'

Lewis stood up and went to stand at the window. 'I dunno.'

'You do, really,' said Libby. 'You wouldn't have asked me if you weren't thinking about telling the police. You would have kept quiet about it all. And what you really think is that the skeleton is the missing owner and your Hampstead friend did away with him. Isn't that right?'

Lewis turned round. 'Yeah. That obvious, is it?'

'I've got sons,' said Libby, with a grin.

Lewis sighed and came back to his seat. 'So what do I do then, Mum?'

Libby laughed. 'Tell the superintendent.'

'The scary super? Blimey.' Lewis shuddered theatrically.

'Is she coming back to talk to you?'

'I expect so. She said she'd need to see me again – or someone would, and there are still loads of 'em all over the wood. Fingertip search, they said.'

'I thought they were digging?'

'Oh, yeah, that too. Gawd, it's like a bloody nightmare.'

'It is a nightmare,' said Libby, patting his arm. 'But think how much better you'll feel when you've told the police everything you know.'

'But I don't actually know anything, do I?'

Libby looked thoughtful. 'How did you buy this place? I mean, obviously not through an estate agent?'

'My mate said he was sellin' it on behalf of this other bloke.'

'The one who'd disappeared?'

'Yeah. I got the deeds and everything.'

'Was it done through a solicitor?'

Lewis looked surprised. ''Course.'

'Then why did you say "under the counter"?'

'Well, it was just, like, hand over the money and we'll hand over the deeds. With a legal document to say it was mine. All very quiet.'

'What about your solicitor?'

'Ah.' Lewis looked away, pink creeping into his cheeks.

Libby sighed. 'You didn't have one.'

'No.'

'Then the first thing you do is to have a solicitor look at the deeds – see if the Land Registry has a record of the transaction.'

'That's what I thought,' said Lewis with a gloomy nod. 'Might not be mine after all.'

'If it isn't, your mate – oh, for goodness' sake, what's his bloody name? Can't keep saying your mate.'

'Tony,' said Lewis.

'Tony what?'

'Just Tony.'

'Oh, all right,' sighed Libby, 'but Tony will have to cough up that money you gave him. How, by the way? Wasn't a cheque, was it?'

'Banker's draft.'

'There you are. The bank will have a record, so he'll have to pay it back.' Libby frowned. 'I must say, it seems a bit careless of him, if he wanted to keep it quiet.'

'It wasn't made out to him,' said Lewis.

'Oh, *Lewis*!' Libby shook her head. 'Honestly! And you didn't smell a rat at the time?'

'S'pose so. I just wanted this place. My mum loves it.'

'Your mum? Is she here?'

'No, but she comes down for weekends. She can't believe it.'

'I bet,' said Libby. 'Well, I think you've just got to come clean about everything to the police. I don't think you've done anything illegal, and then it will be up to them to trace this Tony and your money.'

'You reckon they'll go after my money?'

'Well, it would probably be all part of the investigation, wouldn't it?' said Libby.

Lewis sighed. 'Yeah, all right. I'll ring the scary super this afternoon.'

'Ad calls her Big Bertha,' said Libby. 'Big Bertha the Scary Super. What's her real name?'

'Can't remember.' He looked at her with pleading blue eyes. 'Are you goin' to be here?'

'Even if I was, she wouldn't let me be there when she talked to you,' said Libby. 'What about your mum? Couldn't she come down?'

'I don't want her mixed up in this.'

'Gee, thanks,' said Libby.

Lewis went pink again. 'You know what I mean,' he said. 'Couldn't you hang around until after I've spoken to her?'

'It depends when you get to speak to her. She might not be available. Will you speak to anyone else?'

'I dunno.' Lewis shook himself like a wet dog. 'This is bloody awful.' He stood up. 'Where's Katie with that lunch?'

He strode to the door just as a shout floated up.

'That's Adam,' said Libby.

'Saying lunch is ready, yeah,' said Lewis. 'Coming?'

Downstairs Katie had provided soup, bread, cheese and ham on the kitchen table. Libby looked round admiringly. The kitchen had been part renovated, but there was still a wonderful old kitchen range in a deep fireplace, a wooden airer strung with bunches of herbs and what looked like original Edwardian cupboards along one wall. The table was old, scrubbed and refectory-sized, complemented by a variety of chairs that looked as though they might have come from churches and schools.

'Hello, Ma.' Adam gave her a kiss on the cheek. 'Remember Mog?'

Mog, tall and skinny with rather limp brown hair, shook hands shyly, and sat down at the table. Katie urged them all to follow suit, and soon Lewis, Mog and Adam were deep in discussions about the garden. All worries about the house and the discovery of the skeleton had dropped from Lewis like a cloak, and Libby envied him this ability, whether it was real or assumed.

Katie helped her to soup and told her how she'd come to be working for Lewis.

'We did the catering for that *Housey Housey*,' she said. 'Like outside stuff, when we was at all those different homes.'

'Who's we?' asked Libby.

'Company I worked for. We had one of them vans, and sometimes a double-decker bus. It was all OBs.'

'OBs? Oh, outside broadcasts.'

'That's right. Well, I got to know young Lewis, and his mum come along a couple of times to watch, so I got to know her, too. And then, o' course, he finds out I used to be a seccertary, and he asks if I could help him sort his life out, sort o' thing. So I did.'

'So have you moved down here, too?' asked Libby, between mouthfuls of soup.

'Oh, yes. I don't mind. I've still got me little flat in Leytonstone, and no kids, so I'm fancy free, like.' Katie smiled comfortably. 'I been very lucky. Two good careers, I've had, one working in the bank, and one in catering, and now I can put the whole lot together.' She gazed fondly at Lewis, deep in conversation with Mog and Adam. 'And look after him, the silly bugger.'

'He needs it, doesn't he?' said Libby. 'You know how he bought this house?'

Katie sighed. 'Yeah. I said he was a silly bugger, didn't I? I tried to talk him out of it at the time, but he weren't having any. Didn't even get a survey done.'

'Blimey.' Libby was in awe.

'Oh, yeah. He's made a mint since that *Housey Housey*. Mind you, he didn't tell me how much he paid, but I reckon it must have been less than market value. Stands to reason, havey-cavey business like that.'

'I've tried to persuade him to tell the police about the whole thing,' said Libby, pushing her empty soup bowl away.

Katie shook her head. 'He won't like that. He'll think he's going to lose the house.'

'Exactly. But don't you see, someone, whether it's this Tony he bought it from or someone else, has tried to offload it for some reason. And now the skeleton's been found, that looks suspiciously like the reason, doesn't it?'

'Mmm.' Katie stared at her. ''Course. Makes sense.' She stood up and fetched a cafetière. 'I'll add my two-pennorth and all this afternoon.'

'He must phone the police,' said Libby. 'He can't wait until they contact him.'

At that moment, the phone rang.

Conversation round the table froze as Katie lumbered out into the hall. She came back holding the phone out to Lewis, mouthing 'Police'. He took the phone, glancing at Libby before standing up and moving away from the table. Adam looked at his mother.

'What's going on?' he asked in a low voice.

'I've persuaded him to tell the police whatever he knows,' said Libby. 'That's what he wanted to talk to me about.'

'So what does he know?'

'Oh – who sold him the house. That's all, really.'

'The police will know that already, surely?'

'I would have thought so,' said Libby. How would the police *not* know who owned the house? How it had been sold? They knew Lewis had only recently moved in.

Lewis returned to the table and sat down.

'That super's coming back this afternoon,' he said. 'Wants to talk to me.' He shot another glance at Libby.

'Well, that's good,' she said and stood up. 'I must get back. Thanks for the lunch, Katie. See you on Sunday, Ad?'

Adam nodded, looking at Lewis.

Katie stood up. 'I'll see you out,' she said.

At the front door, she led Libby outside and lowered her voice. 'I'll make sure he tells her everything,' she said. 'Can you come back if he wants to talk to you again?'

'I'll talk to him if he wants to phone me, but I honestly don't see what I can do,' said Libby. 'I'm no private investigator. I'm just Adam's mum.'

Katie's mouth drew down disapprovingly. 'Hmm,' she said. 'Well, I'm going back to London this weekend, so I can't keep an eye on him.'

'Oh, Katie, what do you expect me to do? I don't even know him.'

'He wanted to talk to you.' Katie's mouth was now set in a stubborn line.

'I know, but what Lewis wants he doesn't always have to get,' said Libby. 'He's an ordinary mortal, you know, just like my Adam.'

Katie sighed. 'All right,' she said. 'I'll tell him he can phone you.'

And I bet he will, thought Libby, as she drove back towards Nethergate. All the bloody time.

Chapter Six

BY THE TIME LIBBY met Ben at seven o'clock, Lewis had called at least five times. After the first two calls, Libby had let the answerphone take the messages and wished she'd signed up for caller identification when she missed a call from Ben.

'Sorry about that,' she said now, sitting down opposite him at a table by the empty fireplace. 'What was it you wanted?'

'To see if you wanted to go somewhere else,' he said. 'You could have called me back.'

'I did,' said Libby with a sigh, 'and got your voicemail.'

'Oh.' Ben frowned and pulled his mobile out of his pocket. 'Bugger. So you did. I didn't hear it. Must have been in the shower.'

'So we're even,' said Libby, sipping her lager. 'Ah, I needed that.'

'Why were you call screening, then?' asked Ben.

Resignedly, Libby told him everything that had happened since the morning.

'I have genuinely tried to put him off, Ben, you can ask Adam and this Katie North person. That's why I was trying not to take his calls. He'd already called twice before I stopped answering.'

'What did he say, then?' Despite himself, Ben was looking interested.

'Oh, the superintendent hadn't arrived then. He was just blathering about what he should tell her. But as I said, the police will already know who owned the house previously and they'll probably know all about this seemingly dodgy house purchase, too, so all he's got to do is tell them everything including who this Tony person is so he can't be accused of impeding the investigation.'

'It does sound a bit off, doesn't it?' mused Ben, twirling his glass absently. 'Why on earth would Lewis buy a house like that? Why was he so scared of letting on? What did he think Tony was going to tell the tabloids?'

'I think there must be more to it than he told me,' said Libby. 'After all, the general public know he's gay.'

'But they don't know that's why he got the *Housey Housey* gig, or his own show. It's payola under another name, isn't it?'

'And this Tony didn't want his name revealed. I wonder who he is?'

'I've been racking my brain to think of a high-profile person with media connections in Hampstead,' said Ben.

'We don't know he has media connections, do we?'

'You said he got Lewis on to *Housey Housey* and then leant on someone to get him his own programme.'

'Yes, but that sounds as though he has connections with the Mafia, not the media.' Libby squinted at her glass. 'And I still don't know why he wanted Lewis to have his own show. It couldn't have been for sexual favours, could it? He'd already had those.'

Ben sighed. 'I don't know. And we didn't come here to talk about it, either.'

Libby looked up. 'You wanted to know.'

'I know, I know.' He reached over and patted her hand. 'I'm sorry. I've been a bit pushy, haven't I?'

'Not pushy, exactly.' Libby looked down at his hand. 'I don't want to lose you, Ben.'

He turned over her hand and gripped it. 'I don't want to lose you, either. I'm just not entirely happy with the status quo.'

'Adam says that's the woman's argument.'

'Discussing me with your son, eh?' Ben dropped her hand and leant back.

'Yes, because he guessed how you would feel. No – he actually *knew* how you'd feel. And he told me off.'

'On my side, then, is he?'

'Firmly,' said Libby. 'I always wondered how the kids would

feel if I wanted to get married again.'

'Is that why you've always said you wouldn't?'

'No, I lost faith in marriage. As I said to Adam, my ex and yours both went off with other people, so it's no protection.'

'You don't get married just for protection,' said Ben. 'That's medieval.'

'No profession of commitment, then.'

'It is, Lib. Just because some people change, it doesn't mean they didn't mean it at the time.'

'So what's the point, then? If you're not saying "I will love and stay with you for ever"? You can do that without benefit of the law.'

Ben frowned. 'Why did Harry and Pete get hitched, then?'

'To prove to the world that they meant it?'

'That's one interpretation. Pete wanted to tell the world he loved Harry. And it probably meant more for them to do it than a heterosexual couple.'

'We're talking in circles,' said Libby. 'I love you.' She felt herself going pink. 'But I still don't see the point in getting married. I wish you could talk me round.'

'Perhaps wishing it is the first step?' Ben smiled slightly. 'I'll just have to hope so, won't I? But meanwhile, I think we'd better stick to our own establishments, don't you?'

Libby's mouth fell open in horror. 'You mean –'

'I'll go home every night,' said Ben. 'You can invite me for a meal now and then, of course.'

'That's big of you,' muttered Libby.

'Meanwhile – how about dinner?'

'You mean – er – what do you mean?' Libby scowled at him. 'I don't think you're taking this seriously.'

'Oh, I am, I am. More seriously than you are. And I meant would you like dinner here tonight?'

'Oh.' Mollified, Libby sat back. 'Yes please.'

Since the success of The Pink Geranium, Harry's 'caff' as he called it, the pub, much beloved of calendar makers, had upped its game on the dining front, and now provided home-made food that was beginning to rival the local gastro-pub. Despite the excellence of her steak and ale pie, Libby found the meal hard going. The atmosphere was worse than it had been the very first time they had been out together, much worse, in fact. Libby was still wondering why things had changed so much between them almost without warning, when Ben asked, 'How are young Jane and Terry?'

Libby's heart sank. 'Fine,' she said.

'They're getting married, too, aren't they?' Ben said casually, not looking at her.

'Yes.' Libby refrained from asking how he knew. 'And all you're doing, you know, is causing me to dig my heels in. The more you drop hints, or issue ultimata, the more stubborn I shall be. Exactly as I am about smoking. The more the bloody government preach at me, and ban me from doing things, the more I shall insist on doing them. No one has the right to dictate to me how I live my life. I shall continue to live it according to my own lights.' She sighed, pushed her plate away and stood up. 'It was a lovely meal, thank you, Ben. You must let me buy you dinner some time.' She picked up her basket, noting the expression on his face with satisfaction. 'Good night.'

As she walked down the high street in the gathering gloom she kept her ears pricked for his footsteps behind her, but they never came. By the time she turned into Allhallow's Lane she was feeling slightly embarrassed about her outburst. The lilac hanging over the wall wafted perfume under her nose, and the long racemes dusted her hair as she plodded along towards number 17, a red-brick terraced cottage opposite a tiny green, where Romeo the Renault sat parked under a hawthorn tree, and Sidney the silver tabby regarded the world from the window.

By the time Libby opened the door and stumbled down the step, Sidney was on his favourite stair, trying to tell her that he had been waiting there for her for simply hours.

'Don't lie,' said Libby, slipping her light jacket off and tossing it, with her basket, onto the small table in the window. The lump in her throat was growing bigger and bigger, and she decided the only thing to do was drown it in a large glass of red wine. With a cigarette, she added viciously, even though she hardly ever smoked these days.

Provided with these aids to recovery, she sat down, turned on the television and promptly burst into tears.

The following morning, she packed up several small canvases to take into Nethergate for Guy's gallery-cum-shop. She was always surprised that these paintings sold so well, but Guy wasn't. 'Nethergate,' he always said, 'is a very old-fashioned resort, with what is normally called "a nice Class of Visitor". They much prefer an original to a mass-produced version, even though that might be cheaper. And we keep yours at a reasonable price.'

When she arrived, she found Fran in the shop, sitting beside Sophie, Guy's daughter, going through a magazine. Guy grinned and nodded towards them.

'Wedding magazine,' he explained. 'Sophie thinks it's Christmas.'

'She's pleased, then?'

'Over the moon. She's always liked Fran. I think for a bit she was afraid I was going to team up with you.'

'Gee, thanks,' said Libby, unwrapping brown paper.

'You're too volatile and extrovert for me, she thinks. I need a calming influence.'

'Too much like a bull in a china shop you mean,' muttered Libby.

Guy put his head on one side. 'Sometimes,' he agreed. 'I have heard it said.'

'By Ben and Pete, mainly.' Libby pushed the brown paper and string aside and stood the paintings up. 'There.'

'Very nice,' said Guy approvingly. 'A few different ones this time.'

'Jane and Terry let me use their front windows for a different perspective,' said Libby. 'Now old Mrs Finch has gone, they've been doing up the basement flat, so I'm not in their way.'

'To let?' asked Guy.

'No. They're going to turn Peel House back into one dwelling and ask Jane's mother if she'd like to come and live in the flat. It's got its own entrance and the garden, so she'd be quite comfortable.'

'But I thought she was a dragon? Fran said she was awful.'

'She is. But Jane's thinking ahead. Her mum isn't getting any younger and if she needs care of any sort, Jane's a long way away. Also, she'd be a built-in baby-sitter.'

'Baby? She's not pregnant?' Guy looked aghast.

'No.' Libby giggled. 'But they *are* getting married, and they're not into their dotage yet.'

'They're having the full church do, though, aren't they?' Guy cast a loving glance at his fiancée and daughter. 'Not like us.'

'No.' Libby couldn't help heaving a gusty sigh.

'What's up, Lib?' Guy lifted her chin with a finger. 'Problems?'

'Doesn't matter.' Libby looked at him unwillingly.

'Hmm.' Guy dropped his hand. 'Fran, shall we go and have a coffee? Soph, will you shop-sit for a bit?'

'Sure,' she said, her blonde curtain of hair falling over her eyes. 'Bring me back a latte, will you?'

'Latte,' scoffed Guy. 'Why it can't be plain and simple black or white coffee, I don't know.'

'Nobody of our generation does,' said Fran, tucking her arm through his as they strolled along Harbour Street towards the Blue Anchor café. 'Neither does Mavis, really, but she does her best.'

Mavis was flicking a cloth over the outside tables at the Blue Anchor and greeted them with a gloomy nod and a tin ashtray. Libby glanced guiltily at Guy and Fran and lit up.

'I thought you were stopping,' said Fran, an accusing note in her voice.

'Fran.' Guy dug her in the ribs. 'Come on, then, Lib. Tell us all about it.'

'Three coffees,' said Mavis, appearing with a tray. When Mavis returned to the interior of the café, Libby told Fran and Guy about Ben's reaction to their marriage. Fran was horrified.

'And Terry and Jane make it worse,' said Libby, wiping coffee froth off her top lip.

'Oh, God,' groaned Fran and put her head in her hands. 'I knew I shouldn't have said yes.'

Libby and Guy looked astonished.

'You what?' said Libby. 'Don't be so bloody daft. I told you, you're a different type from me entirely, and what happens to

Ben and me is absolutely nothing to do with you.'

'Quite,' said Guy, looking worried.

'And what about this murder?' said Fran, looking up. 'That can't have helped.'

'Actually, he's quite interested in that,' said Libby. 'I didn't go out looking for it, and I've been trying to stay clear, although I did go and see this Lewis person yesterday.'

Fran sat up straight. 'And?' she said.

Libby looked at her warily, scenting change in the air. 'Don't repeat any of this,' she said slowly, 'because it's completely confidential, but I'll give you the bare bones.'

Guy and Fran groaned together. 'Sorry,' said Libby, and launched into her story.

'The police will have found most of this out anyway,' said Guy, when she'd finished. 'I don't see the need for all this secrecy of the confessional.'

'Me neither. And the identity of his good fairy – no pun intended – will come out, too, as he sold Lewis the house.'

'Who's the body?' said Fran.

'They don't know. They were doing forensics on it, Adam said. I think they thought at first it was very old, but now they think it might be more recent.'

'How recent?'

'Oh, I don't know. Eighteen months?' Libby shook her head. 'The police aren't keeping Adam in their confidence. And he says they've got a scary superintendent they call Big Bertha, who would certainly be immune to any charms of either his or mine.'

'Was it in the wood?' asked Fran.

'The skeleton? Yes, near the edge. Adam and Mog are clearing a path through it. I told you, he wants to turn it into a venue.'

'Not if the entrance is still up that dismal overgrown drive in between those broken gateposts,' said Guy.

'That's the way I go in, but perhaps there's another way.'

'It's not a happy place,' said Fran.

Libby and Guy looked at her.

'No?' said Libby.

'No,' said Fran. 'And Lewis isn't happy, either.'

'How do you know?' said Guy after a pause, while Fran looked out to sea, where the *Dolphin*, or it could have been the *Sparkler*, bobbed slowly round Dragon Island.

'I just do,' said Fran. 'And it's going to get worse.'

Depressed, Libby decided to leave them to it and drive back to Steeple Martin. She was just passing the turn to Steeple Mount when the midday news came on the radio.

'And now, what the police are calling the "unexplained death" in his London home of financier Tony West.'

Chapter Seven

'AD, IS LEWIS THERE?' Libby had barely got through the front door before she was dialling Adam's number.

'No.' Adam sounded perplexed. 'He went off this morning before we got here. Katie won't tell us anything.'

Trying to remember how much Adam knew of Lewis's story, Libby tried another tack. 'Did he talk to the police yesterday?'

'I don't know. Mog and I went back to work and didn't see him for the rest of the afternoon. He's not likely to have told us, anyway, is he?'

'No, I suppose not,' said Libby, and sat down on the stairs.

'What's up, Ma? Is it something to do with what he told you yesterday?'

'In a way, yes,' said Libby, aware of a sinking feeling in her stomach. 'I'm very much afraid your friend Lewis is going to be even deeper in the mire than he was before.'

'What? Why?'

'I think the friend who sold him Creekmarsh has just been found dead,' said Libby, quite certain she was right.

There was a long silence. 'Oh, bugger,' said Adam finally. 'I guess I'd better tell Mog.'

'Yes, I suppose you had,' said Libby. 'I should think there'd be a block on everything to do with the place now.'

'They wouldn't think Lewis would kill this bloke, surely,' Adam said. 'And he couldn't have put the skeleton in the wood, either.'

'I think it's a little more complicated than that,' said Libby. 'If you *do* see him, tell him he can ring me if he wants. And Ad –'

'What?'

'I think I might talk to Fran about it.'

'Ma!' he said warningly.

'No, listen. She said a couple of things this morning about Creekmarsh and Lewis and she doesn't know either of them. I'll have to ask.'

'Well, don't go getting yourselves into trouble again. You know what Ben would say.'

'Yes,' said Libby, gritting her teeth. 'I'd better go now, Ad. And don't stop work yet, the police will tell you if you have to.'

'Oh, thanks, now I've got something to look forward to,' said Adam, and rang off.

Libby sat for a moment, then went and turned on the television and tried to find a news channel. Since Ben had persuaded her to install satellite, this was now easy, but none of the channels seemed to have anything on the death of Tony West. Eventually, however, a photograph flashed up on the screen with his name underneath. Libby recognised it immediately. No wonder Lewis had been keen to keep it under wraps, she thought.

Tony West had been a financier, yes, but also an entrepreneur, his fingers in many media pies, including reality TV. Libby had seen him on various television talk shows, and knew he was reputed to have what used to be known as an eye for the ladies, particularly those with very short skirts and very low tops. Not to mention an eye for the young men, reflected Libby, but she could now see what damage the relationship with Lewis could do to both of them, including the way West had used his influence to get Lewis the job on *Housey Housey* and subsequently his own show.

And now he was dead. And everything was going to come out. And Lewis was going to be destroyed. Of course, she thought, standing up and going into the kitchen, she could be wrong. It could be entirely the wrong Tony. But the coincidences were just too much. She moved the kettle absently on to the hotplate and stood staring out of the window. Sidney was stalking a butterfly, a futile occupation, about which he never learnt. He occasionally caught a blackbird or a mouse, to Libby's horror, particularly as she had to clear up the resulting massacre in the house, but butterflies were far too canny. They led him a pretty chase, although Adam and Dominic said it made him look like a gay ballet dancer.

The kettle began to grumble to itself and Libby warmed the teapot. It was a proper cup of tea moment, not a time for a tea bag in the mug. When she'd poured on the water, she went back to the phone.

'Fran, you know you said Creekmarsh wasn't a happy place? And that Lewis wasn't happy, either? What did you mean?'

There was a short silence. 'I'm not sure,' said Fran eventually. 'It just feels dead. As though the trees are keeping in all the damp and dark and depression.'

Libby shivered. 'It does feel a bit like that,' she said, 'especially going up the drive. The whole area is like it. And although what I've seen of the house is beautiful, in a decaying sort of a way, that's the same.'

'There's been another death, hasn't there?' said Fran.

Libby's heart jumped. 'Yes. Did you see it on the news?'

'I haven't seen the news. But there has, hasn't there?'

'I think so,' said Libby, and explained.

'Yes, that's right. That's him,' said Fran. 'Has Lewis called you?'

'No. Will he?'

'I don't know,' said Fran, 'but I think he's in trouble now.'

'If he wants help, would you be willing?'

Fran sighed. 'Oh, I don't know, Lib. I can't help feeling that we'd be interfering. We know nothing about this. Your only connection is Adam working in the garden. And we don't know any of the police involved.'

'Fran, if he really wants help and he's in trouble, you can't refuse to help him, can you? Not if you've seen something.'

'It's only a feeling, Lib. I haven't seen a hanging man, or anything.'

'But you came up with it spontaneously. Like you used to say, it was just as if you'd always known.'

'All right, all right. If you hear anything else, or Lewis asks you, you can call me. But I really don't want to get involved. Guy and I want to get down to planning our wedding.'

With an effort, Libby accepted the change of subject. 'How exciting,' she said. 'I didn't ask this morning. Any decisions yet?'

'A few,' said Fran. 'Why don't you and Ben come over – oh. No, perhaps not a good idea.'

'No,' said Libby miserably.

'Well, how about I come over this evening and tell you what's been going on so far?' suggested Fran.

'But I only saw you this morning,' said Libby. 'Are you sure you want to see me again? Won't Guy mind?'

Fran laughed. 'Libby, what's got into you? We've seen one another up to four times a day in the past, and as for Guy minding! Since when has that worried you?'

'Oh, it's all this stuff with Ben, I suppose,' sighed Libby.

'I'll tell you what,' said Fran, sounding quite brisk, 'I'll ask Guy to drive over and take Ben for a drink, it's probably just what he needs, and I'll come round to you and we can kill a bottle and discuss wedding plans. How does that sound?'

'Lovely,' said Libby happily.

When Ben phoned later to tell her Guy was taking him out for a drink, she suggested they both come round to Allhallow's Lane later. 'Then Guy can have a coffee before he drives home,' she said.

'So what will you two be talking about?'

'Girly things,' said Libby, feeling the blush creep up her neck. 'You know.'

'Wedding plans?' asked Ben.

'Er – yes.' Libby swallowed. 'Do you mind?'

'Why should I mind? You enjoy yourselves. See you later.'

Libby stood looking at the phone for a good minute after Ben had rung off. She didn't really like this new set-up *at all*.

Fran arrived just before eight, carrying a bottle of wine and a pile of magazines. Libby had heard nothing from Lewis or Adam during the rest of the afternoon, and no more had been added to the television item about the death of Tony West, except to confirm that he was on the board of the television production company behind 'the hit show *Housey Housey*'. Well, that cleared that one up, thought Libby.

Libby poured wine and offered bowls of Bombay mix and peanuts, while Fran spread out magazines and brochures on the floor.

'I thought you were going to have a quiet do?' said Libby, flicking through a series of brochures for country house venues.

'We are,' said Fran, 'but just because it's quiet doesn't mean to say we have to be hole-in-the-corner about it. We think this place is rather nice. Do you know it?'

Libby took the small brochure with a picture of an old oak door on the front. 'Looks more like a house,' she said, opening it. 'Oh, I don't know though. What a great bedroom!'

The photographs showed a four-poster bed in a room with an open fireplace, what looked like a small library and a Tudor hall with a gallery.

'It only accommodates forty guests, though,' said Libby.

'As you so rightly said, we want a quiet do,' said Fran, 'and this is perfect. We can stay there, and there are two or three other guest bedrooms. The kids can fight over who stays, but if you look, there's a minibus service to a nearby hotel if anyone else wants to stay in the vicinity.'

'That'd be me, then,' said Libby. 'It looks lovely, Fran.'

'Actually, Lib,' said Fran, leaning over to top up Libby's glass, 'I thought you might want to stay at the venue.'

'Yes, but there's your children. And Sophie. She'll want to be there, won't she?'

'I'd quite like you to be my attendant. Maid of honour. Bridesmaid. Whatever.' Fran looked down at her hands, and to her surprise Libby saw a faint blush of colour in her cheeks.

'Fran,' she said, suddenly finding it hard to speak. 'Are you sure?'

'Yes, please,' said Fran, looking up. 'It was because of you I met Guy. And he would like Ben to be his best man. Which would have been great if you'd still been together –'

'I think we are still together,' said Libby, 'but I'm not sure we're still on room-sharing terms.'

Fran nodded. 'Yes. Well, we can sort all that out later,' she said. 'We book the place exclusively, so it's up to us who stays and who doesn't.'

'It looks expensive,' said Libby apprehensively.

'Yes.' Fran was amused. 'But you're not paying, so don't worry about it.'

'Fran.' Libby was furiously embarrassed.

'Sorry, sorry.' Fran laughed. 'It was your face. Now have a look at what I want to wear.'

The next hour was spent happily poring over magazines and catalogues of bridal wear, most of it entirely unsuitable for a mature bride, as Fran said, but there were some rather more off-the-wall designs that Libby immediately homed in on. One was a positively medieval dress with a collar that framed the face, photographed on a young woman with distinctly Goth-like make-up.

'You can wear that one,' said Fran. 'Look, they do it in several colours. It would suit you.'

'Me?' said Libby. 'I get to wear a posh frock, too?'

'Well, of course.' Fran looked at her in surprise. 'That's what attendants do, isn't it?'

'What about your daughters? And Sophie?'

'At my age? I want a friend, not a daughter.'

'Oh.' Libby beamed. 'OK then.'

By the time Guy and Ben arrived at a quarter to ten, Libby and Fran had chosen their outfits, the menu and the flowers. Guy laughed.

'Do I get any say in this?' he asked.

'You can change all of it except our outfits,' said Fran, reaching up to give him a kiss. Libby marvelled at how natural and open her friend had become since announcing her engagement. Fran had always been a bit buttoned-up in her opinion.

'Actually, I approve of it all,' said Guy, looking at Fran's notes and handing the brochure to Ben. 'What do you think, mate?'

Libby swallowed hard and got up to fetch glasses. 'Whisky?' she croaked. 'Or coffee, Guy?'

'Scotch'd be lovely, thanks, Lib,' said Ben, not looking at her.

'Coffee, thanks, love,' said Guy.

Ben took the brochure from him.

'This place is great,' he said. 'How did you find it?'

'Internet,' said Fran. 'I just Googled wedding venues in Kent. Most of them were big hotels, or part of chains. I couldn't go to Anderson Place after ...' she trailed off.

'Pete and Harry's do? Or the other business?' Ben squinted at her.

'Both, really,' said Fran, looking embarrassed. 'Harry and Pete's civil partnership was lovely, and that wedding planner – what was her name?'

'Melanie,' supplied Libby.

'She was great. But we don't want quite that level of organisation and grandeur. Do we?' She looked up at Guy, who bent and kissed her.

'No,' he said and, settling on the arm of her chair, grinned happily at the other two.

'And because we got involved in the murder, and it was such a sad story,' continued Fran, 'I just wouldn't feel right going there.'

Libby handed Ben his whisky and went into the kitchen to pour Guy's coffee. Behind her, she could hear the other three talking wedding plans and was surprised to feel a tightening in her chest and throat. It came out of nowhere and threatened to erupt like Vesuvius, leaving her shaking and damp with perspiration. 'Menopause,' she muttered to herself unconvincingly, heaving a huge breath.

'Lib? You OK?' Ben's voice behind her almost undid her again, but she bravely lifted the kettle and poured water into the empty mug. 'Bugger,' she said, reaching for the coffee jar.

'You wool-gathering?' He sounded amused as he came up behind her and put an arm round her. Her throat closed up again and she nodded.

'Here, I'll take that in. He doesn't take milk, does he?' Libby shook her head and reached for the sugar bowl. Keeping her face averted, she didn't see Ben's frown of concern as she handed it to him.

She heard his voice as he gave Guy the mug, and took another deep breath before turning to go back into the sitting room. They were still talking, Ben now sitting on a chair at the small table in the window, while Fran and Guy had moved to the cane sofa. Sidney had turned his back on them all in front of the empty fireplace, his ears flattened to his head. Libby sat in the armchair, grateful that Ben was now partially behind her. Out of the corner of her eye she could see his cream chinos and brown shoes and felt a shaft of pure desire which pooled somewhere below her middle. This, she felt, closing her eyes once more, was a surprise too far. You just do not go weak at the knees over a pair of legs. Not when you are in your mid-fifties.

'Lib?' Fran's voice brought her back to reality. She opened her eyes to see Fran handing her the glass she had left beside the sofa.

'Thanks,' she said, taking a grateful sip and trying not to empty the glass in one go.

Eventually, without Libby taking in a word of the conversation, Guy and Fran left. Libby saw them off, then came slowly back into the sitting room. Sidney had taken her place on the armchair and Ben was sitting on the sofa. She sat down gingerly on the chair vacated by Ben. He looked at her quizzically.

'Why are you sitting over there?'

'Er –' Libby cleared her throat.

'Are you scared to sit next to me?' Ben's voice was soft. Insinuating, even. Libby cleared her throat again.

'And something was wrong earlier, wasn't it?' he continued. 'When you went to get the coffee.'

She swallowed and took yet another deep breath.

'I can't do this,' she managed, and it came out strangled. 'I really can't.'

'Can't do what?' Ben stood up, came and took her hand and led her back to the sofa, where he handed her a new glass of red wine. She held it up and watched the ruby light glowing through it.

'Can't go back to how we were at the beginning.' Libby's throat felt raw and she took a healthy sip of wine.

Ben smiled wryly. 'We haven't. When we first got together we couldn't keep our hands off one another.'

'That was because of – because someone had been killed.'

'Life affirmation.' Ben nodded. 'Yes, we agreed. Then we drifted a bit –'

'Because of my doubts,' Libby said.

'It's always been your doubts, hasn't it?' said Ben gently. Libby nodded. 'And now?' he asked.

That lump was back. Libby didn't dare look at him. 'Erm,' she said.

Ben's arm slipped round her and he gave a squeeze. 'That's not much of an answer.'

'I love you,' said Libby, so quietly that he had to lean in to hear her. 'And I – ah – I –'

'Will marry me?'

Libby's jaw went slack. That wasn't what she intended to say. Ben smiled his wry smile again.

'OK; what, then?'

'I want you,' she whispered.

There was a short silence.

'Well, it's a start,' said Ben, gathering her into his arms.

Chapter Eight

A FRAGILE PEACE HELD the following morning. Libby wasn't stupid enough to believe that things were back to normal, even though for her, at least, it had been a magical night. Ben went back to The Manor without making any arrangements to see her later that day, and she felt more confused than ever.

She pottered about, trying to paint and failing. At last, she called Adam.

'Are you at Creekmarsh?' she asked.

'No.' Adam sounded resigned. 'Lewis is with the police, apparently, and Mog isn't sure that we'll even be paid for the work we've done already, so we're waiting to see.'

'So you've got no work?'

'Mog's got a couple of design jobs he can be getting on with, but I haven't.'

'Are you still staying with him?'

'Yes.' Adam was obviously uncomfortable. 'I gave up the flat in London. It didn't seem worth keeping it on. If I need to, I can always stay with Bel for the odd night.'

As Adam's older sister Belinda tended to be scathing about his lack of commitment to either girlfriends or career plans, Libby wasn't too sure about this.

'You'd better come home, Ad,' she said now. 'You can't stay with Mog indefinitely. His wife will get thoroughly fed up.'

'You sure, Ma? You haven't got much room – and what about Ben?'

Libby was getting sick of being asked about Ben.

'You can store stuff in the shed if necessary,' she said, 'and Ben's not here all the time so it won't bother him.'

'Ri-ight,' said Adam. 'Well, if you're sure. Will it be all right if I come over today? I can get the bus.'

'I'll come and pick you up if you like,' said Libby, wanting something to do. All right, she could clean the house, something she usually neglected until the dust forced itself to her notice, but right now she just wanted to get out and *do* something.

'Are you sure? It would be a help with all the stuff I've got.'

Libby's heart sank. Just how much stuff?

'That's fine, darling,' she said bravely. 'Tell me where Mog's house is and I'll be over in about an hour, if that's all right.'

'Leave it a bit longer, Ma, if you don't mind. I've got to pack.'

That, too, sounded ominous, thought Libby, as she switched off the phone. What had she let herself in for? Still, you always had to provide a home for your children, didn't you? And the deserting Derek and his pneumatic Marion were hardly the father and stepmother to do that.

Adam's stuff wasn't as bad as she had expected, extending merely to two large rucksacks and a couple of boxes. Mog helped get them into the boot, and Fiona, heavily pregnant, stood around smiling helpfully and holding her back. Libby thanked them both for looking after Adam, and Mog apologised gruffly for the unexpected lack of work. Adam said cheerfully it didn't matter, just to let him know when there was some.

'So what will you do now?' asked Libby, as they drove out of Canterbury. She saw Adam's shrug out of the corner of her eye, and set her mouth firmly. 'You've got to do something, Ad,' she said. 'You can't just sit around waiting for something to turn up.'

Adam sighed heavily. 'If you're going to start lecturing before I've moved in, Ma, then I've changed my mind.'

'For goodness' sake, Adam, don't be so pathetic,' she said with some asperity. 'I'm entitled to say anything I want to you, you're my son.'

Adam lapsed into a silence that lasted almost until the bend in the road took them into Steeple Martin.

'Actually, I was going to do some work for Lewis,' he said in a small voice. 'But it looks as though that's not on, now.'

Libby risked a quick look at his profile, while she waited to turn right into Allhallow's Lane.

'Why? Just because he's being interviewed by the police? That doesn't mean he has anything to do with this body, or the murder of Tony West.'

'But his career'll be down the tubes, won't it?' Adam sighed again.

Libby pulled the car over onto the bit of green opposite her cottage. 'I don't know, and neither do you. Just wait until you hear from him.'

'Or you do,' said Adam, getting out and going to open the boot. 'I bet he calls you.'

The answerphone light was winking when they struggled through the narrow door of number 17.

'Go on,' said Adam, nodding towards it. 'I bet it's him.'

And he was right.

'Could you give me a call, Libby? Sorry to bother you. And tell Ad I'm sorry.'

Adam pulled down the corners of his mouth. 'Hmm,' he said, before lugging one of the rucksacks upstairs.

Libby went and put the kettle on and dug around for biscuits. Somewhere she had some of the home-made ginger ones Belinda had taught her to make, containing lethal amounts of golden syrup. When Adam came back down he immediately took two from the plate, his good temper restored.

'Have you phoned him yet?' he asked.

'No, I thought I'd wait until you were here,' said Libby. 'Do you want to take the tea into the garden? It's a lovely day.'

When they were settled at the slightly unstable table under the cherry tree, Libby keyed in Lewis's number. He answered almost instantly.

'Libby, I'm sorry about this,' he said, his voice sounding strained.

'Where are you?'

'At home. They let me go.' He gave a short laugh. 'I suppose you heard?'

'About Tony West? Yes.'

'Tony? I didn't mean –' he paused. 'I meant about me being

questioned by the police.'

'I heard about that, too, Lewis, but it didn't take much detective ability to put two and two together when Mr West's death was announced on the radio yesterday.'

'Yeah. Well, that's why they wanted me, see. They know all about it. More'n I do, really. How's Ad?'

'He's fine.' Libby pointed to the phone and raised her eyebrows at Adam. He shook his head. 'It's a pity they've had to stop work on the garden, that's all.'

'They've what?' Lewis's voice rose sharply. 'Why?'

'Well,' said Libby, choosing her words carefully, 'they couldn't work in the wood, and there was no guarantee that any further work would be called for, or …'

'Paid for?' Lewis was a shrewd East End boy. 'I know, I know. Well, you tell 'em, there'll be a cheque in the post tonight – or, if Mog gives me his bank details, I'll transfer the money straight away. And yes, I do want them to carry on. I want that parterre garden finished this summer, and I know it'll take time.'

'But what about the house? Is it all kosher?'

'It turns out, yes. Me owning it, anyway. Look, I'll tell you all about it. Can I buy you a drink or summat?'

Libby flashed another glance at Adam. 'Come over here for supper,' she said. 'Ad will be here. Anything you don't eat?'

'Come on, Ad, he's going to keep you on,' she said after switching off, watching Adam's mutinous face. 'And pay you up to date.'

Adam's face cleared. 'What about the police?'

'I doubt if you'll be able to go back into the wood yet, but he wants you to finish the parterre.' She smiled. 'It turns out the house *is* legally his after all. At least, I think that's what he meant. And could you ask Mog to give him a ring because he'd like to pay the money straight into the account.'

A little later, leaving Adam to sort out the guest room and pack things away in the ancient shed, where he grumbled about damp and mould, she went into the village to see Bob the butcher, and then to Ahmed and Ali's eight-til-late. Standing on the pavement between the two shops, she frowned. Should she ask Ben? Check whether he intended to come tonight? Conscious of a slight rolling in her stomach and an accelerated heart rate, she pulled out her mobile and pressed speed dial. It went straight to voicemail and she swore under her breath.

As she plodded back up Allhallow's Lane, her mobile rang.

'Hi, Lib. You called?'

'Did you not listen to the message?'

'No – I just saw one missed call and it was you. What's up?'

Libby explained, slowing to a halt under the lilac tree. The scent was calming.

'Right,' said Ben. 'So basically, this Lewis wants to talk to you about the murder and the house? And Adam's moved in?'

Libby's heart sank. 'Only temporarily,' she said. 'Just until things are sorted out.'

'Well, you won't want me there this evening, that's for sure,' he said. 'Mum'll be happy to see a bit more of me. I'll call you tomorrow.'

'OK. Ben –'

'Speak to you then. Bye, love.'

Libby was left holding a dead mobile to her ear and feeling as though she might burst into tears. Again.

Lewis had said he would arrive around seven, and by 6.30 Libby had all the food ready and waiting and she and Adam were decently clothed and watching the local news together. There was a brief mention of the Creekmarsh case, but it had obviously been relegated to the 'other news'. Adam reached for the remote and switched off.

'So tell me what's up with Ben,' he said. 'Why isn't he coming tonight?'

Libby sighed and explained to the best of her ability, waiting for the inevitable 'I told you so'. It didn't come.

'He's a prat, Ma,' said Adam, getting up to give her a hug. 'Nice bloke and all that, but a prat.'

'I thought you were on his side?'

'In a way, but he's using emotional blackmail now, and that's wrong.'

Libby thought about it. 'I suppose he is,' she said. 'How horrible. I'd never have thought it of him.'

'I don't suppose he sees it like that,' said Adam, quite the wise young judge. 'He just doesn't want to lay up any more grief for himself if you're not going to commit to a life together. Sensible, in a way.' He turned away and poured drinks for them both.

Libby looked at him in horror. 'Now you've completely confused me,' she said. 'He's a blackmailing prat, but a sensible one?'

He handed her a glass with a cheerful smile. 'Yup. Cheers!'

The knocker rapped loudly.

'That's Lewis,' said Adam. 'I'll get it.'

This evening Lewis Osbourne-Walker was far from the ebullient young presenter of television's most popular home design programme. His spiky blonde hair drooped, and his cherubic face had a distinct lack of the angelic about it.

'Sit down,' said Adam, indicating the chair. 'Drink?'

'Got any water?'

'Plenty in the tap,' said Adam.

Lewis grimaced. 'Yeah. Sorry. Prat, aren't I?'

Libby and Adam exchanged amused glances.

''Course not.' Adam made a face. 'Tap water – juice?' He cocked an eyebrow at his mother.

'Apple juice,' said Libby, 'or tonic water?'

'Tonic water'd be nice,' said Lewis, brightening.

When they were seated, Lewis leant back in the armchair and closed his eyes. Libby and Adam exchanged another significant look.

'Come on, then, Lewis, tell us all about it,' said Adam. 'What's been going on?'

Chapter Nine

LEWIS OPENED HIS EYES and looked nervously from Adam to Libby.

'They found Tony yesterday morning.' He took a sip of his tonic water. 'In his bedroom.'

'Yes, it said that on television,' said Libby.

'And my prints were all over it.'

Libby and Adam looked at one another.

'How did they have your prints?'

'They asked for them yesterday.'

'Tell us from the beginning, Lewis. What happened when you went to talk to the police yesterday morning?' said Libby.

He sighed. 'They asked who I bought the house from, and in the end, of course, I had to tell 'em, didn't I? I said Tony. Because I don't actually know *who* owned it. So this other copper who was with Big Bertha leant over, like, and whispered in her ear. Then she went out of the room.'

'And?' prompted Adam.

'Then she came back and asked me how well I'd known Tony.' Lewis reddened. 'So I said he was a mate, like. Then they asked me if they could take fingerprints. I couldn't say no, could I?'

'And after that?'

'They went on questioning me. They gave me some lunch and then this bloke from London appeared and he and Big Bertha interviewed me together. Then, o' course, they tells me about Tony and my prints being there. And that Tony didn't hold title – or something – to my house. It belonged to some famous bloke. Well, I knew that. Not that he was famous, though.'

'Who was the famous bloke?' asked Adam.

'Some actor. Can't remember, although they did tell me.'

'And they confirmed that he was missing, as Tony told you?' said Libby.

'Yeah. They think the skeleton is him.'

'So did you,' said Libby.

'Yeah, well, now they can do whatsit – DNA – on him. It.'

'At least you couldn't have killed him,' said Adam.

'They don't know that,' said Lewis gloomily. 'They reckon I must've known him and killed him and then tried to buy the house so no one would ever find him.'

'Ah,' said Adam.

'How did you first find the house?' asked Libby.

'Tony brought me down here once,' said Lewis. 'Took me into the house. Said it belonged to a friend who'd asked him to look after it. He wanted some details copied for the Hampstead place, he said, but I don't believe it. He wanted to get me down here. He knew I'd fall for the place, being a common cockney bloke with whatsits of grandeur.'

'Delusions,' said Adam helpfully.

'That's them,' Lewis nodded.

'So how, if the house still belonged to this missing person, did Tony manage to sell it to you legally?'

'He had something to show he could do it. Some legal thing. Power something.'

'Power of attorney?' Libby's eyebrows shot up. 'Why?'

'How do I know?' said Lewis pettishly. 'He just did.'

'Was he a relative?'

'Look, Lib,' said Lewis, blowing out a sigh, 'I don't know any more than they told me, which wasn't much, except to tell me I could go back home and it was mine.'

'But you're still a suspect?'

'I'm not sure. Wouldn't they have made me pay bail if I was?'

'I don't know.' Libby looked at Adam. 'Who would know?'

'That Ian person,' suggested Adam promptly. 'He'd know. He'd know about Big Bertha, too.'

'I can't ring Ian!' said Libby, scandalised.

'Fran could.'

Libby chewed her lip. 'All right,' she said. 'I'll call her after we've eaten.' She looked at Lewis. 'So what happens next?'

'They said to keep in touch and let them know my movements. Can't leave the country, that sort of thing.'

'Well, they have got a potential double murder on their hands,' said Libby. 'You can't blame them.'

'If they really thought you could have been behind the skeleton's burial, why didn't they tell you this missing person's name?' said Adam.

'They did, I told you. I just can't remember.'

'Honestly, Lewis. How can you *not* remember?'

'It was all so muddled. And I was bloody scared.' He looked belligerent.

'So would I have been, Ma,' said Adam.

'I know, but that name is really important.' Libby sighed and stood up. 'Come on, let's eat. You don't mind the kitchen, do you, Lewis?'

They managed to stay off the subject of the murders while they ate, and Lewis professed Libby to be almost as good a cook as Katie. Adam grinned and told him of all the disasters that had happened in Libby's kitchen over the years. 'She's only just got the hang of it,' he laughed.

'Cheek,' she said, good-humouredly. 'Actually, Lewis, I was going to ask you if you like vegetarian food?'

Lewis looked down at his plate, surprised. 'Yeah, but this wasn't –'

'No, no, it's just that our friends Harry and Peter have a veggie restaurant in the village called The Pink Geranium. Harry's the chef. They do a lot of Mexican food. I thought you might like to try it sometime.'

His face brightened. 'They the mates you told me about, Ad?'

Adam nodded. 'Nice blokes. Pete's some kind of hotshot journalist so he's often in London, but he works from home mostly.'

'Journalist?' Lewis looked wary.

'Not that sort,' comforted Libby. 'Political and features,

mainly. No sludge gathering.'

'Oh. Well, I'd love to give it a try if you'll come with me.' He looked at them both like a particularly soulful spaniel.

''Course we will,' grinned Adam.

'Come on then,' said Libby. 'If you've finished we'll go into the sitting room and I'll call Fran.'

Fran, as Libby had predicted, was not happy about calling Ian. Part of it was embarrassment, Ian having been a former suitor who lost out to Guy, and the other part was Fran's unwillingness to butt into the investigation.

'All right,' huffed Libby, eventually. 'Give me his number and I'll call him. I'll tell him about the wedding, which will be much better than him just finding out.'

Fran demurred, but in the end decided to give Libby the number. 'I feel a terrible coward not facing up to telling him, but there's no real reason why I should, is there?'

'None at all, but I can be concerned about him. I can even sympathise and hint about the problems it's causing with Ben,' said Libby.

'Oh, *Libby*!' Fran almost shouted. 'Don't you dare. If you're going to say that sort of thing I shan't give you the number.'

'Sorry, sorry.' Libby gave the phone a shamefaced look. 'I didn't mean it.'

'All right. But promise you won't.'

'Promise.'

'OK. I'll text you the number when I've found it.'

'Lovely, thanks –' said Libby, but Fran had gone.

'You do put your foot in it sometimes, Ma,' said Adam.

Libby sighed. 'I know. I don't think before I speak half the time, do I?'

The number came through very soon afterwards and after pouring herself a large glass of wine, Libby took a deep breath and punched it in.

'Connell,' said a gruff voice on the first ring.

'Ian?' said Libby. 'I'm sorry to disturb you. It's Libby Sarjeant. Are you in the middle of something?'

'Libby?' Ian sounded surprised. 'No – well, I'm in the middle of paperwork and I should have gone home hours ago.

What's up?'

'Ah – well,' said Libby, not sure how to begin now the moment had come. 'Had you heard about Fran?'

'She and Guy are getting married, I understand.' Ian's voice didn't change. He couldn't be that upset.

'Yes. I thought you might not know,' said Libby sheepishly.

'So you thought you'd enlighten me? Very kind.' He sounded amused. 'But not necessary. Things get around very quickly in a small place like Nethergate.'

'Then you'll know all about the Creekmarsh business?'

There was a pause. 'Of course. Libby, what's this about? You didn't ring up about Fran at all, did you? You know I can't tell you anything.'

'I know, I know,' said Libby, 'just, I wanted to know, as they've let my friend Lewis go, is he bailed? They didn't ask him for any money.'

'Your *friend*?' said Ian. Libby saw Lewis and Adam flinch as the voice thundered out of the receiver. 'What the hell are you getting into now?'

'Nothing, Ian, honestly,' said Libby, crossing her eyes at the boys. Lewis giggled. 'Lewis is actually a friend of Adam's. My son? He's been doing the –'

'Garden, yes, I know. He and his friend found the skeleton. I didn't connect the two names, more fool me. There can't be many Sarjeants with a J around.'

'Right.' Libby let out a breath. 'So, you see, I've got a legitimate interest.'

'And you shouldn't be talking to me about it,' said Ian, 'but as it happens, your friend hasn't been bailed. They'll want to speak to him again, probably several times, but once they found that the sale of Creekmarsh was legitimate –'

'Was it power of attorney?' interrupted Libby.

'Yes.' Ian was beginning to sound even more irritated.

'Right. Oh, just one more thing,' said Libby, ignoring the spluttering at the other end, 'who was the actor West had power of attorney for?'

'Oh, you don't know that, eh? Antennae slipping are they? Surely your friend Lewis knows?'

'He says he can't remember.'

'Oh, come now, Libby. I don't believe that for a second. Now you just tell him to do exactly as Superintendent Bertram tells him and not to go investigating on his own. Or rather,' said Ian, taking a deep breath, 'getting you to do it for him.'

'OK, Ian, I get the picture. And thanks.'

She looked over at the boys and sipped her wine. 'He wouldn't tell me. Said he didn't believe you couldn't remember, but that you aren't on bail. And warned me off.'

'I gathered that,' said Adam. 'You can't blame the poor bloke.'

'And I found out that Big Bertha's name is really Bertram.'

Adam shrugged. 'Well, you can see how she got the name, can't you?'

'Anyway, Lewis, you're a free man. And the missing actor –'

'Is Gerald Shepherd. I've just remembered.'

Chapter Ten

'GERALD SHEPHERD?' REPEATED LIBBY.

'Who's he?' asked Adam.

'He was huge in the seventies and eighties,' said Libby. 'You'd know his face. Mainly television and films, but he did quite a bit on stage, too. He had that detective show *Flanagan's Army*.'

'Oh, him! Wow. He really is famous.'

'Was.' Libby turned to Lewis. 'Why had you forgotten?'

'Honestly, Lib, I don't know. The name went over my head. I know now, of course, but at the time it didn't mean anything. I was just panicked.'

'I can't see how it didn't mean anything,' said Libby, frowning at him. 'Surely you remember the scandal a few years ago?'

'Scandal? No.' Lewis shook his head and Adam looked interested.

'He disappeared with his daughter-in-law and has never been seen since.'

'Bloody hell,' said Adam. 'But he must have been ancient.'

'In his sixties I should imagine. The daughter-in-law, or maybe she was the son's girlfriend, was in her twenties as I remember.'

'Dirty old man,' said Lewis, wrinkling his nose. 'No, I don't remember, sorry.'

'I think drugs were involved somewhere along the line, too,' said Libby. 'I'll look it up tomorrow.'

'Look it up where?' said Adam.

'Google it, of course,' said Libby loftily.

'Well, where does this leave us?' asked Lewis. 'What

happens next?'

'You wait for more questions from the police, and I'll look up the background. There isn't anything else we can do. As I said, I've been warned off.'

'So if the skeleton is this Gerald Shepherd, that means the daughter-in-law chopped him?'

'Possibly, but I don't see how they'll ever prove that, even if they could find the daughter-in-law. And I don't see what it's got to do with Tony West, either.'

'Perhaps he was her father?' suggested Adam.

'That's an idea,' said Libby.

Lewis shook his head. 'Didn't have any children. His wife didn't want any, he said.'

'That's a point,' said Libby. 'Where was his wife when he was found?'

'New York,' said Lewis. 'Shopping.'

'Ah.'

A silence fell.

'He still could have been her father,' said Adam. 'By someone else.'

'Yes, he could.' Libby looked thoughtfully at her son. 'But it still doesn't explain why he had the power of attorney. And isn't there something about registering it with the Office of the Public Guardian?'

'The what?' said Adam and Lewis together.

'I may have got it wrong,' said Libby, frowning, 'but I'm pretty sure the old Enduring Power of Attorney has been replaced by something else, so presumably the police will be looking at the date it was registered. And if Gerald Shepherd couldn't be found, was it legal to sell his house?'

'God, I don't know,' said Lewis. 'All I know is the police said Creekmarsh is mine. If Tony had no right to sell it surely the solicitor would have found out?'

'Yes, but you said you didn't have one. So Tony's solicitor could have been bent and glossed over it. Presumably the police have checked the Land Registry or they wouldn't have said it was legally yours.'

'Doesn't it sound,' said Adam slowly, 'as if someone was

trying to offload Creekmarsh?'

Lewis and Libby looked at him in surprise.

'Of course!' said Libby. 'That's what it is, Lewis! Either Tony West or Gerald Shepherd or both were trying to get rid of the place because they didn't want to be associated with it and anything that might be found there.'

'Right!' Lewis high-fived Adam. 'You're brilliant, mate.'

'Of course.' Adam beamed at them both.

'Well, we still need to find the connection between West and Shepherd,' said Libby. 'I'll get on to it in the morning.'

'Hey, hey, Ma.' Adam stood up. 'No investigating. Remember? You said it yourself.'

'It's only for interest's sake,' said Libby, opening her eyes wide at him. 'And Lewis wants to know.'

'But you told him not five minutes ago that all he could do was wait. And what did that Connell tell you? Keep out.'

'As I said,' said Libby, looking uncomfortable, 'it's just for interest.'

'Hmm,' Adam said and left the room in search of beer.

'Will you tell the police all this, Libby?' asked Lewis in a low voice.

'It's not my place and they wouldn't listen anyway,' said Libby. 'Besides, you can bet that if we've pieced all this together they certainly have. They'll have known all about the sale of the property the minute you mentioned not having been here long, and with their resources everything else would have been laid on a plate for them. I strongly suspect West's solicitor of being bent. I should think he's going to have a lot of explaining to do.'

Lewis was frowning. 'You said daughter-in-law. So what about the son? There must have been one.'

'Yes.' Libby stared at him. 'Of course. I don't remember anything about the son. I don't remember anything about the daughter-in-law, come to that, just that it was she he ran off with. I'll find out tomorrow.'

Lewis looked uncertainly towards the kitchen door. 'Won't Adam be cross?'

Libby laughed. 'He's my youngest son, Lewis, not my

keeper.'

'No, course.' He shrugged. 'He seems very grown up to me.'

'Not to me, he doesn't,' muttered Libby.

Just then the wonder boy strolled in carrying a bottle of beer. 'Have you been talking about me?' he asked with a grin.

'Yes,' said Libby, 'but don't get bigheaded about it.'

'I think I'd better get back,' said Lewis standing up. 'Katie's out there all on her own, and it can be a bit – well –'

'Creepy,' supplied Adam.

'Only because of what's been happening.' Lewis was defensive. 'Thanks for a great meal, Libby. If you pick a date I'll treat you both at your mate Harry's next.'

'You're on,' said Adam, shaking his hand. 'And we'll be back at work soon, will we?'

'Yeah. Mog said he'd pick you up on the way tomorrow. Didn't he ring you?'

'No. I'll give him a ring in a minute.' Adam opened the front door and Sidney shot out.

'Is he all right in the street?' said Lewis anxiously, looking back at Libby.

'Not much of a street, really, is it?' she said. 'He's fine. He'll be over the back and across to the wood in no time.'

When Lewis had gone, Libby went through to clear up in the kitchen while Adam called Mog. She thought she heard raised voices, but when Adam joined her he had a smile on his face.

'Now I know why Mog didn't ring,' he said. 'Fiona's had the baby.'

'No!' Libby sat down on the edge of the table. 'I didn't think she was due yet. What was it?'

'A boy, and no, it wasn't due for a couple of weeks, but it's all great. Started while we were loading up the car, actually, but she didn't want to say.'

'Aah!' Libby gave her son a hug. 'So now what will you do?'

'Can I get a bus to Creekmarsh from here? Mog said I could make a start on the parterre.'

'Do you know how? And it's Saturday tomorrow. Are you supposed to be going in to work?'

'Ma! 'Course I know what to do. We're preparing the ground

first, anyway. And I want to go in. So how do I get there?'

'You could borrow Romeo. I expect I could ask Ben for a lift if I was stuck,' said Libby doubtfully.

'Thanks, Ma,' said Adam, giving her a hug. 'You're a gem.'

'I know,' sighed Libby. 'A positive jewel.'

The following morning, after Adam had left in high spirits, Libby tidied up the cottage and booted up the computer. Within minutes she was reading the reports of Gerald Shepherd's disappearance.

After the heyday of the seventies and eighties, it seemed, Shepherd had almost fallen into obscurity. A handsome man with distinguished grey hair, he had suddenly reappeared in a political thriller, *Collateral Damage*, in the mid-nineties. His subsequent celebrity had affected his family adversely, however, his wife leaving with a younger actor to go to America, and his son turning to drugs. The son had, however, made an effort to turn his life around and became something of a celebrity himself, attracting a very attractive young model turned singer, whom he married after a whirlwind romance played out very much in the public eye. All three Shepherds remained popular, although less noticeable, until the son, Kenneth, was recruited for a reality show called *Dungeon Trial*. Libby's mental ears pricked up.

It was while he was incarcerated in the fastness of the show's castle that it became apparent that Gerald and Cynthia, known as Cindy, were closer than they should have been. When Kenneth was released from his dungeon, they had vanished. It was a nine-days' wonder in the media, then the next scandal hit the red tops and the next outrage hit the broadsheets and the whole debacle disappeared from view.

Libby sat back and frowned. So where was Kenneth now? And why on earth hadn't he had the power of attorney?

She typed Kenneth Shepherd into the search engine, but the only results were those which she had already seen. She tried Cindy Shepherd, but only came up with the girl's maiden name, which she had kept for career purposes after her marriage. Trying Cindy Dale didn't come up with much either, just lists of her appearances as first a glamour model, then a rather unsuccessful singer with an equally unsuccessful girl band.

Libby typed Dungeon Trial into the search engine. The reality show had started at around the same time as most of the others of the same type, but had foundered earlier. And to her disappointment, the production company behind it wasn't even the same one that produced *Housey Housey*, so the hope of a possible link to Tony West was demolished. She sighed and sat back in her chair. What she needed was a good long chat with a friendly policeman.

Her eye fell on a packet on the arm of the sofa. She let out an exasperated sigh. After all the trouble she'd gone to making him sandwiches, Adam had left them behind. Hoping, no doubt, to cadge some more of Katie's cooking. Ah well, she thought, switching off the computer and standing up, it wouldn't hurt to pop them over to Creekmarsh, would it?

'Oh, bugger,' she said out loud. Adam had gone off with the car. She tried to convince herself it was emergency enough to call Ben and ask for a lift, and although a week ago she would have done so, now she thought better of it.

However, she could call Lewis and tell him. Why wasn't she calling Adam, she wondered, as she keyed in Lewis's number? They were his sandwiches.

'Do you want me to call him?' Lewis asked when she'd told him.

'No, it's OK, I can't get out there because he's got the car. I just wondered if there was any chance Katie could give him a spot of lunch. Sorry to be a nuisance.'

'You're not, don't be daft. Problem is, Katie's not here today, so I'm fending for myself as well. Tell you what, how about I come and pick you up and bring you over here? You can make me some sandwiches, too!'

'Cheek!' Libby laughed. 'It seems a convoluted way round the problem, but OK. I'll bring a picnic.'

'Great, I'll be there about half eleven.' Lewis hesitated. 'D'you look up that stuff?'

'About Shepherd? Yes. I'll tell you when I see you. Or you could Google him yourself.'

'Dunno what I'd be looking for.' Lewis sounded

uncomfortable. 'Look, I'll see you later.'

Libby smiled at the receiver and went back into the kitchen to make more sandwiches. If anyone had asked her, she couldn't have said why she wanted to go back to Creekmarsh; all she knew was something was drawing her there. She paused, loaf in one hand, knife in the other. She wasn't getting like Fran, was she? A shiver went through her and she shook herself.

But when she'd packed up her picnic and put on some make-up, she called Fran while she waited for Lewis and told her everything that had been happening.

'Thoughts?' she said when she finished and Fran had been silent for a long time.

'It's all a bit odd.' Libby heard her take a breath. 'I know I said I didn't want to get involved, but I suppose I couldn't come out and have a look, could I?'

'Why not?' Libby was conscious of relief. 'Come out today. I'm going for lunch.' She explained about the sandwiches.

'I'll come over about one, then, shall I? Then I can drive you home.'

'Brilliant. See you later.'

Lewis was delighted to hear of Fran's visit and promised a guided tour of the house and grounds.

'I haven't had that,' said Libby indignantly.

'For both of you, of course,' said Lewis in surprise. 'I was going to take you round today, anyway. The police seem to have gone now.'

Libby nodded absently and stared out of the windscreen. They were just passing the turning for Steeple Mount, and Libby could see the woods on the hill that masked Tyne Hall and its chapel. She shivered slightly.

'What's up?' Lewis shot her a quick look. 'You're not cold?'

'No.' Libby pointed. 'That's where they used to hold Black Masses and where someone we knew was murdered. There's a chapel behind those woods.'

'Wow. You do see life round here, don't you? What happened?'

'Fran knows more about it than I do,' said Libby. 'Her aunt was murdered.'

'Blimey,' said Lewis, looking at her again and swerving.

'Eyes on the road, Mr Osbourne-Walker,' said Libby, who returned her attention to the scenery while she told him of her findings on the Internet.

Adam met them as they turned into the drive. Lewis opened the window.

'Sorry, mate, nothing I could do about it,' said Adam.

'About what?'

'That bloody Big Bertha. She's in there now. With a search warrant.'

Chapter Eleven

Wɪᴛʜᴏᴜᴛ ᴀɴᴏᴛʜᴇʀ ᴡᴏʀᴅ, Lᴇᴡɪs accelerated up the drive and came to a gravel-spraying halt. He disappeared inside leaving the car door open and Libby to her own devices. She climbed out slowly, clutching her basket as Adam caught up.

'What's going on, Ad?'

'I don't know, Ma. They turned up about twenty minutes ago. I tried Lewis's mobile, but it was switched off.'

'He was driving, that's why,' said Libby, remembering seeing the phone on the dashboard.

'Yeah, I know. Anyway, I tried to stop them, but they had a warrant. That woman is a nightmare.'

'But why? They don't think Lewis has any connection to the skeleton or Tony West's death.'

'No, but Tony West sold this place to Lewis. They must think there are traces of him or what's-his-name –'

'Gerald Shepherd,' put in Libby.

'Yeah, him.'

'But they must have already searched the house,' said Libby, frowning. 'When the skeleton was found.'

'I don't think they did,' said Adam, shaking his head. 'Remember, at first they didn't think it was a recent body.'

'Oh, yes, that reminds me, how old do they think it is?'

'I don't know. When did Shepherd and the girl go missing?'

'About three years ago, I think,' said Libby. 'You still think it's him?'

'It would make sense, wouldn't it?'

'But they haven't released anything about it?' said Libby.

'Don't think so,' said Adam.

'What shall we do with this?' asked Libby, waving her

basket at him. 'I suppose we can't take it into the kitchen?'

'Don't see why not,' said Adam, grinning. 'Give us a chance to see what's going on.'

Libby eyed him warily. 'All right. Come on, then,' she said, indicating that he should take the lead.

There appeared to be no one anywhere downstairs. Murmured voices could be heard from the solar, where Libby guessed Lewis was having to answer more of Superintendent Bertram's questions. She unloaded sandwiches, cheese and fruit onto the kitchen table, and sat down.

'I suppose now we wait,' she said.

'Yeah.' Adam looked up at the ceiling. 'Can't really go poking upstairs, can we? And I ought to get back to the parterre. D'you want to come and see it?'

'Not right now,' said Libby. 'I'll wait for Lewis.'

And Big Bertha, she added mentally. Why she wanted to see her she couldn't have said, but then again, she had curiosity programmed into her character, so thought her nearest and dearest, those very same nearest and dearest who fondly referred to her as 'the bull in the china shop'.

She looked towards the kitchen door and felt her heart jump in shock. There was someone standing there.

The woman surveyed Libby as dispassionately as she might a cabbage on a vegetable stall. 'And you are?' she said in a voice like a cheese grater.

'Libby Sarjeant,' Libby said, and cleared her throat. 'With a J. Who are you?'

The woman looked startled, as if she wasn't used to being questioned. Or going unrecognised. Libby took in the slender, petite stature, the bright blonde hair, over made-up face and the too-short skirt of the black suit.

'Superintendent Bertram, CID.' The woman snapped it out and Libby's mouth dropped open. *This* was Big Bertha? 'What are you doing here?' Bertram walked to the table and looked down at Libby from eyes heavy with eyeliner.

'I beg your pardon?' Libby pushed back her chair and stood up, all of five feet three inches, but able now to tower over Superintendent Bertram, who scowled up at her.

'This is a crime scene.'

'I thought the gardens were a crime scene, not the house.' Libby wasn't going to back down.

'Why are you here?' Bertram didn't comment on Libby's assumption, which made her quite sure she was right.

'I'm a friend of Lewis Osbourne-Walker's. He brought me here ten minutes ago when we learnt from my son that you had broken into his home while he was absent.'

Bertram looked furious. 'We did not "break in". We had a search warrant.'

'Why?'

This time Bertram looked simply astonished. Before she could recover, Libby sat down again, happy to have had the upper hand, if only for a few minutes.

'Ms Sarjeant,' began Bertram.

'Mrs,' Libby corrected, and smiled. Bertram heaved a sigh.

'Very well, Mrs,' she said. 'A search has to be carried out thoroughly on these premises and no unauthorised persons are allowed here.'

'Authorised by whom?' asked Libby pleasantly. 'After all, it still belongs to Mr Osbourne-Walker. I know you've checked the legality of that, and as far as I can ascertain he isn't a suspect. I have his authority to be here, and I don't believe I need yours.'

Bertram's eyes narrowed. 'I know who you are,' she said slowly.

'Oh?' said Libby, still smiling, but with a sinking feeling.

'I believe you know DCI Murray?' Bertram smiled; at least Libby thought it was a smile. 'And DI Connell.'

'Yes.' Libby nodded, still pleasantly.

Bertram placed her hands on the table and leant forward. 'Let me warn you, Mrs Sarjeant. You will not be allowed to get in my way or hamper this investigation, with or without psychic intervention.'

'Oh, you've got that quite wrong,' said Libby, keeping the smile fixed with difficulty. 'I don't do psychic intervention.'

Bertram straightened up, obviously puzzled.

'No,' said a voice behind her, 'that's me.'

Bertram whirled and Libby stood up again.

'Fran!' she said.

Fran came into the room and allowed herself to be hugged by Libby, while a scowling Bertram looked on.

'This is Mrs Castle,' said Libby. 'She knows DCI Murray and DI Connell, too.'

Bertram bit her lip, still scowling. She looked from Libby to Fran and back again.

'Just keep out of my way,' she said, and stalked to the door brushing rudely against Fran as she went.

'Wow,' said Fran. 'Who's she?'

Libby explained, leading the way back to the table. 'Would you like tea?' she asked. 'I think I know where everything is.'

'Thanks,' said Fran looking round the huge kitchen. 'So this is Creekmarsh.'

Libby switched on the kettle and went to find milk in the stylish silver refrigerator.

'This is Creekmarsh,' she confirmed. 'What do you think?'

Fran was silent for a moment. 'I'm not sure,' she said finally. 'There's a good deal of unhappiness here, isn't there?'

'Do you mean current unhappiness? Or sort of still-in-the-walls unhappiness?'

'Both.' Fran was looking at the ceiling. 'How old was Tony West?'

'Eh?' Now it was Libby's turn to look startled. 'No idea. Why?'

'Oh, nothing.' Fran shook her head. 'Has that woman finished with your friend Lewis?'

'I don't know. She must have if she came down here. I suppose he's upstairs overseeing the search.'

'They do miss things, you know,' said Fran, remembering her own visit to a murder scene eighteen months ago where she had uncovered evidence which at the time seemed irrelevant, but had eventually led to the solution of that and a previous murder.

'You won't be able to go over this place,' warned Libby. 'You saw what she was like.'

'I know,' said Fran serenely, 'but it's not being protected as a crime scene, is it? So Lewis will let me have a look.'

'When they've gone, yes,' said Libby. 'I do hope they clean up after themselves.'

'Oh, I expect they will. It isn't as if they can just walk away with crime scene tape across the door, is it? Lewis is still living here.'

'Will he much longer, do you think?' mused Libby, as they heard hurrying steps on the stairs.

'Lewis.' Libby went to him and put a hand on his arm. 'Come and meet Fran Castle.'

Fran stood up and shook hands. Lewis looked grey and dishevelled.

'What have they been doing to you?' asked Libby, handing a mug to Fran, then pouring one, unasked, for Lewis.

'Oh, nothing. They're just turning over everything.' Lewis pushed his hands through his spiky hair, which accounted for the dishevelment, thought Libby. 'And that fucking woman –' he stopped and looked guiltily at Fran. Not at her, Libby noticed. 'Sorry,' he went on. 'But she's turning me into a wreck.'

'Not a pleasant lady,' agreed Libby. 'We've just met her.'

'You have? Both of you?'

'I only saw her briefly.' Fran gave Libby an amused look. 'I think she was getting the worst of an encounter with Mrs Sarjeant here.'

'Ri-ight.' Lewis nodded. 'That's why she was in an even fouler temper when she came back into the room.'

'She didn't tell you she'd met me?' Libby grinned. 'I thought she was impressed.'

'I think she was.' Lewis picked up his mug and grinned back. 'Cow.' He leant forward and poked at the covered plate in front of him. 'Is this sandwiches?'

'It is. Shall I call Adam?'

'I'll do it.' Lewis stood up. 'I know where he is, you don't.'

He strode out of the kitchen. Fran watched.

'He isn't quite what I expected,' she said.

'No. He's not as openly camp as you might expect, and he's a genuinely nice bloke,' said Libby. 'And at the moment he's feeling really bad because he thinks he's been let down by Tony West, which he has, and now he feels guilty for thinking that because West's dead.'

'Nothing to do with him, though,' said Fran.

'Really?'

Fran turned to look at her friend. 'As far as I can see,' she said, 'but I'd like a look over the house and grounds when the police have gone, all the same.'

When all the sandwiches, fruit and cheese, supplemented by a very good white wine produced by Lewis, had gone Libby loaded the dishwasher, packed her own things in her basket and suggested they start the tour with a visit to the parterre, where Adam had vanished the minute the clearing up began.

Lewis led the way across the front lawn, which Libby hadn't seen before. She was pleasantly surprised at the open aspect, rather than the rather gloomy side approach with which she was more familiar. At the side, an arched door was set in an old wall. Beyond this worked Adam, singing along to his MP3 player. Libby and Fran watched him playing with small sticks and pieces of string while Lewis went and stood in front of him to catch his attention.

Adam explained the thinking behind the restoration of the parterre, and showed them where he and Mog had excavated the original outlines of the garden. Fran wandered away.

'Can we see the wood now?' she asked, when Adam had finished his explanation.

Lewis and Adam exchanged glances.

'I suppose so,' said Lewis, 'although there's still tape over the path.'

'I'd just like to see where Adam found the bones. Not close up. Just in general.' Fran turned and began to leave the garden, going, Libby noticed, in the right direction.

'OK.' Lewis sighed, patted Adam on the shoulder and followed.

'Why did she come?' Adam asked Libby with a frown.

'She felt something I think. I told you yesterday. She's intrigued despite herself. And if it helps Lewis, what harm is there?'

'None,' said Adam, 'but I just don't want you getting involved and Ben blaming me for it.'

'Not much chance of that,' said Libby, and ignoring Adam's enquiring gaze, she set off to follow Lewis and Fran.

She caught them up at the other side of the house by the smaller lawn which led to the wood. She could see the blue and white tape fluttering in the slight breeze and looked round nervously for signs that the police were still there.

'No,' said Lewis. 'Madam's gone, taking her bully boys with her. They didn't find anything.'

Fran nodded and went on towards the wood. Libby put a restraining hand on Lewis's arm and watched. After a moment, Fran stepped neatly round the last section of tape and disappeared.

'Come on,' said Lewis, 'we'd better see what she's up to.'

'Oh, she'll be fine,' said Libby. 'She won't disturb anything.' But she followed Lewis into the wood, where they found Fran staring thoughtfully at the ground a little way beyond the earth displaced by Adam's digger.

'This area's been searched, hasn't it?' she asked Lewis.

'They did a fingertip search through the whole wood.'

'But they didn't dig any more?'

'All round the site of the skeleton, yes.' Lewis waved his arm towards the swathe of disturbed ground. Fran nodded.

'How old was Tony?' she asked Lewis.

'You asked me that,' said Libby.

'But Lewis will know.'

He shrugged. 'Late forties? We never talked about it. No reason.'

Fran looked round at the wood.

'They won't find anything else here,' she said. 'Not unless they dig up the whole wood.'

'Would they find something then?' Libby asked.

'Possibly. I expect the bones have been scattered by now.'

'What about clothing?'

Fran shrugged. 'I don't know. I can't see any.'

'What does she mean?' whispered Lewis. 'Can't *see* any?'

'In her mind,' said Libby. 'Come on, you were interested in what she might find out.'

'Now I'm not sure,' muttered Lewis. 'She's a bit scary.'

'But not a fake,' insisted Libby. 'Quite genuine and very ambivalent about this strange gift she's got.'

Fran came back to them. 'May I see the house now, Lewis?' she asked. 'I think there might be something there.'

Without a word, Lewis led them back to the house and upstairs to the solar. Fran stood in the middle of it looking round with pleasure.

'The only stuff left behind after old Shepherd did his vanishing act were a few letters and photographs,' said Lewis. 'The police have been through the lot, but there wasn't anything there. They were all too old.'

'Have they started looking for the relatives?' asked Fran.

'There would only be the son, Kenneth, and the daughter-in-law, Cindy Dale. The one he was supposed to have run off with,' said Libby.

'And you said about three years ago?'

'I think so.'

Fran turned and looked straight at Lewis. 'Then that body is not Gerald Shepherd,' she said.

Chapter Twelve

L EWIS GAPED. 'NOT –?'

'No.' Fran shook her head. 'Could I see the letters and photographs he left behind? If the police haven't kept them?'

Recovering, Lewis went to a large, carved oak chest under the window. 'Here,' he said holding out a folder. 'The police put them in that.'

Fran took the folder to the little side table and began to leaf through the contents. Libby went and looked over her shoulder. The letters seemed to be purely personal ones, mainly from friends, with the occasional scrawled message from Kenneth, usually asking for money.

'These must be from before he pulled himself together and married Cindy,' said Libby, handing over those Fran had finished with to Lewis.

'And long before *Dungeon Trial*,' he said. 'I thought there might be something there.'

'A connection to Tony West? Yes, so did I,' said Libby, 'but he wasn't connected to the programme at all.'

'I still don't understand why he was able to sell me the house,' said Lewis, sitting down in one of the large leather armchairs. 'Why did he have that thing?'

'Power of attorney? I don't know. That's what the police are trying to find out, I expect.'

'But why,' said Fran, turning suddenly, 'did they turn up today with a search warrant? They must have discovered something. They hadn't searched before.'

'I dunno.' Lewis shrugged. 'Big Bertha kept asking me about Tony this morning. Nothing about old whatsit.'

'What sort of thing was she asking about?'

'Same old, same old. How long had I known him, how did we meet, when did I first see this place, what did we talk about. I ask you! What sort of a question is that?'

'What did you say?' asked Libby.

'When we first got together nothing! It was more action, if you know what I mean.'

Libby looked at Fran and grinned. 'I'm sure,' she said, 'but what about later?'

'Gawd, you're as bad as she is,' said Lewis.

'It was your idea to ask me here,' said Libby. 'We'll go if you like.'

Lewis shifted uncomfortably in his chair. 'No. Sorry. I don't know exactly. We talked about my career, then he got me on *Housey Housey*, and I reckon he leant on someone for that. Then he got me me own show, and he leant a bit harder. That wasn't why someone knocked him off, was it?'

'Because he wangled you into television? I shouldn't have thought so,' said Libby.

'But it all seems tied up with me and this place,' wailed Lewis. 'I love it, but I wish I'd never seen it.'

Fran gave him a look that reminded Libby of her old headmistress.

'Have a look at these photographs,' she said, pushing them under his nose, 'and try and be helpful.'

Lewis, looking surprised, took them.

'Recognise anybody?' Fran was watching him.

'No.' He shook his head. 'These are all old. They must belong to old whatsit.'

'Gerald Shepherd,' said Libby with a sigh.

'Must try and remember,' he said, a little shamefaced. 'Like the dog.'

'Eh?'

'German Shepherd,' he said with a grin. 'Then I'll remember.'

'These would have been here when Shepherd still lived here,' said Fran, effectively calling the meeting to order, 'but do we know whether he was living here when he disappeared?'

'I never thought of that!' said Libby. 'Was he, Lewis?'

'No idea,' said Lewis, looking surprised. 'I mean, I didn't know anything about him until the other day, did I?'

'Hmm.' Fran took the photographs back and flicked through them.

'May I see?' asked Libby.

Fran handed them over. 'See if there's anyone you recognise in them,' she said.

'Should I?'

'I don't know. You might do.'

Libby frowned and began looking through the photographs. Some were studio prints of Gerald Shepherd, obviously taken in the era when it was considered the done thing to be seen at an improbable angle with the light behind you, and some slightly dog-eared black and white prints of young people on a beach. There were a few in colour taken in the eighties, by the look of the clothes. Shepherd appeared in a few, two of which where he had his arm loosely round the shoulders of a young man with a beard.

'Only Shepherd himself,' said Libby, handing them back to Fran.

'Neither of you recognised the man with him?' Fran held up the colour prints.

Lewis shook his head. 'No,' said Libby. 'Is it his son? Kenneth?'

'I had a look on the Internet before I came over,' said Fran, 'and Kenneth was only about thirty when his father disappeared, so it can't be.' She looked at the pictures again. 'Would it be all right if I borrowed these?' she asked Lewis.

'Yeah, if you want. I don't need them, do I?'

'Do you think there's a connection with these and the skeleton?' asked Libby. 'The police obviously didn't, or they'd have taken them away.'

'They took some other stuff away,' said Lewis. 'There were some photo albums in the loft. Well, attic, I suppose. Did you want to have a look up there? Or anywhere else in the house?'

'If you don't mind,' said Fran. 'Coming, Lib?'

The house was a strange mixture of immaculate restoration and neglect. As Libby had already discovered, the kitchen was half and half.

'Who did it all?' asked Libby, as they scrambled through the dusty attics.

'German Shepherd started the restoration years ago, but let it go. No one had been living in it when I bought it.' He frowned. 'Not even Tony.'

Fran turned from an inspection of an interesting box which had, however, nothing inside it, and looked at him. 'When did he first bring you down here to see it?'

'While I was doing *Housey Housey*. He thought it might make a project for the show.'

'Did he say he owned it?'

Lewis thought back. 'I don't think so. I just assumed he did.'

'But you didn't do it on the show?'

'No. It was too big, really. I just never heard any more about it. Then he mentioned it again not so long back and I said I'd like to buy it. Well, you know the rest.'

'Did he suggest you bought it, or did you?' asked Libby.

Lewis screwed up his face. 'Gawd, Libby, you're at it again. I dunno. Let me think.' He sat down on an unstable-looking chair. 'What it was, he said did I remember this place, and I said 'course I did, I'd loved it, and he said the owner wanted to sell, a quick sale, and he was to do it on behalf of him. The owner, that is.'

'So it was his suggestion?' said Libby.

'I s'pose so. I didn't think about it at the time. I handed over the money and signed all the bits and pieces and that was that.'

'Libby said you had a threatening message,' said Fran. 'Why do you think that was?'

'I dunno. I didn't get the telly jobs legit, that's all I can think of. I still reckon Tony sent it.'

'Did you tell the police about it?'

He shook his head. 'I should have done, shouldn't I?'

'They might have been able to find out where it came from if it wasn't Tony,' said Libby.

'Have you finished in here?' Lewis stood up. 'Can we move on? It's a bit spooky.'

Fran was quiet as they toured the rest of the house. Part of one of the wings was in such a state of disrepair they could go no further than the hallway, and they returned to the solar.

'Is there any information on the history of the house?' asked Fran.

'What, deeds and things? I've got those somewhere.' Lewis went to his ornate desk.

'No, I mean any booklets or reference works.'

'Oh.' Lewis frowned. 'Local library? It's never been open to the public, so I don't suppose anyone thought of doing a book.'

'There must be archive material somewhere,' said Fran. 'Household accounts books, that sort of thing.'

Lewis's eyes opened wide. 'Really? Why? Why would anyone want them?'

'Big houses usually kept them. Housekeeper's day books and laundry lists. They're valuable social history.'

'County archive,' said Libby. 'You could look there. Say you're writing a history of the house.'

'Why would you want them, though?' asked Lewis. 'Stuff that happened years ago don't have anything to do with Tony or that bleedin' skeleton.'

'It might,' said Fran, looking stubborn. 'Do you mind if I try and find out?'

He shrugged. ''Course not. Do you need my permission, or something?'

'I don't think so, but if anyone asks I'll refer them to you, OK?'

'OK.'

'What about Gerald Shepherd's will?' asked Libby. 'I just thought of that.'

'Was it found?' asked Fran.

'Gawd knows,' said Lewis, looking even more bewildered. 'What's that got to do with it?'

'It might explain Tony West's right to have the Lasting Power of Attorney,' said Fran.

'Oh, is that what it is now?' said Libby. 'Or will it stay Enduring because it was done before the new law?'

Fran shrugged. 'Don't know,' she said, 'I only know the term because Guy and I have been making new wills and sorting out our own powers of attorney.'

'Gosh,' said Libby, 'aren't you sensible?'

Fran glared and Lewis looked embarrassed.

'Fran's getting married,' explained Libby, 'so she and her fiancé are planning.'

'Ah!' Lewis looked relieved. 'Sorry I can't offer you Creekmarsh as a venue,' he said, 'but I don't suppose I'll be able to get it up and running for ages.'

'Kind of you,' said Fran, 'but we've found a place already. If it's not booked up,' she added gloomily.

'I thought you'd already booked it?' Libby was surprised.

'We thought so, but according to their system, we'd only made an enquiry. Guy's waiting to hear.'

'Bummer,' said Lewis.

'Fran,' said Libby suddenly, 'why did you say that body isn't Gerald Shepherd?'

'Oh, you know,' said Fran vaguely.

'You just knew it wasn't,' Libby nodded. 'OK.'

'You can't be sure,' said Lewis.

'Of course not,' said Fran. 'Are you ready to go, Lib?'

Lewis and Libby, both flustered, stood up quickly.

'Seen enough then?' asked Lewis.

Fran smiled, still vaguely.

'Obviously she has,' said Libby, with a disgruntled look at her friend. 'I'll just collect my basket from the kitchen.'

'Yeah, thanks for the picnic,' said Lewis, as he followed them down the stairs. 'I'll have to forage for myself tonight.'

'Will Katie not be back then?' asked Libby.

'I haven't heard,' said Lewis. 'I knew she was going to London, but she's not answering her phone.'

'Is that at her flat in Leytonstone?'

'Yeah. She told you about that?'

'Yes. She told me how she'd worked in a bank and then in outside catering, hadn't any children but enjoyed her job with you. Pocket biography.'

'Yeah.' Lewis frowned. 'Can't imagine her without kids, can you? Perfect mum, I'd have thought.'

'Perhaps she's a perfect auntie,' said Libby. 'Has she got

family?'

'No idea,' said Lewis, looking surprised. 'She's never mentioned any.'

'Oh, well,' said Libby with a shrug, 'I expect she'll turn up. She struck me as being very reliable and responsible.'

'Always has been.' Lewis saw them to the door.

'How did you meet Katie?' asked Fran suddenly.

'I told Lib, she was doing OB catering on that *Housey Housey* show.'

'Right. And you got that job through Tony West?'

'Yes.'

'Did he know her?'

'Blimey! No idea.' Lewis laughed. 'He does now, since she's been with me.' He caught his breath. 'Did, I mean.'

'Whose idea was it she worked with you?'

There was a short silence.

'Tony's, I think,' said Lewis finally. 'But only because she and me'd got on.'

'She told me you asked her because you and your mum got on with her,' said Libby.

'Well, yeah, but I'm pretty sure it was Tony's idea.'

'Right.' Fran smiled brightly. 'Well, thanks for showing me round, Lewis. If I think of anything that might be of use, I'll let you know.'

It wasn't until they were on the main road back to Steeple Martin that Libby turned to her friend.

'So what was that all about?' she said. 'You got something, didn't you? Lewis was terribly confused.'

'Hmm,' said Fran.

'Oh, come on, Fran. You asked to go there. And what was it had you so convinced that the skeleton isn't Gerald Shepherd?'

'Because Gerald Shepherd is still alive,' said Fran.

Chapter Thirteen

LIBBY GAPED.

'Don't ask me how I know,' said Fran irritably.

'I wasn't going to. I was going to ask when you found out.'

'I didn't "find out".' Fran let out a gusty sigh. 'It's been hovering away at the corner of my consciousness all day.' She hit the steering wheel with a frustrated hand. 'I do *wish* I could do this properly.'

'You mean – to order? Focusing on items?'

Fran nodded.

'But you can. You've done it before, haven't you? With the Anderson Place business?'

'It was almost by accident, though, wasn't it?' said Fran. 'Anyway, I tried just now with the photographs and all that happened was it reinforced the feeling that Gerald is still alive.'

'Nothing about the other people in them?'

'I've *told* you.' Fran sounded even more irritated. 'Honestly, Lib, I don't need this.'

'You asked to come to Creekmarsh.'

'Also,' Fran went on, as though Libby hadn't spoken, 'did you notice what Lewis said when he was telling us how Tony West had offered him the house?'

'What do you mean?'

'He said the owner wanted a quick sale.'

Libby frowned. 'So?'

'Making it sound as though the owner was still alive.'

'Oh! I see. Was he lying? Did he think the owner was dead, or did he actually *know* the owner was still alive?'

'That's what I think,' said Fran. 'Tony West knew the owner was still alive.'

Libby thought for a moment. 'What about the girl? Cindy Dale?'

'I don't know,' said Fran. 'I haven't thought about her.'

'And Kenneth? He would be the owner if Gerald Shepherd was dead, wouldn't he?'

'Exactly.' Fran was triumphant. 'So Shepherd must be alive.'

'Do we tell anyone?' asked Libby.

'The police will find out themselves, they always do. And I can't see that woman Bertram listening to us.'

'I've just thought,' said Libby a few moments later as they were driving down the hill into Steeple Martin. 'Didn't they say the body was of a man between thirty and fifty?'

'Who's they?' asked Fran, slowing down past the pub and The Pink Geranium.

'On the radio – or the television, can't remember. But that's what it said. So it couldn't have been Gerald Shepherd anyway.' Libby turned excitedly to Fran. 'You're right.'

Fran looked sideways at her. 'So I needn't have bothered?'

Libby subsided. 'Well, you didn't know what you were going to come up with, did you? You could have come up with something even more startling.'

Fran made a sound that could have been agreement but sounded rather more disgruntled, and she turned into Allhallow's Lane.

'Do you want tea?' asked Libby as they pulled up outside number 17.

Fran sighed. 'Yes, please, and a bit of normality.'

'And no more grumps,' added Libby to herself.

The day having turned rather grey and chilly, they had tea in the front room. Sidney reluctantly moved up to allow Libby to sit beside him on the sofa, turning his back to her and flattening his ears.

'What will you do if you can't have that hotel?' she asked Fran, deciding not to go any further down the murder route.

Fran shrugged. 'Find somewhere else, I suppose,' she said. 'We might have to wait longer, though. People book so far in advance.'

'Or you could get married sooner. I bet there are places with vacancies in the next month.'

Fran looked up, interested. 'Of course,' she said. 'Once it gets to a couple of months before, no one's going to book a wedding, are they?'

'It might be difficult to get a registrar, though,' warned Libby, 'but you could always try. When had you intended to do the deed?'

'October, we hoped, so it wouldn't be bringing it forward too much.' Fran fished in her bag. 'Do you mind if I call Guy?'

'Go ahead,' said Libby, amused at the sight of her friend evincing such enthusiasm.

While Fran was talking, she turned on the television with the sound down to see if she could locate a mid-afternoon news bulletin. When she did, almost immediately a picture of the outside of Creekmarsh flashed up on the screen. Fran had seen it and switched off her mobile. Libby turned up the sound.

'... gave a statement at lunchtime today,' the announcer was saying, 'which indicated that the remains found in the grounds of a house in Kent match the DNA of vanished actor Gerald Shepherd.'

Fran and Libby gasped together. A picture of Shepherd appeared on the screen.

'Shepherd disappeared just over three years ago,' continued the announcer, while a series of publicity stills of Shepherd were shown. 'He was famous for his portrayal ...'

Libby turned the sound down. 'We know all that,' she said. 'What's going on?'

Fran shook her head, frowning. 'I don't know. He's alive, I'd swear it.'

'Is it a bluff, do you think?' asked Libby.

'I don't think the police are allowed to bluff,' said Fran. 'And why, anyway?'

Libby's phone rang. 'Lewis, I bet,' she said, going to answer it.

'Did you hear that police statement?' Lewis sounded agitated.

'Yes,' said Libby, 'we just saw it on television.'

'So it's that Gerald Shepherd all along. Your mate got it

wrong.'

'I don't think so,' said Libby cautiously. 'There must be an explanation.'

'Well, until old German Shepherd turns up alive and well we ain't got one,' said Lewis. 'I'll see you, Lib.'

'He doesn't sound too impressed,' said Libby, going back to the sofa. 'What do we do now?'

Fran sighed. 'Why do we have to do anything? The police think it's Shepherd. They'll presumably investigate further and get to the bottom of it.'

'But they'll be looking in the wrong direction,' protested Libby. 'If it isn't Gerald, they need to find out who it *really* is. They'll be looking into Gerald's past instead.'

Fran closed her eyes. 'So what do you want to do?' she asked in a resigned voice.

'Find out who it is, of course,' said Libby.

'And how do you propose to do that? And what about Ben?'

'I don't know,' said Libby, frowning.

'The how? Or Ben?'

'Both,' admitted Libby. 'I'll just have to play it by ear.'

Fran opened her eyes and leant forward. 'There's no way you can find out who those bones belonged to without a forensic anthropologist, Libby. And the police are stretched financially as it is. They probably won't investigate any further, they'll simply find some contributory evidence and thankfully close the file.'

'Without finding out who did it?' asked Libby, shocked.

'If it isn't Shepherd, they can't, can they?'

'Heavens, how complicated,' said Libby, starting to search for a cigarette. 'Sorry, Fran, but I really need one.' She found a packet in the log basket and lit up. 'They'll start a hunt for Kenneth and Cindy, won't they? They'll have to. Because Kenneth would be Gerald's heir.'

'Not to Creekmarsh any more,' said Fran.

'No, but if Tony West had the power of attorney legally, as it seems he had, the money must be somewhere.'

'Unless he spent it.'

'No, he wouldn't be able to do that,' said Libby, 'it would have to go into a client account, or something.'

92

'Well, I'm sure we can leave the police to find out,' said Fran. 'We can't.'

For a moment Libby looked mutinous, but then she sighed and leant back. 'You're right, of course.' She smiled. 'What did Guy say?'

'Oh –' Fran coloured slightly, 'he thought it was a great idea and said he'll get on to it straight away.'

'So we could have a July wedding? Or even a June one?' Libby grinned. 'Better get a move on with those outfits, then!'

Later, after Fran had gone home and before Adam appeared, Libby rang Ben.

'Would you like to come to supper this evening?' she asked.

'I'd love to. Just us, or will there be any waifs and strays?'

Libby gritted her teeth. 'Just us, unless Ad's staying in,' she said.

'Sevenish, then?' said Ben. 'I'll see you then.'

Adam was quite happy to rustle himself up a snack when he came in, saying he was going to meet a couple of old school friends in Canterbury and would go in by bus. Libby had a long bath, tried to tame her rusty hair and put on her favourite velvet skirt and floaty blouse.

'Wow!' said Adam when she came downstairs. 'I'm tempted to hang around and see Ben's reaction.'

'Oh, stop it, Ad.' Libby tied an apron over her finery and fetched a basket of vegetables. 'Do you want to help me do these?'

'Ah. No, I'd better be off after all.' Adam came to give her a kiss. 'Be good, Ma.'

'Always am,' she said as he left the cottage. 'Sadly.'

When Ben arrived, chicken was simmering in a cream sauce and vegetables waited in a steamer.

'You look gorgeous,' he said, kissing her cheek and handing over a bottle of wine.

'Thank you,' said Libby, 'so do you.'

'So, how have you been getting on with the investigation?' asked Ben, as Libby poured drinks. She winced.

'We're not,' she said, handing him a glass. 'The police think they know who the body is, so that's that.'

Ben raised his eyebrows. 'But what about this other murder in London? I thought that was connected?'

So he'd been following it, thought Libby.

'Yes, I suppose it is, but it's nothing to do with us,' she said.

'But it is to do with Adam's employer.'

'Well, yes.' She wriggled in her chair. 'Look, Ben, we don't have to talk about murders. I just wanted to see you.'

He stood up and came to sit beside her. 'And I wanted to see you,' he said. 'I don't like this situation.'

Libby opened her mouth to tell him that he'd started it and thought better of it.

'Yes,' he said, reading her mind, 'I know I started it, so can we just talk it through now and see where we go from here?'

Libby stared at him, then stood up. 'I'm just going to put the vegetables on,' she said.

When she came back, Ben had topped up their drinks and taken off his jacket.

'What do you want to say?' Libby sat down beside him again and picked up her glass.

He looked amused. 'What I'd like to say is "will you marry me?" but I won't.'

Libby choked on a mouthful of scotch. He patted her on the back. 'Instead, I'll say please will you continue to be my significant other because I love you and I miss you. And I would like to move in with you permanently, as you don't want to move to The Manor – and I can quite see why – but if you'd rather I didn't, then I suppose we'll have to go back to the way we were.' He shifted position in order to drape an arm round her shoulders and give her a squeeze. 'I know I was sounding pushy and dictatorial, and I know it all sounded like blackmail, but I realised that we're not kids with our whole lives ahead of us, who could say "there's no future in this" and move on to someone else.'

'So we'll have to settle for us?' Libby frowned at him.

'I didn't mean that,' Ben sighed. 'I meant that I've found my future, there's no point in looking for anything else.'

'Me?' asked Libby hesitantly.

'Of course, you,' said Ben. 'Now shut up and let me kiss

you.'

It was much later when Libby suddenly sat up in bed and let out an exclamation.

'What?' Ben mumbled.

'I've got it,' said Libby, throwing the duvet back.

'Got what?' Ben sat up. 'And where are you going?'

'I'm going to phone Fran,' she said.

'It's gone eleven, Libby, and I thought you weren't involved in this investigation?'

'I'm not,' Libby said and grinned over her shoulder at him. 'I'll be back in a minute.'

Fran sounded no more awake than Ben had and twice as exasperated, but Libby took no notice.

'It's obvious when you think about it,' she said. 'I don't know why you didn't.'

'What's obvious, and why should I think of it?'

'The skeleton. The DNA. It's Kenneth.'

Chapter Fourteen

THERE WAS A SILENCE while Fran tried to wake up. Libby sighed impatiently and began to tap her fingers on the receiver.

'All right, all right, I'm awake now.' Fran paused. 'Of course, you could be right.'

'Of course I'm right,' crowed Libby. 'It's so bloody obvious I don't know why the police didn't think of it.'

'They probably did,' said Fran slowly, 'when you realise they had given the age of the skeleton as a man between thirty and fifty. Gerald doesn't fit into that age range.'

Libby deflated. 'Oh.'

'So that means they must have ruled Kenneth out.'

'What?'

'It's just as obvious, Libby. Creekmarsh belonged to Gerald Shepherd. He's disappeared, and apparently now, so has his son. Nothing's been heard of him for a couple of years, has it?'

'Don't know,' said Libby. 'He made enquiries when his father and Cindy went AWOL, but I don't know what happened after that.'

'Well, then, the police would know that, so they would look into the possibility that the body was his.' Fran yawned. 'Look, let's talk about this in the morning.'

'But you said I was probably right.'

'I said you *could* be, Lib. It doesn't feel right to me. Let me sleep on it. Go back to bed.'

Libby crawled back under the duvet and tentatively reached for Ben.

'That didn't take long.' His voice was blurred with sleep.

'No,' said Libby and, smiling, closed her eyes.

Sunday dawned sunny and Libby was filled with optimism.

Adam and Ben were both still asleep when she came downstairs to Sidney's importunings, and after she'd fed him, she went into the garden to wait for the kettle to boil.

A soft breeze drifted through the branches of the cherry tree, now alive with bright green leaves, the white blossom only a memory, and multi-coloured aquilegia waved along the bottom of the large choisya. Sidney had disappeared over the back fence into The Manor woods, and Libby could hear a distant lawn mower. Sniffing, she agreed with Chesterton's dog Quoodle; there was a definite smell about Sunday morning.

She made tea and took hers upstairs with Ben's.

'This is nice,' he said, struggling to an upright position and leaning forward to kiss her.

'It is, isn't it?' she said, her stomach melting with the pleasure of just seeing him there, propped up against the white pillows.

'Come back to bed, then.' He turned back a corner of the duvet and waggled his eyebrows at her. She giggled.

'Drink your tea first,' she said. 'Or it will go cold.'

It did.

'And now,' said Libby, some time later, 'I shall have to make more tea and go and see if Ali and Ahmed are open this morning.'

'Why?' asked Ben lazily. 'It's Sunday.'

'And I promised Ad a proper Sunday lunch, which I completely forgot about. So I'll have to go and see what Ahmed can rustle up.'

'He might have a frozen chicken,' said Ben doubtfully, 'but what about vegetables?'

'I might have to cadge off Pete and Harry or your mum,' said Libby. 'Do you think they'd mind?'

'I'll give Mum a ring,' said Ben, swinging his legs out of bed. 'Where are my trousers?'

'Do you have to put your trousers on to phone your mum?' Libby snickered. 'Will she be shocked?'

'Idiot. My phone's in the pocket.'

When Libby returned from the bathroom to get dressed, Ben was back in bed.

'We've all been invited to lunch at The Manor,' he said, holding out a hand. 'So you can come back to bed again. We've got some time to make up.'

'Did you force your mum into it?' asked Libby suspiciously.

'No, she was delighted to ask us. It gives her a chance to cook properly, she said. You know how she loves entertaining.'

'Cooking, yes. I wouldn't say she liked entertaining as in dinner parties.'

Ben grinned. 'No. I can't see my mum in a glam frock serving goat's cheese on a raspberry coulis, can you?'

Libby grinned back and let her dressing gown fall to the floor. 'No, thank goodness,' she said, and dived back under the duvet.

By the time Adam appeared, Ben and Libby were in the garden, respectably dressed and in deep conversation about summer flowering perennials.

'Morning, Ma,' he said, pushing a hand through tangled hair. ''Lo, Ben. Is there any tea?'

'You can make some,' said Libby. 'Hangover?'

'No,' said Adam with some surprise. 'I got a lift home from someone and he didn't want to be late, so I was in by about half twelve. You were already asleep.'

'Well, good,' said Libby, avoiding Ben's eye, 'because Hetty's invited us up to The Manor for lunch.'

'Hey, great,' said Adam, brightening. 'But I thought you were going to do lunch?'

'I was, but now Hetty's invited us. I expect she wants to see you.'

'She's got a soft spot for you, you know,' said Ben, sitting down on one of the slightly unstable garden chairs.

Adam looked down at his feet. 'Yeah, well,' he said.

'Go on, then, have a shower and I'll make you some tea,' said Libby, giving him a fond push towards the cottage.

It was a shock later, when Libby turned on the radio while clearing up the kitchen from the previous evening, which unaccountably hadn't been done, to hear that the midday news bulletin contained a reference to both the discovery of the Creekmarsh skeleton, although without naming the house, and

Tony West's murder. Scraping the remains of the chicken into the bin, Libby realised she hadn't once thought about 'the investigation' since Ben had arrived. She smiled a secret little smile.

Promptly at one o'clock, Ben, Libby and Adam presented themselves at The Manor. Hetty greeted them without fuss and showed them into the sitting room, where Ben's father Greg sat, frailer than ever, but ever the courteous host. Lunch was served at the huge table in the kitchen. Adam's eyes gleamed at the enormous rib of beef, the tureens of vegetables, Hetty's special gravy and horseradish sauce.

'Enough to feed an army as usual,' said Ben, grinning at his mother, who wielded a skilful carving knife.

'Plenty to see us through the week,' said Hetty. 'Take some 'ome cold, gal, put it in 'is sandwiches.' She nodded towards Adam, who beamed back at her.

'Will you be needing sandwiches next week, Ad? Or will Katie be back?'

'Who's Katie?' asked Ben.

'She's, like, Lewis's sort of housekeeper-secretary,' said Adam, helping himself to roast parsnips. 'She's been away since – well, I don't really know. She wasn't there yesterday.'

'She's just gone home for the weekend,' said Libby. 'Lewis said she'd gone to London.'

'So what's he like then, this Lewis Wotsit?' asked Hetty.

After lunch, Libby offered to help with the clearing up, and, as usual, Hetty said it would all go in the dishwasher – she gave it a pat – and she preferred to do her pots herself.

Adam, perfectly at home at The Manor, wandered into the library, which, he told them, was the perfect setting for a murder and wondered why Ben and Libby both told him to shut up.

'Actually, Ad, I was going to ask your advice about something,' Ben went on.

'*My* advice?' Adam looked shocked.

'You must have picked up a certain amount working with Mog?'

'Well, yes, I suppose so,' said Adam, glancing nervously at his mother.

'I need a bit of advice on what to do with that bit of the old lawn that goes down to the wood,' said Ben, putting an arm round Adam's shoulders. 'Would you come and have a look at it?'

They disappeared through the French windows and Libby watched, an amused expression on her face.

'There now,' said Hetty, coming in with a tea tray. 'I didn't make coffee. Thought you'd like a cuppa.'

'Lovely, thanks, Hetty,' said Libby, who was still full of Cabernet Sauvignon. 'Does Ben really need Adam's advice on the garden?'

Hetty looked up. 'If it's that bit down by the woods, yes, he does. Can't decide whether to chop the lot down, put up a fence or what. Not much fer 'im to do round 'ere, really.' She passed Libby a cup. 'So things working out for you again?'

'Er –' said Libby.

'Just our Ben's not bin happy this week. And I reckoned it had something to do with you. And that Fran and Guy getting married.'

Libby sighed. 'Yes,' she said. 'That's it exactly. And Guy wants Ben as best man, and Fran wants me as – well – attendant, I suppose. All very difficult.'

'And you still don't want to get married?'

'Oh, Het, I'm not sure. I love Ben, but marriage hasn't done well by either of us in the past, has it?'

'Neither it did with that Fran, nor that Guy. They was both married before, and they're taking the chance.'

'I know.' Libby looked down at her cup. 'Would you be happier if we got married?'

Hetty shrugged. 'Don't make no difference to me,' she said. 'Don't know why you don't just live together. Most folks do.'

'Ben's said he'd like to move in with me,' said Libby. 'Not,' she added hastily, 'that it isn't lovely here –'

'But it ain't your own.' Hetty nodded. 'Be Ben's one day, though.'

'Don't talk about it,' said Libby.

'Have to. My Greg's not going to last much longer – it's a wonder he's held on as long as he has – and I ain't no spring chicken. Got power of attorney for both of us, has Ben. 'Course, there'll be our Susan to think about too, but she's got her own place.'

'Power of attorney? Gosh, has he?' said Libby. 'I didn't know that.'

'No reason you should. Just being sensible, case anything happens. I remember what it was like when I took over here.' Hetty stared broodingly at the carpet.

'It must have been so hard for you,' said Libby gently, after a moment.

Hetty pulled herself together. 'Yeah, well, had to be done, didn't it?' She poured more tea into her cup and looked enquiringly at Libby, who shook her head. 'You have to get things in order, gal, so as your kids don't have a mess to clear up. Don't mean you're going to die next week, just that it's all clear and they don't have nothing to worry about when the time comes. Hard enough without all that.'

Libby nodded, feeling her throat constrict at the thought of this doughty old woman who had had so much to contend with throughout her life, and who still worked so hard, being so concerned to leave everyone happy.

Hetty looked at her watch. 'Time for Greg's medicine,' she said, 'but he's dozed off in the sitting room, so I'll leave him to it for a bit.'

'How is he?' asked Libby, a question she rarely asked because she was always afraid of the answer.

'Up and down. Likes a bit of company, you could see that, couldn't you?' Hetty's faded eyes twinkled. 'Likes you, he does. And that Adam. He's a caution, that boy.'

The caution then reappeared at the French windows with Ben in tow and immediately began regaling Hetty and Libby with his thoughts on The Manor grounds. Ben shrugged and smiled at Libby, coming to sit on the arm of her chair. Hetty offered tea and she and Adam settled down to talk about gardens.

'He knows what he's doing,' Ben murmured to Libby. 'How long has he been working with Mog?'

'Not long. He's helped him out with odd jobs before, but this is the first major thing he's done. I wonder if he'll make it into a career?'

'Well, he's learnt an awful lot in a short time, so he must be interested,' said Ben.

Adam's pocket began to sing 'Yellow Submarine' and he fished his mobile out of his pocket.

'Sorry, Hetty,' he said, 'just better see what this is.'

He stood up and went to the windows, listening, then turned to Libby with an astonished look on his face.

'It's Lewis,' he said. 'Cindy Dale's just turned up.'

Chapter Fifteen

'CINDY WHO?' BEN ASKED.

'Gerald Shepherd's daughter-in-law,' said Libby. 'What else, Ad?'

'He's had to go. She's in the room with him, apparently.' He looked hopeful. 'Do we go?'

Ben groaned. Libby shook her head. 'No. I'm sure we'll hear all about it soon. You will, tomorrow, anyway.'

'Don't you go getting involved, young Adam,' said Hetty. 'Leave it to yer ma.'

Ben groaned again and put his head in his hands.

Libby laughed. 'Oh, Het! You couldn't have said anything worse.'

'Well, you won't let it alone whatever anyone says,' said Hetty reasonably, 'so might as well let you get on with it.'

Ben looked up reproachfully. 'Oh, Mum. I expected you at least to be on my side.'

Hetty grunted. ''Course I am. But she won't take no notice of me.'

'Let's forget it,' said Libby, feeling a blush creep up her neck. 'Nothing to do with us.'

'Not what you said last night at half past eleven,' grumbled Ben.

Adam's eyes widened. 'Hey – too much information!'

Libby's blush got deeper. 'Is there any more tea, Hetty?' she asked desperately.

Hetty cocked an eye at her and nodded. 'Go and put the kettle on, gal,' she said.

Despite her determination not to discuss the Creekmarsh case, Libby thought about it while she carried the tray through to the kitchen and put the big kettle back on the Aga. Something else had occurred to her, triggered by the reappearance of Cindy Dale, a hugely surprising event in itself.

If Tony West had been proved to have legal power of attorney, when had it been implemented? Gerald Shepherd had been missing for three years, so it must have been done before he went, which argued a degree of forethought not substantiated by the public version of the story, that Cindy and Gerald went off together while Kenneth was in *Dungeon Trial*. She frowned. Now she really did want to meet Cindy Dale and find out what actually happened, although the police would probably be crawling all over her for the next few days. Libby warmed the pot thoughtfully and wondered when Cindy had turned up at Creekmarsh. And, whenever she'd appeared, why?

The rest of the afternoon passed without embarrassment or incident, and on the way back to Allhallow's Lane, Ben suggested he and Libby should call in to see his cousin Peter and Harry. Adam said he would go back to the cottage before going to the pub.

Peter and Harry were in a Sunday afternoon state of sloth. Libby sank into her usual sagging armchair and refused tea.

'We're awash with Hetty's PG tips, thanks,' she said.

'Drinky-poos, then?' said Harry, pulling his towelling robe more firmly round his waist.

'Oh, go on, then,' said Libby with a grin. 'May I have a whisky?'

Harry poured whisky for Libby and gin and tonics for himself, Peter and Ben. Ben, perched on the arm of the sofa, was deep in conversation with his cousin about other members of the family, notably Peter's mother Millie, Hetty's sister, who now lived in a comfortable home for the slightly insane, as Peter put it. Millie had suffered a complete nervous breakdown some years before, and although at first she had been able to live in her own home with a suitable carer, this was no longer an option. The last time Libby had seen her was at Peter and Harry's civil partnership celebrations, at which she had surprised everybody by behaving impeccably, although with no idea where she was or what was going on.

'How is she?' Libby muttered to Harry. 'I don't like to pry.'

'Pry away, ducks,' said Harry. 'She's as fit as a fiddle and will probably outlive us all. Pete's big problem at the moment is what to do with Steeple Farm.'

'Why is that a problem? Can't he sell it?'

'He hasn't got power of attorney,' said Harry.

'Blimey O'Reilly,' said Libby. 'All I seem to hear about these days is power of attorney. First this bloody Creekmarsh case, then Hetty this afternoon and now you.'

'You asked,' said Harry, affronted.

'Sorry, Harry.' Libby reached over and patted his knee. 'It's just such a coincidence. Tell me why Pete hasn't got power of attorney?'

'Because Millie went loopy before he could get it. You can't do it unless the donor, as they're called, is aware of what's going on. And after she flipped, she wasn't. So he and James will have to wait until she pops off, I suppose.'

'You do sound callous,' said Libby.

Harry shrugged, causing his robe to gape alarmingly. 'Got to be sensible,' he said. 'And she doesn't know what's going on, does she? Anyway, it's not as if either we or James need the money.'

'So what's Pete worrying about, then?'

'It's standing empty, and Pete feels guilty. He thinks we should let it out, but it would need a lot spent on it first.'

'Really? I thought Millie had already spent a lot on it? She ripped out the old kitchen and put in that new one, didn't she?'

'Which is already dated and, as you well know, doesn't suit the house at all. Mind you, I don't suppose tenants would worry about that. No, it's health and safety. A lot of the furniture would have to be replaced with fire-retardant stuff, and the insurance would be prohibitive. It's bad enough anyway, as it's thatched.'

'Oh, I see. What a waste of a lovely old house,' said Libby wistfully.

'Here! That's it!' said Harry, patting her cheek. 'You and Ben can go and live there and do it up for us.'

'Oh, gee, thanks,' said Libby. 'I couldn't live with that

kitchen.' She sipped her whisky. 'I suppose it was all the fuss with Millie that made Hetty sort out their powers of attorney with Ben.'

''Spect so,' said Harry, 'but what about this Creekmarsh business? Why don't I know anything about it?'

'You've heard it on the news, haven't you?'

'All I've heard is a skeleton in some big garden.'

'That's the one. Creekmarsh, over the other side of Nethergate.'

'Yes, and I know Ad's been working there. How is the dear boy?'

'Lovely, thanks. Creekmarsh's owner fancies him.'

Harry looked interested. 'Oh, yeah? Male, this owner?'

'Don't get excited. Ad and I are bringing him to dinner at the caff sometime this week. You can look him over. Lewis Osbourne-Walker if you've heard of him.'

'Known as Osbourne-something-else in the community,' grinned Harry, 'but as he's mates with you I suppose he isn't.'

'No, he isn't. He's just a bit confused, having a lot of money quite suddenly and then being mixed up in what looks like a double murder.'

'A *double* murder?'

'Oh, bother.' Libby shook her head. 'I didn't mean to say that. The police haven't linked the two as far as the public are concerned, but yes. Two.'

'Poor sod. So it's his garden on the news. They haven't said so, have they?'

'I don't think so, and I'm truly surprised that it hasn't leaked to the media. If they connect poor Lewis to either of the murders then it will, obviously.'

'And *is* he connected?'

'Sort of,' said Libby uncomfortably, looking across at Ben.

'Ah,' said Harry, following her gaze. 'Not happy about it?'

'Well, not really. I think we've sorted it out now, though.'

'Sorted it out? The murder?'

'No –' Libby hesitated. 'Did I tell you Fran and Guy are getting married?'

'It filtered through,' said Harry. 'And that's our Ben's

problem, is it? Wants to follow suit?'

'How did you feel two years ago when Peter suggested it to you? You came and talked to me about it.'

'Two blokes are somewhat different from the conventional couple, dear heart.' Harry slid off the arm of her chair and took her empty glass. 'Refill time.'

The conversation became general, and Libby made a resolution to make time this week for a good long chat with Harry, who had been her confidant ever since she had moved to the village, and she his. He could be abrasive and brash, but was surprisingly softhearted and understanding, and adored all his new extended family, in which he included Libby and all three of her children. His own background he never revealed, although Peter had hinted at a troubled childhood.

Later that evening, as Ben and Libby walked home in the twilight, Ben himself mentioned Steeple Farm.

'Harry was telling me about Pete's problems with it,' nodded Libby.

'Pete and James,' said Ben. 'It's left to them equally. James doesn't want to live there, which you can understand, him being a young-man-about-Canterbury.'

'I always thought he would move there, for some reason.'

'They talked about it, but not an option, really.'

'And they can't let it because it's not up to elf-an-safety?'

'Exactly. When Millie did it up, she only did the cosmetic part she wanted herself.'

'That awful kitchen,' said Libby.

'Yes, and you haven't seen the rest of the house.'

'Is it dreadful?'

'Decoratively, yes. Completely out of keeping with the building itself. It could fairly easily be put back together again, though, but Pete and James don't want to spend a fortune getting it ready to let if they're just going to sell it when Millie dies.'

'So Harry was saying. I'd love to have a look round. Do you think they'd let me?'

They stopped outside number 17, and Ben looked at her.

'I was just going to suggest it,' he said. 'I wondered what you'd think about living there?'

Chapter Sixteen

LIBBY WAS SO STARTLED she dropped the key. Ben bent to pick it up with a rueful smile and opened the door. Sidney greeted them from his favourite place halfway up the stairs and Libby stumbled on the step.

'Careful,' warned Ben. 'It's only visitors who are supposed to do that.'

Libby preceded him into the sitting room and carried on to the kitchen. Sidney had been at the bread bin again. As she absentmindedly wiped muddy paw prints from the sink and the work surface, she marvelled at Harry's prescience, then looked up and stared through to the conservatory. Or was it prescience? Had Peter and Ben already discussed this possibility? The more she thought about it, still wiping the now clean bread bin, the more likely it seemed.

'Penny for them?' said Ben from behind her. She turned round.

'Have you and Peter talked about this?' The words came out as an accusation, which was not what she wanted, but too late now. Ben's eyes narrowed.

'Why do you say that?'

'Because Harry made the same suggestion. He was joking, I'm pretty sure, but it's such a coincidence.'

Ben sighed. 'Yes. Pete mentioned it a few weeks back.' He held up a hand. 'Hear me out. He was simply saying he wondered if I wanted to carry on living at The Manor, it was nothing to do with you.'

'No?'

'Well, not until he said you might be happier living somewhere new to both of us.'

'Ah.' Libby turned back to the bread bin.

'Do you want a drink?' Ben came up beside her.

'We've been drinking all day,' said Libby. 'I'd prefer coffee, I think.' She filled the kettle and pushed it onto the Rayburn. 'Come and sit down. You'd better tell me all about it.'

'That's all there is, really,' said Ben, leading the way into the sitting room and sitting on one of the upright chairs by the table in the window. Libby frowned. This was not a good sign.

'Pete suggested – what? You might like to rent it? Or do it up, like Harry said?'

'Is that what Harry said?' Ben looked interested. 'Because that was the idea. It was fairly vague, but Pete said if I wanted my own home rather than The Manor, wouldn't it be a good idea? Especially if you would feel happier in a home that was "ours" rather than mine or yours.'

Libby was silent for a moment. 'I can see his point,' she said eventually. 'I really would not like to live at The Manor.'

'Because of my mum and dad?'

'Obviously. But it also feels too big. I know you grew up there and it's your family home, but what on earth would we do with all those rooms if – when – it becomes yours?'

'It isn't entailed, you know. I could sell it.' Ben leant his elbows on his knees and looked at the floor. 'And I have asked if I could move in with you permanently. Even though this house is so small.'

'What's that got to do with anything?'

'I mean,' said Ben with a sigh, 'I'm perfectly happy to continue our relationship on your terms. Just I'd prefer we were actually together as a couple.'

Libby was silent once more. This was simply going over old ground. Slowly, she went back to the kitchen and poured hot water into a cafetière. Looking back over her shoulder to where Ben sat, still gazing at the floor, his curly grey hair just beginning to show signs of thinning, her heart squeezed within her. She turned back, assembled mugs, milk and cafetière on a tray and went back into the sitting room.

'We've been round and round this subject over the last few days, haven't we?' she said, putting the tray down carefully.

'And last night I thought we'd resolved it. We've both given way and reached a compromise. I agreed we should live together properly and you agreed to come here. Should we not leave it there for a while and get used to it?'

Ben looked up and smiled. 'But we are used to it. The only difference will be me coming here after work and not going to The Manor before work.'

'Hmm.' Libby poured coffee. 'All your stuff will be here, though.'

'Yes, and perhaps that's another reason to think of Pete's offer.'

'How would it work, though? If you do it up, will Pete pay you for it?'

'I think his idea is that I – we – live in it rent free while we do it up, then when Millie dies we buy it as sitting tenants.'

'Because he can't sell it while she's alive.'

Ben nodded. 'That's why Mum made sure about hers and Dad's power of attorney, so I can deal with anything I need to while they're still here.'

'I thought that was how it was,' said Libby. 'But what about this place?'

'You could hang on to it. Escape route,' said Ben, picking up his mug.

Libby made a face. 'That's not very optimistic,' she said.

'Well, we could live here while we do up Steeple Farm. You've been inside, haven't you?'

'Yes, when Millie gave me breakfast. It gave me the creeps a bit.'

'Did it?' Ben looked up. 'Inside?'

'No, the outside. It's a picture-book place, but those eyes ...'

'Eyes?'

Libby shivered. 'The windows under the eaves.'

Ben frowned. 'I always thought they were picturesque.'

'Well, I'll have to have a proper look, won't I,' said Libby. 'When can we go?'

Ben gave her a relieved smile. 'As soon as you like,' he said.

As soon as you like turned out to be Monday afternoon, when Ben had finished his not-too-onerous duties on The Manor estate. In the morning, however, after Libby had done a little desultory housework, she was determined to find out more about Cindy Dale. She had given Adam strict instructions to ring her if he had any news and given him sandwiches again in case Katie hadn't returned from her weekend away. She switched on the computer and found a couple of local news sites. There was nothing about either murder. In desperation, she called Lewis's number.

'Libby.'

'Yes. Hi, Lewis. Just wanted to know how you were.' Libby squirmed. She was being unwarrantably nosy, and Lewis didn't exactly sound friendly.

'I'm fine. As a matter of fact, I've got someone with me just now –'

'Cindy?' breathed Libby.

'Yes. Adam was going to ring you.'

'To tell me?'

'Ye-es,' he said slowly.

'Right.' Libby cheered up. 'I gave Ad sandwiches again in case Katie hadn't come back, but I can't bring any more today. I'm going out.'

'Yes, Katie's back. You can't come out?'

'Did you want me to?'

'Adam will ring you,' said Lewis briskly. 'Got to go now, Lib.'

Libby switched off and sat back in her chair. So what was that all about? Was Lewis warning her off? Bit of a cheek after having invited her into the case. Or did he still want help? Was that why Adam was going to ring her?

A few moments later the phone rang.

'Ma, it's me. Lewis asked me to call.'

'Yes?' Libby wasn't going to say she'd been hassling Lewis.

'That Cindy Dale's here and Lewis doesn't know what to do with her.'

'Has he told the police?'

'Oh, yes. And they've been to talk to her. Trouble is, she's staying here. I don't think Katie's best pleased, and Lewis certainly isn't.'

'So why did he want you to call me?'

'Motherly advice.' Libby could tell he was grinning.

'Is he going to get me up to speed?'

'Yes, but not while Cindy's around. Could we take him to Harry's tonight?'

'It's Monday – he's not open.'

'Oh, bugger. What else can you suggest?'

'I can't come over this afternoon, even if I had the car. Ben and I are going out.' She hadn't said anything to Adam about Steeple Farm.

'OK. Could he come over tonight to the house? Would Ben mind?'

'Not sure,' said Libby, thinking furiously. 'Let me have a word with him and I'll get back to you.'

Before she could lose her nerve, she punched in Ben's mobile number, hoping he wasn't at that moment up to his thighs in farmyard mud.

'Lib? What's up?'

'Are you busy?'

'Not dreadfully. Looking at the tenants' milk quotas. Why?'

'You know Lewis Osbourne-Walker works for house makeover programmes?'

'Ye-es.'

'And he was a professional before that?'

'I didn't, but it follows.'

'I wondered if we might ask him to have a look at Steeple Farm?'

There was a short silence, then Ben burst out laughing. 'OK, OK,' he said. 'It's the naffest excuse I've heard, but OK.'

'Really?' Libby was stunned. 'You don't mind?'

'If it means you're going to look more favourably on the Steeple Farm project, of course I don't mind. We're going at two-ish, aren't we? So ask him to come over at half past.'

'This afternoon?' she squeaked.

'I thought that was what you wanted.'

'Well, yes, but –'

'That's all right, then. I'll see you at lunchtime.'

Libby sat back in her chair, still astonished. Shaking her

head, she hit Adam's number on speed dial and waited for him to pick up.

'Ma?'

'Ask Lewis if he can come to Steeple Farm this afternoon at half past two. Tell him it's a bona fide house job.'

'Eh? Isn't that where Mad Millie lived?'

'It is. Peter needs it done up.' Libby crossed her fingers. That was what she would tell Lewis, too.

'Really? You're not bamming?'

'No, it's true. Ben and I will be there. Do you know where it is to give him directions?'

'He can look up the postcode and use the satnav,' said Adam. 'Can I come with him?'

'You'll be working.'

'Not much to do now I've mapped out the parterre. Not until Mog comes back. If Lewis says yes, can I?'

He sounds like a ten-year-old again, thought Libby, with a sharp stab of nostalgia. 'Yes, of course, if Lewis doesn't mind. How's Katie, by the way?'

'Fine. Well, a bit down about Tony, 'cos Lewis told you she knew him, didn't he? Not well, but he got her the job with me. Otherwise she's OK. Not happy about this Cindy, though.'

'No, you said. What's she like? Cindy?'

'Odd,' said Adam. 'I dunno what I expected, but she definitely isn't it.'

'Tell me later,' said Libby.

'We both will,' said Adam, obviously now in high spirits. 'See ya.'

Libby called Ben back to tell him the good news, then called Fran to give her an update.

'By the way,' said Fran when she finished exclaiming over Libby's news, 'that hotel had a wedding cancellation, including celebrant, on the third week in June. We've taken it.'

'My God!' said Libby, winded. 'That's only a few weeks away. How –'

'Will we do it?' Fran laughed. 'Not much to do. We're going to ring or email everyone this afternoon, then make sure we can get the outfits ready in time. That's about it.'

'Have you booked Ben and me into the hotel itself?'

'We've taken all the rooms, so yes. Are you going to be together?'

'I told you.' Libby felt herself blushing again. 'We've sorted it out.'

'Not marriage, though,' said Fran.

'Not marriage, no. Not yet anyway,' said Libby, surprising herself.

'Well! So there's hope?'

'Don't know,' said Libby. 'We'll see.' She took a deep breath. 'So. Is Guy excited? Are *you* excited?'

'Yes to both questions.' Fran certainly sounded as though she was fizzing. 'I'm sure this is the way to do it – quickly, with no long waits while everything gets boring.'

'I think you're right,' said Libby. 'How's Sophie? And your three?'

'I've already called Jeremy. He wasn't overjoyed as it was still only four o'clock New York time, but he's coming over. *With* the girlfriend.'

'Coo! You've never met her, have you?'

'No. I haven't told the girls yet, because I know they'll both moan at me and call me selfish.'

'Then tell them they're the selfish ones and hang up,' said Libby.

'I might well do that,' said Fran, which made Libby raise her eyebrows. 'Sophie's just thrilled about the whole thing, and is likely to outshine everybody.'

'That's good. Is she giving her dad away?'

Fran laughed again. 'No, but I suppose she could be his "best woman", couldn't she? You were for Pete and Harry.'

'Excellent idea,' crowed Libby. 'See? All organised. Now I'd better go and get Ben's lunch before we go and see Steeple Farm.'

'Good luck,' said Fran.

I'll need it, thought Libby, and she went into the kitchen.

Chapter Seventeen

STEEPLE FARM WAS AT the other end of the village. The lane turned right from the main Nethergate road and wound up between high banks until, as Libby had thought before, they could have been miles from civilisation. No traffic noise reached them, apart from the sound of a distant tractor. Libby looked up at the house and realised that the two dormer windows with eyebrows of thatch no longer looked like evil eyes.

Ben opened the heavy oak door onto the anachronistic hallway, with its thick red carpet, walls painted cream, gilt touches in the wall lights, switches and chain-store picture frames. A teak telephone table, complete with cushioned seat and space for directories, stood by the stairs. They exchanged rueful glances.

'This hall is flagged, isn't it?' asked Libby. 'She didn't have it pulled up?'

'No. It's still in the kitchen, too, underneath the vinyl.' Ben pulled a face and led the way into the pale wood and stainless steel kitchen Libby remembered so well.

'Is the larder still here?' asked Libby, opening the door to what once would have been a boot room. Still was, with old coats and rubber boots forlornly abandoned years ago, by the looks of it.

'Over here.' Ben opened a door. 'She seems to have kept it as a junk store.'

'There must be other places in the house more suitable,' said Libby. 'I've always wanted a larder.'

'So you're thinking of it favourably?' Ben closed the door and took her by the shoulders.

'Maybe,' said Libby cautiously. 'It'll take a lot of thinking through.'

Ben nodded, satisfied, and let her go. They spent the next half hour wandering through the house and exclaiming, usually at the gross excesses of Millie's taste.

'I can't believe she gave birth to Peter and James,' said Ben, gazing up at a particularly hideous lampshade. 'Were they changelings, do you suppose?'

'She told me she'd done all this after their father died. I suppose they took after him.'

'I don't remember him that well. He was quiet and adored Millie, I know that much.'

A shout floated up to them through the open casement window and Libby leant out under the thatch. Lewis and Adam stared up at her.

'Door's open,' she called back. 'Come in and we'll be down.'

'I haven't said anything about the possibility of us moving here,' she whispered to Ben as they went towards the stairs. 'Just that Peter wants it done up.'

Ben raised an eyebrow, but nodded.

'Cor!' said Lewis, wandering through the downstairs. 'Great house, pissin' awful décor.'

Libby laughed. 'It's Ben's aunt you're talking about here,' she said. 'Come and meet him.'

Lewis and Ben shook hands warily as Adam burst through from the back of the house.

'This is a great place, Ma,' he said. 'Masses of room. You should live here.'

Libby opened her mouth and shut it again, shooting a warning look at Ben, who smirked.

'So have a wander round, Lewis, and then tell us what you'd do with it,' she continued. 'Shall we have a look round outside, Ad?'

She, Ben and Adam went out through the boot room and into the overgrown garden, beyond which was what looked like a paddock.

'It used to be a farm, didn't it?' she asked, leaning her arms on the five-bar gate into the paddock. 'Did they sell the rest off?'

'Let,' said Ben. 'They still have a tenant farmer, like we do at The Manor. If we put the land up for sale some developer would leap in and apply for planning permission.'

'They wouldn't get it, surely?' said Libby, shocked.

Ben shrugged. 'They might, although at the moment no one would buy or develop it with the economic situation as it is.'

'Huge bloody garage,' said Adam coming round the side of the house and brushing off cobwebs. 'Part of it's set up as a workshop.'

'Is it unlocked?' said Ben in surprise.

'Yeah. Well, I got in. Doesn't seem to be much in there to pinch.'

Ben went off to investigate and Adam joined his mother at the gate.

'This is exactly the sort of place where I wanted to live when I was a child,' said Libby dreamily. 'Put a pony in that paddock and I'd have been in heaven.'

Adam looked at her with his head on one side. 'And you'd still like to, wouldn't you?'

'Well, yes,' said Libby, with a nervous laugh. 'I mean, who wouldn't.'

'I just wondered why you and Ben were here instead of Pete,' said Adam.

'Because of asking Lewis, of course,' said Libby, looking at him with wide eyes.

'Oh, right.' Adam nodded and looked across the paddock to the stand of trees beyond.

Libby frowned at him suspiciously and turned to go back in the house. She found Lewis and Ben sitting at the kitchen table discussing floors.

'What do you think, Lewis?' she said, sitting down.

'It's a great house, and in terrific condition. Little bit of damp here and there, but whoever looked after it before all this bloody tat –' he waved a dismissive hand '– knew what they were doing. Just needs a cosmetic overhaul, except in here, of course. I reckon they've wrecked a good bit of the original room putting this lot in.' He looked round and shook his head. 'You wouldn't credit it, would you?'

'The original fittings went to the owner's son,' said Ben. 'He's got the dresser and the Aga, and the big kitchen table.'

'Lucky bugger. Is he the one who wants this place put back to rights?'

Ben nodded. 'Do you want to take it on?'

Lewis looked uncomfortable. 'I don't really do this sort of stuff these days,' he said. Then he grinned. 'But I could be project manager, if you like. I reckon I'll have the time for a bit, won't I? My show will be on hold until I'm in the clear, and we aren't due to start filming anyway for another couple of months. What do you think?'

'Sounds good,' said Ben slowly, 'but I'll have to talk to Peter, obviously.'

'Oh, yeah, fine,' said Lewis. 'Just let me know soon as, eh?' He stood up. 'Come on, Ad, I'd better get back to Miss Droopy Drawers.'

'Is that Cindy Dale?'

'Yeah. You must come over and meet her, Lib. I'd got quite the wrong idea about everything, you know, and I think the public had when all that business blew up.'

'I thought you wanted to talk to me today,' said Libby. 'That was one of the reasons I asked you out here.'

'You don't want me to take on this house?' Lewis looked puzzled.

'Yes, of course, but –'

'Not the right time now, anyway,' said Lewis. 'Tomorrow.'

'All right,' said Libby, with a quick look at Ben, who gazed studiously out of the window. 'Perhaps tomorrow morning. Oh, and you said you wanted to go to Harry's restaurant, didn't you? How about the four of us go tomorrow evening. Ben? Would that be OK?'

Ben smiled and nodded. 'We could talk about this place, couldn't we?' he said craftily.

'Great,' said Lewis, beaming. 'Tell me what time when you come over in the morning.' He stopped on his way to the door and looked serious. 'You will come, won't you?'

'Yes,' said Libby, 'I'll come.'

Surprisingly, Ben had no objections. Throughout the evening

they talked about Steeple Farm and what it could be like. Ben's memories of it as a child were vague, but very much as a typical country farmhouse.

'The only room I remember being different was the sitting room,' he said at one point. 'Millie must have persuaded my uncle to let her decorate it. It had silver embossed wallpaper on the chimney breast and bamboo paper in the recesses. I think she boarded up the fireplace and put in a gas fire.'

'It hasn't changed much now,' said Libby. 'Except the wallpaper's different and there's a television in front of the fireplace.'

'It's a pity,' said Ben, 'that we didn't get together sooner. It would have been a wonderful place to bring up children.'

'If we'd got together sooner Millie would still be at Steeple Farm,' said Libby, 'but I see what you mean. I said that to Adam this afternoon. It was the sort of place I dreamt about when I was a girl reading horsey books.'

'Didn't you dream about places like The Manor?' said Ben.

'No, they weren't homely enough. In the books I read, they always belonged to the snotty family with the daughter who won everything at the Pony Club competitions and came a cropper in the end.'

'That was our Susan, then,' laughed Ben, 'although you wouldn't have said we were a snotty family, would you?'

'Not with your mother,' grinned Libby, 'anything but.'

The following morning Adam went off in the Renault and Ben lent Libby the Land Rover.

'It's really not difficult to drive,' he said. 'Just remember there are more gears than your car has.'

Libby looked down nervously from the driving seat. 'It seems very high,' she said.

'Then you can see over hedges,' grinned Ben. 'Go on, off you go. I'll see you later.'

'Will you book a table for tonight and ring me so I can tell Lewis?'

'Yes,' said Ben with a sigh. 'Now stop dithering and go.'

Libby drove slowly and carefully towards Nethergate, infuriating several other drivers. Pulling up on the Creekmarsh drive and letting out a great sigh of relief, she found her shoulders ached from tension. Lewis came out to meet her and helped her down.

'It's like driving a bloody lorry,' she said, stumbling against him. 'And I've got to drive it back.'

'Come and have a cuppa,' said Lewis, tucking her arm into his. 'Katie's got the kettle on.'

Katie didn't look particularly down, thought Libby, when they went into the kitchen. Tired, perhaps, but otherwise just as Libby had last seen her.

'Nice to see you again, lovey,' she said. 'Been a bit much, all this, hasn't it?'

'Certainly has,' said Libby, sitting at the table. 'Did you have a good weekend at home?'

Katie turned back to the kettle. 'Oh, yes,' she said. 'Caught up with a few things and had a good dust round, you know.'

'Do you want to come upstairs and meet Cindy,' asked Lewis, who had been hovering by the door, 'or drink your tea down here?'

'I'd rather have my tea here,' said Libby, 'and anyway, I want to hear about her before I meet her. You haven't said much, either you or Ad, except that she wasn't what you'd expected.'

There was a snort from the other side of the table. Libby and Lewis looked at Katie's uncompromising back. 'Doesn't like her,' mouthed Lewis. Libby controlled a strong desire to giggle.

Lewis came and sat down at the table. 'Well,' he began, 'I thought she –'

'Oh, I'm sorry,' said a quiet voice from the doorway. 'I didn't know you had company.'

Lewis, Libby and Katie turned towards the door, and Cindy Dale came into the room.

Chapter Eighteen

LIBBY STARED. CINDY GAVE her a shy smile, hesitating by the table.

'Come and sit down,' said Lewis, pulling out a chair. 'Katie's just making tea. This is my friend Libby. She's Adam's mother.'

Katie almost slammed three mugs down in front of them and stomped away to the fridge.

'Hello,' said Cindy. Her voice was light, her vowels home counties. Stranger and stranger, thought Libby. 'Adam's nice. You must be proud of him.'

'I am, yes. I'm proud of all my children.'

'How many do you have? Is Adam the oldest?' Cindy leant forward, wide, confiding grey eyes staring into Libby's own.

'No, the youngest. Belinda's the middle one, and Dominic's the eldest.'

'What lovely names,' said Cindy, a trace of wistfulness in her voice. As Katie poured tea into the mugs, Cindy looked up, pushed a lock of mouse-brown hair behind an ear and smiled. 'Thank you, Katie,' she said.

Katie grunted and with thinned lips went out of the kitchen.

'She doesn't like me,' said Cindy.

Lewis cleared his throat. 'I'm sure she does, she's just – er – a bit – um –'

'She was like that with me at first.' Libby rushed in to avoid the difficult moment and Lewis looked grateful.

'Oh? Have you known her long?'

'Er – no, not long,' said Libby, feeling a bit pink. 'She'll be fine in a day or so. Are you staying that long?' Oh, bugger, she thought. I shouldn't have said that.

'I don't really know,' said Cindy, turning the grey eyes towards Lewis, who was studying knotholes in the table.

'Oh.' Libby was at a loss. She didn't know why Cindy was here, what she'd told Lewis or the police and, most importantly, why she was so different from the picture painted of her by the media three years before. This was no glamour model. This was a girl who wouldn't have been out of place in the pony books Libby had been remembering. She wore a loose shirt over jeans, had thick, straight hair and wore no make-up on her high-cheekboned face. Libby tried to remember if there'd been any photographs on the various sites she'd turned up on the search engine. She didn't think there had been, but the descriptions of Cindy as a model turned singer had suggested a very different type of person than the calm, quiet girl who sat opposite her now.

'Is the house much changed?' she asked, and cursed herself again. 'Sorry. That was insensitive of me.'

Cindy's smile was sad. 'Oh, yes, of course,' she said. 'Lewis has done quite a bit more than we ever got round to.'

We? Libby risked a glance at Lewis, who was now concentrating on a new knothole. 'I suppose he would, being a television DIY expert,' she said out loud, and wondered how on earth she was going to get out of this conversation. With relief, she heard her mobile trilling from inside her basket.

'Ben? Oh, great. Yes, I'll tell him. No, I didn't crash it. I might on the way back, though.' She turned to Lewis. 'Ben's booked our table for eight, if that's OK?' She smiled at Cindy. 'Sorry we're taking him away from you this evening.'

Cindy looked startled. Lewis cleared his throat, looking relieved. Libby realised he hadn't relished telling his house guest that she was to be left alone. Well, she thought, if you turn up out of the blue, you can hardly expect to be entertained the whole time, can you? Out loud, she said, 'I'd better go and find Adam and let him know. I'll see you in a bit, Lewis.' She held out her hand to Cindy. 'Nice to meet you,' she said.

Cindy put a soft hand into hers and smiled. 'Yes,' she said. 'It was.'

Outside, Libby realised she had no idea which part of the

garden Adam was working on, and as she didn't want go back in and ask, she had to go exploring.

The gardens were extensive. She found her way first to the parterre, where Adam wasn't, then following the downward slope of a meadow with a ha-ha halfway down, which would doubtless one day be another lawn, found herself by the edge of the creek, or the inlet, she remembered. And there, just to her right, stood the weatherboarded building which must be the sailing club. Moored alongside a pontoon, several small boats bobbed and swung contentedly, like so many seabirds. Finding an ancient wooden bench, Libby sat down and contemplated the view.

The river was at its widest here, and almost dead ahead was the sea. On the opposite bank, she could see trees, a church spire and a couple of houses with riverside access. Expensive, she thought. But no more expensive than this place. She turned to look back and discovered that the house couldn't be seen from here. So this place couldn't be seen from the house either. She turned back towards the river and the sailing club. An ideal place for concealing activities, it would be, supposing you needed to. She stood up and made for the lane which ran alongside the meadow and took her down to the pontoon.

Sure enough a small notice attached to the door, which was firmly padlocked, announced it to be the Creekmarsh Sailing Club, Private, Members Only. Not many members, thought Libby, looking at the collection of small boats, although perhaps there were other moorings. She wondered if Gerald Shepherd, or any former owners of Creekmarsh, had sailed from here, or used it, perhaps, as a secret way of ingress or egress. It looked possible that the estate owned the land, which probably meant that the sailing club leased the building and the moorings. She must ask Lewis. Whom she now heard calling her name.

'Over here,' she shouted, waving at the small figure at the top of the meadow. She watched as he trotted down to meet her, his unnatural tension of earlier now replaced with his usual ebullience.

'Watcher doing all the way down here?' he asked breathlessly, as he came up beside her.

'Exploring,' grinned Libby. 'I started looking for Adam by the parterre, and just carried on in this direction.' She pointed towards the Creekmarsh Sailing Club. 'Ben used to sail here with a friend in his schoolboy days. Do you own the land?'

'I dunno.' He walked forward curiously. 'Never thought about it. The land goes right down to the river, so I suppose I do.' He nodded towards the sailing club. 'D'you reckon that's illegal?'

'The building? No, I should think they lease the land and the moorings from the estate. You'd better check with your solicitor.'

Lewis groaned. 'Bloody solicitors again. You wouldn't believe what's been happening.'

'No, so why don't you tell me.' She led him to the bench and sat down. 'You were going to before Cindy interrupted us.'

'Ears of a bat, that girl,' growled Lewis. 'Bet she heard.'

'You don't like her either, then?'

'Oh, I dunno.' Lewis sighed. 'It's just such a shock, her walking in like that. *She's* such a shock, herself. Don't get me wrong,' he added hastily, 'she ain't done anything awful, like, but it's got everyone confused.'

'Tell me how it happened,' said Libby. 'From the beginning.'

'Well,' said Lewis, leaning back and turning his face up to the sun, which was just emerging from the overhanging trees on the other side of the lane. 'Sunday afternoon, see, and I was up there all on me own. Katie wasn't back, and I didn't know when she'd turn up, so when I heard the front door open, I thought it was her and just sort of yelled out.'

'Wasn't it locked?'

'Oh, yeah, that's why I thought it was Katie, see, 'cos she's got her own key. Anyway, there's no answer, so I goes to the stairs and there's this girl standing looking up at me. "Who are you?" she says. So I thought, bloody hell, what a cheek, and I goes haring down the stairs. "Excuse me," I says, "but who are *you*? I just happen to be the owner of this place." So she looks real surprised, like, and takes a step back. "But it belongs to Gerald," she says. "Not any more, it don't," I says, "and who are you anyway?" So she tells me and you could have knocked me

124

down with a feather.'

'I bet,' murmured Libby.

'So anyway, I takes her into the kitchen and makes her a cuppa – for shock, you know – and tell her the whole story. All about how Tony sold the house to me with his power of wotsit, then about the body in the garden. Then she sort of puts her head in her hands and starts crying.' He shook his head. 'I didn't know what to do.'

'So what *did* you do?'

'Well, I'm shocked, like, 'cos of thinking that she'd run off with old German Shepherd, and then she explains. And, cor, Lib, it just shows how the papers can get stuff wrong.'

'So what does she say happened, then?'

'This is the bit that explains a lot.' Lewis turned to face her and leant forward. 'See, Lib, we was all wondering about that power –'

'Of attorney,' supplied Libby.

'Yeah, because how come Tony had it? When old Shepherd had done a runner three years before? Well, it turns out that he had the beginnings of that thing, you know,' he clicked his fingers, annoyed, 'where your memory goes.'

'Alzheimer's disease?'

'That's the one. And he knows it, so he gets this all set up with Tony.'

'How did he know Tony?'

'I dunno. Tony's got – had – all sorts of connections in the entertainment business, like I told you, so I expect that's how. Anyway, then Cindy and Kenneth come down here to look after him, like, but then Ken gets this *Dungeon Trial* gig, so Cindy and Shepherd are left down here on their own. And then Shepherd starts trying it on.'

'Ah!' said Libby.

'Well, yeah, but then he starts getting violent, and she gets scared, so she runs off. She tells Tony, who seems to have been a bit like a dad to her, and he tells her Shepherd's looking for her. Next thing is, she hears Ken's come out of his dungeon so she goes back, sort of secretly, like, and finds Ken's come to all these wrong conclusions. Then o' course, Shepherd turns up and has a fit, and knocks old Ken cold. So Tony turns up – always there, the bugger, ain't he? – and tells her to run away, like, because if she's found there she'll be for it, too, and she goes off somewhere, she hasn't said where, and a couple of days later Tony sends her a false passport and says she can lie low for a bit, and he's got all her real papers, birth certificate and wotnot so she can return when she likes.'

'I don't get it,' said Libby, frowning. 'Why on earth would Tony tell her to run away? She had nothing to do with it, and surely they could have proved Shepherd killed his son?'

'Don't ask me,' said Lewis with a shrug, 'except that Tony was going to cover it up, like, to protect German Shepherd, I expect, so he wanted her out of the way.'

'She'd be the heir, though, wouldn't she, if Gerald died? As Kenneth's widow? Is that why she came back?'

'I reckon so,' Lewis nodded. 'She still had her keys, see. She heard about the skeleton in the garden on the news – she's been living in Spain lately – and realised old Ken'd been dug up. Then, o' course, she heard about the theory that she and Shepherd had run away together.'

'And she hadn't heard it before?' Libby's eyes were wide with disbelief. 'That's ridiculous. It was all over the media. She couldn't have missed it, even if she'd gone straight to Spain. Besides, it hasn't been confirmed by the police that it's Kenneth's body. Did she say it was Kenneth?'

'That's what she says, anyway, and that's what she told the coppers. That Big Bertha – cor, she weren't 'arf mad!'

'Why? No one's found out where Shepherd is now, have they? According to Cindy, all she's got to do is find him. Does Cindy know where?'

'She says not,' said Lewis, getting up and stretching. 'Didn't know the house was sold, either. So she's sort of in limbo. I reckon she was expecting to inherit it one day and when she heard about old Ken's body –'

'On the news which she didn't listen to or read three years ago,' said Libby.

'Look, it's her story, not mine. 'Course it don't sound right, but old Bertha's looking into it, so I expect she'll get to the bottom of it.'

'So why's Cindy still here?'

'Well,' said Lewis, looking uncomfortable, 'I didn't like to ask her to go. She did live here once.'

'But not now,' said Libby. 'Honestly, Lewis, you're too soft-hearted for your own good. You'll have to tell her to go. You wait, she'll start taking over before you know it.'

'That's what Katie says. Cor, she right had the hump when she got back and found her here.'

'Did she know who she was?' Libby frowned. 'She wouldn't have met her before.'

'Katie turned up Monday morning, walked into the kitchen and there was Cindy doing herself some breakfast. I was up in me bedroom, and I didn't hear about it until I came down and Cindy tells me. And Katie's in a right hump with me, as I said.'

'Why, though? It doesn't make any difference to her, does it?'

'No, it's this taking over thing. Cindy's got a bit of the old lady of the manor about her, see? Treats Katie like the faithful old family wotsit.'

'Retainer.'

'One of them, yeah. Anyway, the faithful old retainer's got lunch ready. Going to stay?'

'No, I won't, thanks, Lewis. I can't say I took to Miss Cindy Dale, either. But she's so different from what I imagined.'

'Yeah, no tits and teeth, eh? Me and all. You'd better say hello to Adam, though, hadn't you, or he'll be miffed with me for not letting him know you've been here.'

They walked up to the house through the parterre and found Adam coming to meet them.

'Hi, Ma,' he said. 'Lewis, I think you'd better go in. Cindy's looking as sick as a parrot. Big Bertha's back.'

Chapter Nineteen

WITH AN EXPRESSION OF horror on his face, Lewis shot into the house. Adam made a face at his mother and began to walk her towards the Land Rover.

'So, you met her?'

Libby nodded.

'What did you make of her, then?'

'She's obviously very different from how we all thought she'd be, and she's telling a very strange, and, frankly, unbelievable story.'

'I thought Lewis believed it.'

'Well, I've put some doubts in his mind now. What does Big Bertha want?'

'Goodness knows. To talk to Cindy, I expect.'

'What I can't understand,' said Libby, turning round with her hand on the driver's door, 'is why a superintendent is out on the ground, so to speak.'

'Huh?'

'They're usually sitting behind a desk directing operations.'

'Not on telly, they're not.'

'If you think about it, most of the TV detectives are inspectors,' said Libby. 'Like Ian, or Donnie Murray.'

'Donnie?'

'Don't you remember? When DCI Murray came to see *The Hop Pickers*, his wife called him Donnie. You were all there.'

'God, Ma, that was years ago.'

'Two years, that's all. Anyway, that's all beside the point. Superintendent Bertram is coming out and questioning suspects. I wonder why?'

'You have the strangest mind,' said Adam, frowning at his

mother. 'That isn't important, surely? You said Cindy's story was unbelievable, so that's the strangest thing.'

'Perhaps.' Libby turned and climbed into the Land Rover. 'See you later. Ben's booked a table at Harry's for eight.'

'I'll be home before that,' said Adam, 'unless you're throwing me out.'

'Stoopid,' said Libby, and ruffled his hair. 'See you.'

But Cindy's truly was an unbelievable story, she thought as she drove past Steeple Mount without even thinking about the grisly chapel. Especially when you remembered that Fran wasn't certain the skeleton was Kenneth. Libby pulled the Land Rover into a gateway and thought. Then, carefully, she turned back the way she had come and drove down into Nethergate.

Fran was in the gallery with Sophie and professed herself ready for a cup of tea. Sophie happily agreed to shop-sit, and Libby walked purposefully down Harbour Street to The Blue Anchor.

'We could have had a cup of tea at home,' said Fran.

'But I can smoke here,' said Libby, pulling a battered packet out of her basket. 'I still haven't *quite* given up.'

'So what's the problem?'

While Mavis went to fetch their tea, Libby told her Cindy's story.

'And I thought, well, if it wasn't Kenneth in the wood, the girl must be lying. And if she's lying about that, what else is she lying about?'

'Look, I know I said I didn't think it was Kenneth, but I'm not infallible. It seems most likely it *is* him, after all.'

'Yes, I know, that's why even I managed to work it out. If it's got Shepherd's DNA it seems there's only two people it could be, Shepherd himself or Kenneth.'

'It's not Shepherd.' Fran shook her head. 'But I'm concerned about why I thought it wasn't Kenneth. As you said, who else could it be?'

'How is DNA extracted from a skeleton?' asked Libby after a moment.

'I don't know!' Fran looked startled.

'And the other question,' said Libby, looking excited, 'is how

129

did they get Shepherd's DNA?'

Fran paused in the act of raising her mug to her lips, an arrested expression on her face.

'I mean, he's not around now, and Lewis has cleared out most of the stuff that was left behind.'

'Except those albums, but they couldn't get DNA off those, could they?'

'Did they find something in the attic, do you think?' Libby squinted against cigarette smoke.

'Even if they did, they couldn't be sure it was Shepherd's.' Fran frowned. 'This is very peculiar. It could be anybody.'

'I wonder if Lewis knows how they got the DNA? They asked him if he'd ever met Shepherd, didn't they?'

'Did they? I suppose if they asked him if there had been anything of Shepherd's left in the house ... they would have wanted to rule him out, wouldn't they?'

Libby nodded. 'Exactly what I was thinking.' She stubbed out her cigarette in Mavis's tin ashtray. 'I shall ask him tonight.'

'Tonight?'

'He's coming over and Adam, Ben and I are taking him to The Pink Geranium.'

'You've got very friendly with him.'

Libby grinned. 'He fancies Ad, so he's treating me like a mother-substitute.'

'Don't you mind him fancying Ad?'

'No, why should I? Ad's over twenty-one, and if he decides he wants to try something different, who am I to stand in his way?'

Fran looked uncertain.

'Anyway, he's coming over tonight so I'll ask him about the DNA. He's also coming to talk about something else.' Libby stopped and looked down at the table.

'Oh?'

Libby fidgeted. 'Well, I suppose I can tell you about it, but you're not to say anything to anyone else.'

'Not even Guy?'

'Oh, I suppose he's all right. But no one else.'

Fran made a comical face. 'Cross my heart,' she said.

So Libby told her all about Steeple Farm and Ben's suggestion.

'I thought you didn't like it,' said Fran.

'I didn't when Millie lived there, but it's the cosmetics I didn't like, not the building. And if Lewis oversees the prettification it'll be back to a real old Kentish farmhouse.'

'You're happy at number 17, though.'

'I always have been, but if Ben and I live together Steeple Farm would be more practical. And there'll be more room for the children to come and stay.'

The corners of Fran's mouth were turned down, and now Libby was worried. 'What's the matter?'

'I can't see it, that's all,' she said. 'Sorry.'

'Oh.' Libby was nonplussed. 'What does that mean if we go ahead with it?'

'I don't know,' Fran sighed. 'Oh, don't take any notice. I expect I've started being wrong again. I haven't had any practice recently.'

'All right,' said Libby slowly.

'And now I'd better get back to the shop,' said Fran, standing up. 'Sophie's very good about taking over, but she's only been back from uni a week or so, and all we've had her doing is working.'

Libby stood up and picked up her basket. 'What about your lot? Told the girls yet?'

Fran laughed. 'I sent them an email invitation. So far there's been a stony silence. I'm waiting for one or both of them to turn up on my doorstep in high dudgeon.'

Libby arrived back in Steeple Martin at about half past two and drove the Land Rover up to The Manor. Popping her head round the door she called for Hetty, who looked out from the kitchen.

'Just leaving the Land Rover for Ben,' she said.

'Righto, gal. D'you want a cuppa?'

'No, thanks, Het, I won't,' said Libby, reflecting that she'd been drinking tea all day. 'I'll get off home. Got some catching up to do.'

'Oh, ah.' Hetty nodded. 'Two men in the house now. Makes

131

a difference.'

Libby smiled ruefully. 'Certainly does,' she said.

In fact, it was the washing she was finding hardest to cope with, she thought as she walked back down The Manor drive, never having mastered Ben's shortcut through The Manor woods. Adam seemed to generate five times more washing than she did herself, and the thought of having to take on Ben's as well was daunting. She took a deep breath and put her shoulders back. No quitting now, she told herself. You've more or less committed to this new life. The one thing she wasn't going to do though, she thought, fitting the key into the lock of number 17, was sell her cottage.

Ben and she were happily ensconced on the sofa in the window of The Pink Geranium while Adam bothered Harry in the kitchen when Lewis arrived. Adam brought Harry out to be introduced and Libby, amused, watched them size one another up.

'Nice bloke,' said Lewis after Harry had left them with menus. 'Does his own cooking?'

'Oh, yes,' said Adam. 'I've helped in the kitchen sometimes.'

'Jack of all trades, you are, mate,' said Lewis, giving him an affectionate thump on the arm. Adam grinned and buried his face in the menu.

Over pre-dinner drinks, Ben asked Lewis if he'd had any thoughts on Steeple Farm.

'A few,' he said, 'but we've had the cops over again today, and I've not had much time to think about anything.'

'What did they want?' asked Libby. 'Ad said he hadn't heard anything.'

'More questions for Cindy,' said Lewis. 'I don't think they believe her story either.'

'Why? They didn't let you stay while they talked to her, did they?'

'No, 'course not, but she didn't look very happy when they left.'

'Do you know why the superintendent is taking such an active role?' asked Libby. 'It's not normal.'

'How should I know? Perhaps she's one of these people who

can't delegate.'

'I didn't think they had a choice in the police force,' said Ben.

'I didn't either,' said Libby. 'Now, Lewis, the other thing I wanted to ask you –'

'Was what?' said Lewis, looking resigned.

'Are you wishing you hadn't asked me to look into this?' Libby frowned at him.

'Was that the other question?' asked Lewis, and Ben and Adam burst out laughing.

'No! Honestly, men,' said Libby, picking up her menu.

'Oh, go on, Lib.' Lewis leant across and patted her hand. 'I was joking. What was the question?'

'How did they get Gerald Shepherd's DNA?'

A silence fell.

'What the hell do you want to know that for?' asked Ben finally.

'A theory,' said Libby stubbornly.

'Oh, God, here we go again,' said Ben and picked up his own menu.

Lewis shot a worried look at Adam, then turned to Libby. 'Why?' he asked.

'I wondered how they knew the skeleton had the same DNA as Gerald Shepherd if he's disappeared. Could be dead for all we know.'

'He is if he *is* the skeleton.'

'Wrong age group,' said Libby. 'But somehow, they got hold of his DNA because they would have thought first of all that the body was his and they needed to know if it was.'

'I told you, they came and searched the house –' began Lewis.

'I was there. They hadn't searched it before, had they?'

'No. But I remember you saying they'd check his DNA the first time we had a chat about it.' Lewis was now looking very puzzled.

'Well, I didn't know much about it all, then, did I? But now, I wonder how they got it? It couldn't be from a hairbrush, or a toothbrush, because all of that had gone.' Libby turned again to

Lewis. 'Was any of that sort of personal stuff still there when you moved in?'

'No.' Lewis frowned. 'There wasn't much the first time I saw it, either. So it had been cleaned out by then.'

'When Tony West took you to see it?'

'Yes! You know all this, Lib.'

'I know, I know.' Libby sighed. 'It's just so annoying when you can't get to the bottom of something and there are no helpful police to ask.'

Ben patted her hand. 'Just as well,' he said. 'You'd only go blundering in and get yourself hit over the head again.'

Lewis looked horrified. 'Hit over the head?'

'I wasn't,' said Libby. 'I was sort of kidnapped.'

Lewis goggled.

'Nothing would have happened to us,' Libby continued, 'we just had to be got out of the way.'

'Us?' Lewis's voice went up an octave.

'Fran was with me,' said Libby. 'But we were OK. You can see that, can't you?'

'Oh, yes,' said Lewis, looking depressed. Adam gave him a nudge.

'Come on, mate, don't let it get you down. I told you Ma was mad. Just ignore her and choose your food. I can recommend the Quesadillas de Hongos.'

'Huh?'

'Mushrooms,' chorused the other three, as Donna came up to take their order.

Lewis cheered up during the meal, despite only drinking fizzy water. The conversation turned to Steeple Farm and, finally, Ben confessed to Lewis and Adam his thoughts on moving into it with Libby.

'I guessed as much,' said Adam triumphantly. 'When Ma was standing there looking all moony at that paddock.'

Libby sighed. 'I wasn't moony.'

'You'll love it, Ma. You always wanted a country cottage.'

'I've got one,' said Libby. 'Number 17 is a cottage in the country, isn't it?'

'In a village, yes,' said Adam.

'Exactly. I didn't want to be isolated.'

'Steeple Farm isn't isolated,' said Ben.

'I know.' Libby turned to him. 'It's a lovely house, Ben. And when Lewis has finished with it, it'll be even better.'

'Hey! That's great,' said Lewis, scooping up the last of his refried beans. 'I'd love to do it for you, Lib. You wouldn't like it to be a project on the prog, would you?'

Ben and Libby looked at each other.

'I thought you were worried about that? Doing another series, I mean?' said Libby.

'No one's said I'm not,' said Lewis with a grin. 'If I got in touch with the producer and suggested Steeple Farm I'd know, wouldn't I?'

'I'm not sure,' said Ben. 'I don't know that Peter would be comfortable with it.'

'And there's the privacy aspect,' said Libby.

'Oh, right.' Lewis looked disappointed. 'Well, if you change your minds –'

'We'll tell you,' said Libby. 'But you're still happy to oversee the project?'

Lewis brightened. 'Oh, yeah. Give me something to do apart from worrying meself sick over all this murder stuff.'

Harry came out to join them for a drink at the end of the meal, and Libby was amused at his avuncular treatment of both Adam and Lewis, who was plainly fascinated.

'Quite the father figure, isn't he?' murmured Ben. 'Is that what marriage does for you?'

'Makes you into a father?' Libby twinkled at him. 'It did for you!'

Later, over a nightcap in the sitting room of number 17 Ben returned to the subject of Steeple Farm.

'You're still not convinced, are you?' he said.

Libby looked uncomfortable. 'It's such a big step.'

'But you like the house, now?'

'Oh, yes.' Libby smiled. 'Adam's right, it is a dream place.'

'But you still like this house.'

'I *love* this house,' admitted Libby. 'Although I've still got a rubbishy cane sofa and odd chairs round the kitchen table it's exactly how I want it, and I've even got the conservatory for my painting. Not,' she added guiltily, 'that I'm doing much of that at the moment.'

Ben looked at her with his head on one side. 'Then had we better give Steeple Farm a miss?' he said. 'I'd hate to drag you away from here and have you resent me for it.'

'You said I could keep this place anyway,' said Libby, prevaricating.

Ben nodded. 'So what do you want to do?'

Libby sighed heavily. 'This is so sudden,' she said.

'Hardly sudden,' laughed Ben. 'I've been suggesting we live together properly for ages.'

'I know, but moving. That's what's so sudden.'

'I'll tell you what,' said Ben, 'we'll let Lewis carry on with the project anyway, and make a decision at the end.'

'Who's going to pay?' asked Libby. 'Peter doesn't want to.'

'I will. I'll get it back when Pete eventually sells it, or if we do decide to live in it, all well and good.'

Libby flung her arms round him. 'Oh, Ben,' she said. 'I do love you.'

'Thank goodness for that,' said Ben.

Chapter Twenty

'WHAT WAS THAT PROGRAMME Gerald Shepherd did in the nineties?' asked Fran.

Libby frowned at the telephone. 'Why do you want to know?'

'I thought I'd see if it was on DVD.'

'But why?'

'I want to know what he looked like in later life.'

'There's sure to be photographs on the Internet,' said Libby.

'No, I want to see him in action,' insisted Fran. 'So, what was it?'

'It comes up if you Google him,' said Libby. 'It was a political thriller.'

'Got it,' said Fran. '*Collateral Damage*. That's what it was. Thanks, Lib. I'll get on to it.'

Still frowning, Libby switched off the phone. Fran was obviously getting interested in the Creekmarsh murder, which wasn't, possibly, A Good Thing. Guy would be expecting her to concentrate on their rapidly approaching wedding, his attitude to the women's shared investigations being much like Ben's.

But Fran's interest would only be piqued if she thought there was something to be uncovered. If her mind had told her something was wrong. Otherwise, she would back away from any involvement, unsure of her own gift, if that's what it was. To Fran it often appeared more of a curse. Libby sighed and went to fetch a duster. Last night, after Ben had made his suggestion about staying put for the time being, she'd taken a critical look round this cottage she loved so much and noticed the dust and hidden cobwebs. Time for a bit of a clean-up.

As she worked, her mind disassociated from her physical

actions, she thought through what she knew of the Creekmarsh murder. Or murders, probably. First, Adam had dug up part of a skeleton. Next, the police had discovered it to be approximately three years old and to match Gerald Shepherd's DNA, although how they obtained that Libby didn't know.

Next, Lewis had confessed that Tony West had sold him Creekmarsh with power of attorney for Gerald Shepherd. This had to have been obtained over three years ago, since that was the time Shepherd and his daughter-in-law had gone missing. Libby, from what Lewis had said, was sure that Lewis had been almost coerced into buying the place, presumably to offload it. It looked to be a long-term plan if Tony West's manipulation of Lewis's career was any guide, although his presence on *Housey Housey* may well have been simply as a reward for sexual favours, the offloading of Creekmarsh Place being an inspiration that came later, when Lewis's money came rolling in.

Meanwhile, Tony West himself was killed in his bedroom in Hampstead. Although Lewis had been questioned, it appeared the police didn't think he was connected, even though his fingerprints were found. Old, though, Libby thought, probably overlaid by others. So someone had wanted to cover up West's involvement with Shepherd, although they must have known it would come out when Lewis was questioned.

Then Cindy Dale had turned up – or Cindy Shepherd, as Libby supposed she was – with her story of Kenneth being killed by his father. It was perfectly feasible, given the DNA clue, but where was Gerald now? Fran was certain he was alive. Kenneth she wasn't so sure about, and if Fran wasn't sure you could almost be certain she was wrong.

This brought Libby up short. Fran had said she couldn't see Libby at Steeple Farm. At least, that was what it seemed like. But just because she couldn't see it didn't mean it wouldn't happen, thought Libby, taking a deep breath and pushing the thought away. If she could actually *see* Libby in three years' time still living at number 17, that would be different.

Still, unless the original DNA sample was faulty, it looked as though this skeleton had to be Kenneth on two counts. One, Fran was certain Gerald was alive and two, Kenneth, not Gerald, fell into the age group predicted by the DNA. Libby thought about the DNA. If it was wrong, then whose could it have been? And anyway, the police didn't get that sort of thing wrong, did they? They must have been sure they had bona fide samples of Gerald Shepherd's DNA. They wouldn't have made a mistake.

So now the police must be looking for Gerald Shepherd. No death certificate had been found, and Libby assumed the police would have checked with whatever was Somerset House these days. Central Records Office? And there was the Office of the Public Guardian, of course, where the power of attorney would be lodged. The police would have checked all of those.

But Cindy – a name which didn't suit her – thought Libby, had said he was suffering from the onset of Alzheimer's Disease. Surely he would have needed to be taken care of somewhere. Wouldn't there be records? And why didn't Cindy know? There were too many questions about Cindy. Where had she been, why had she come forward now and why hadn't she reported her father-in-law as a murderer in the first place.

Because, thought Libby, sitting down at the table still clasping a damp cloth, she must have been scared of Gerald. He'd killed Kenneth; if she reappeared she would still be a threat and he might have gone after her. Libby shook her head. No, that didn't work, because if Gerald had Alzheimer's he would have got progressively worse, so no threat at all. He probably wouldn't even remember her. But it could still be the reason she didn't come back to England until the discovery of Kenneth's body made her realise she could still inherit the estate. She didn't know Creekmarsh had been sold, but she could still be in line to inherit the proceeds of the sale.

Anyway, thought Libby, absently rubbing the damp cloth over the window frame, it still doesn't explain why she ran away in the first place. Except – of course. She stopped rubbing the window frame and smacked the table. If Tony was covering up for Gerald, he'd want her out of the way in case she told the police the truth.

The phone rang again.

''Ere, Libby, it's all go round here.' It was Lewis.

'What's happened now?'

'Cindy's discovered Tony's dead. Gawd, I haven't heard so much weepin' and wailin' in years. Katie's going round all tight-lipped 'cos I can hardly turn the kid out now, can I?'

'Didn't she know he was dead? Didn't you tell her that first day? Hadn't she tried to contact him before she came back?'

'No, she says he always said not to come back unless he said so, so she was afraid he'd stop her. And I thought I had told her, but I can't have done.'

'Bit of an evil genius our Tony, wasn't he?' said Libby. 'Is that why she stayed away, do you think? Because she was scared of Tony?' Libby hadn't thought of that one until now.

'Could be,' said Lewis slowly. 'He could be a bit scary.'

In fact, thought Libby, how convinced was everybody that Cindy was telling the truth about Kenneth's murderer? Could it have been Tony himself who killed him? If the body was Kenneth, of course. She must find out about that DNA.

'So what did you want, Lewis? Or was it just a sympathetic ear?'

He laughed. 'That an' all,' he said. 'No, I wanted to say thanks for last night. I was supposed to be taking you, not the other way round.'

'Pleasure,' said Libby. 'We enjoyed your company. Had Cindy waited up for you?'

'No, but Katie had. Apparently they had a row. I think Katie must've told Cindy where to get off ordering her about.'

'Quite right, too,' said Libby. 'Even if Cindy had still been the heir apparent, Katie isn't her servant.'

'Even I don't treat Katie like she does,' said Lewis. 'Anyway, Cindy'd gone off to bed in a huff, and this morning the police are back asking about Tony. And off she goes. Hysterics.'

'I still don't know why didn't she know before. When the police first questioned her it would have come up, surely?'

'I said, I thought she did know. When she was talking about him, it didn't occur to me she wouldn't have known. She'd told the police about him, an' all, and I suppose they thought she knew, too. They'd been checking when she come over here. Flights and that.'

'And when did she come?'

'Sunday, like she said. I reckon they'll have her for false passport and that.'

'I expect so, unless they think it's mitigating circumstances. No,' said Libby, catching herself up, 'of course they won't. She's going to be done as an accessory to murder and obstructing the police, isn't she?'

'S'pose so. Can't think why she come back. She must've known she'd be in trouble.'

'Perhaps Creekmarsh was enough of an incentive.'

'Yeah, but if old German Shepherd is still alive it wouldn't be hers anyway. Or the money. Not until he was dead.'

'Have they found a will?'

'They wouldn't tell me, would they? And I reckon if he made one, Tony would have it.'

'What about the solicitor who drew up the power of attorney? He probably drew up a will as well.'

'Don't ask me! How do I know? I'm sick of the whole thing now. I just want shot of the police, shot of Cindy and get on with me own life.'

'OK, OK,' said Libby, 'you don't want me ferreting about any more.'

'Oh, I didn't mean that, Libby,' he said, sounding awkward. 'You been great, but what you said at the beginning was right. The police always get there in the end, don't they? They'll find German Shepherd and that'll be that. Then they'll leave me alone.'

'Meanwhile, you must get rid of Cindy,' said Libby. 'Tell her she's got to go.'

'I can't!' Lewis wailed. 'I don't know how.'

'Then ask Katie to do it, she'd love to.'

'No, Cindy would just come straight to me. You could do it.'

Libby laughed. 'The same thing would apply. She wouldn't believe me and go straight to you.'

'You could come and back me up while I do it. If Katie does, Cindy'll just say she's been influencing me or something. She won't say that about you.'

'Oh, all right, I'll come. When do you want me?'

'Soon as you like,' said Lewis, sounding more like himself. 'Although I suppose we'll have to let her find herself somewhere to stay.'

'I'll help with that,' said Libby. 'Look, I'm going to have something to eat, then I'll be over.'

After lunch, Libby borrowed the Land Rover again and set off for Creekmarsh. The weather had turned and drizzly rain shrouded the hedgerows in a faint mist. The wipers screeched across the windscreen and Libby turned them off in disgust. She wasn't looking forward to a confrontation with Cindy Dale, and wondered what the outcome would be. Would she go? She presumably wouldn't be allowed to go back to Spain. She wouldn't have either her false passport or her real one, which hadn't yet been found, as far as Libby knew, although the police may have found all sorts of things by now. She sighed and wished Ian Connell had been on the investigating team.

As she turned into the Creekmarsh lane, she was surprised to find herself at the end of a queue of traffic. Was it a sailing day? she wondered. She gave up trying to edge along towards the gates and drew in to the lay-by near the church. It would be quicker to walk.

When she reached the drive she realised why the cars were there. Reporters. Not too many, as yet, but then, Lewis had said nothing about them on the phone, so this was presumably a recent leak, or even press conference. The rest of the horde would be here soon, she thought. The rusty gates were closed, and beyond them stood Adam, looking scared but determined, with a mobile to his ear. He looked relieved to see Libby, who pushed her way to the front of the crowd and slipped through the small gap he opened for her, practically being flattened by the press behind her.

'I've asked Lewis to call the police. Apparently they held a press conference because something had leaked about Shepherd owning this place. That had been kept quiet until now.'

Libby looked back at the crowd of reporters and photographers. They knew about the body being dug up and Shepherd's DNA. Why had the police kept quiet about the location, and, if they had, why had they now revealed it?

Chapter Twenty-one

THE ANSWER WAS SOON revealed. As Libby and Adam walked towards the house, a commotion behind them caused them to stop and look back. In quick succession came two police cars, a long black saloon and the familiar van belonging to Kent and Coast Television. Adam went reluctantly back down the drive and unlocked the gates. The police were more successful at holding back the crowds than he had been, and while the black saloon and one of the police cars drove up to the house, the other stayed at the gates. 'To repel boarders,' said Libby as she and Adam, unchallenged, followed the police into the house.

'Who was that in the unmarked police car?' asked Libby, as they hesitated in the hall.

'I couldn't see,' said Adam. 'Big Bertha, I suppose.'

'Still don't know why she's been so hands-on,' muttered Libby, and she turned to greet Katie who had emerged from the kitchen wiping her hands on a tea towel.

'Hello, lovey,' she said. 'What do they want now?'

'Don't know,' said Adam. 'I asked Lewis to call them because of the reporters turning up, but I didn't expect all this.'

Katie shrugged. 'Come and have a cuppa,' she said. 'We'll find out soon enough.'

Lewis appeared a few moments later looking scared.

'They're arresting Cindy,' he said.

'Really? What for?' asked Libby. 'I mean, which bit? False documents, leaving the scene of a crime, accessory, what?'

'False documents, I think,' said Lewis.

'They've only got her word for it about Ken's murder,' said Adam. 'I expect this is to get her into custody so they can have another go at her.'

'Serve her right,' said Katie, pouring boiling water into the big brown Betty teapot. 'Stuck-up little cow.'

No one reprimanded her, but Libby did feel a little sorry for Cindy. Although how she could have expected to get away with coming back to claim an inheritance under the circumstances seemed incredibly naïve.

'What about the press?' she asked. 'How did they get to hear about it?'

'Nobody seems to know, but it was hearing about Cindy's return apparently, and someone linked her up to Kenneth.'

'But Creekmarsh? The police haven't let that out,' said Adam.

'Same source I suppose,' said Libby. 'Somebody knows what's going on.' She looked over her shoulder. 'They'll probably think it's one of us.'

'It isn't criminal, though,' said Lewis.

'It wasn't you, was it?' Libby narrowed her eyes at him.

''Course not.' Lewis was indignant. 'D'you think I want a bunch of bloody reporters camping on my doorstep?'

'No,' conceded Libby, looking up at the sound of footsteps on the stairs. They all turned.

Cindy, accompanied by two plainclothes and one uniformed officer, was coming down like a French aristo to the tumbrel. As she was escorted outside, Lewis rose and went to the door. After a moment, one of the plainclothes officers came back.

'Thank you, Mr Osbourne-Walker,' he said. 'I expect we'll be in touch.'

'What about Miss Dale?' said Lewis. 'I mean, she doesn't live here or anything. Where will she go after?'

'I don't think she'll be going anywhere soon,' said the officer. 'We'll be in touch.'

A silence fell after the officer left, until Libby said, 'Do you think they'll look for evidence to connect her to Kenneth's death?'

'Oh, Ma, of course they will. I bet they go through Tony West's place with a toothcomb looking for clues. After all, she knew him well enough for him to get her away after Kenneth's murder.'

'They've already gone through his place,' said Lewis. 'They'd have found anything there was to find by now.'

'What do you suppose he did with her real passport and stuff?' said Libby. 'And Gerald's whereabouts? He must have known that as well.'

Lewis shrugged. 'Bank safe somewhere?'

'He'd have had documents relating to it,' said Libby, shaking her head. 'Well, it all comes down to Tony West in the end, doesn't it? I wonder why he did it?'

'Dunno. He didn't seem a soft sort of bugger to me,' said Lewis. 'Cruel but fair, as someone said.'

'Devious, if you ask me,' said Adam. 'What do you think, Katie? You knew him.'

Katie had been sitting at the end of the table, her head bowed over her mug of tea. She looked up and Libby was surprised to see real grief in her eyes.

'He was good to me,' she said shortly. She stood up and took her mug to the sink, rinsed it out and left the room by the back door.

'He got her the job with you, didn't he?' said Libby. Lewis nodded. 'So he knew her before then?'

'Yeah, I think so. Not well, though. He got to know her better after she started working for me.'

'Were you still –' Adam stopped, going bright red.

Lewis grinned at him. 'Shagging? No, mate. Not regular, anyway. Once or twice.' He leant over and patted Adam's arm. 'Now you're shocked, aren't you?'

Adam shook his head, blush subsiding. 'I just wondered how often you saw him after you moved in here.'

'Few times. He knew the house, see? He come down to have a look round if I wasn't sure about how I ought to do things.'

'And he didn't say anything about Gerald Shepherd?' said Libby.

'No.' Lewis shrugged again. 'Just as how he knew the house, like.'

'Hmm,' said Libby thoughtfully. Then she stood up. 'Well, as you don't need me to help you get rid of Cindy, I'll be off. See you later, Ad.'

'OK, Ma.' He, too, stood up. 'I promise I'll sort out some transport of my own. I know you don't like driving the Land Rover.'

'You can always stay here,' said Lewis, following them to the door. 'I've said so before. Then you wouldn't have to keep going backwards and forwards.'

'You're all right, Lewis, thanks. I quite like being at home with Ma.' Adam gave Lewis a grin. 'See you later, Ma.'

Libby was shepherded through the gates and the rabble of the media by the two policemen on duty. Outside the Kent and Coast Television vehicle she caught sight of Campbell McLean, the reporter she'd met during last summer's murder investigation into the body on the island. He, luckily, either didn't see or recognise her, and she drove safely away towards home.

The red answerphone light was winking when she got in. Pressing the button she listened to the message while unwrapping her cape from around her shoulders. One day, she thought, she really must invest in a more conventional coat.

'Libby,' said the answerphone, 'I found the DVD in Canterbury. Do you want to see it? And Guy says there was something on the radio about Cindy Dale and Creekmarsh while I was out. What's going on?'

Libby sat down on the cane sofa and lit a cigarette. Sidney jumped up beside her. After a short period of stroking and bonding, he jumped down again and Libby picked up the phone.

'I wouldn't mind seeing the DVD, but I'm still not sure why you wanted to. You really went all the way into Canterbury just to buy it?'

'Well, they wouldn't have it in any of our shops,' said Fran. 'And I bought a couple of other things as well, so it wasn't a waste of time. Shall I bring it over?'

'Do you and Guy want to come to supper, then?' said Libby. 'Might as well make an evening of it. The boys can go to the pub with Adam.'

'I'll check with Guy,' said Fran. 'Now tell me what was going on at Creekmarsh.'

Libby filled in the details and waited for Fran to pronounce.

'Did you think any more about the day books or housekeeper's records?' she said finally.

'You said you were going to research those,' said Libby. 'You asked Lewis's permission.'

'Yes,' said Fran vaguely, 'but I thought … with Cindy –'

'You thought she might be looking?'

'It stands to reason, doesn't it? She's looking for her passport and certificates. She might have found them somewhere.'

'But she hasn't. And I think the police would have found them if she had because they would have gone through her belongings.'

'OK.' Fran now sounded brisk. 'I'll check with Guy about tonight and ring you back.'

She did, within a few minutes, and Libby called Ben to let him know and ask him to beg some vegetables from his mother as once again, she'd forgotten to go shopping. 'Tomorrow,' she told herself, picking up her basket and heading off to the eight-til-late.

Fran and Guy arrived at seven and by half past the four of them and Adam were sitting round the kitchen table.

'Tell me again why we're being packed off to the pub?' said Adam, spearing a large potato.

'We're going to watch a DVD of Gerald Shepherd. You'd be bored,' said his mother. Ben and Guy exchanged eye-rolling glances.

'Why?' asked Adam.

'Just to see what he's like,' said Fran, sipping wine.

'What he *was* like,' said Adam. 'That serial was on when I was at school.'

'Isn't he dead?' said Guy. 'You said what he *is* like.'

'No, he's not dead.' Fran shook her head. 'I think he's in a home somewhere.'

Libby raised her eyebrows but said nothing.

When the men had left them to the washing-up, Libby asked her question.

'In a home?'

'He'd have to be. To be cared for. And Tony West would know where.'

'Yes, I thought of that. That he'd know where Gerald was.'

'And that, of course, is why Creekmarsh had to be sold.'

'Is it? I thought it was to get rid of it so any stray bodies wouldn't be associated with the Shepherd family.'

'There was that aspect, but think about it. What else?'

'I don't know. What else?'

'The funds to keep Gerald in a home.'

'Oh!' Libby stopped washing plates and stared at her friend. 'Of course!' She placed the plate thoughtfully in the draining rack. 'But if he was in a home, how did West persuade the staff to keep quiet?'

'Money? Or perhaps he put him there under a false name. Seems he had no trouble finding false papers for Cindy Dale.'

Libby emptied the sink and dried her hands. 'You're very sure about this,' she said, and picked up the wine bottle. Fran picked up the glasses.

'My brain's sure,' she said. 'I don't know why. It is logical, of course, but why I'm so certain – well.' She grinned at Libby. 'You know what I'm like.'

Collateral Damage was a political thriller with Gerald Shepherd as a manipulative back-room wheeler and dealer who almost brings down the government of the day.

'Not a very nice character,' said Libby, pausing the film while she topped up glasses.

'No, but very charismatic,' said Fran. 'Quite the charmer.'

'In a non-charming way,' agreed Libby, and un-paused the film.

'So,' she said when it had finished. 'Did that help at all?'

'Not really,' said Fran with a sigh. 'But I enjoyed it.'

'So did I.' Libby took a thoughtful sip. 'I can see why Cindy might have had an affair with him despite him being so much older.'

'But she says she didn't,' Fran reminded her. 'You said Lewis told you –'

'That he tried it on. I know. But the public thought they'd run away together, and you can see why. Except that Cindy isn't the glamour model I thought she'd be.'

'I wonder where the investigation will go now?' mused Fran.

'They really ought to concentrate on Tony West.'

'Because no one knows why he was killed?'

'It was obviously something to with Creekmarsh,' said Fran, 'but what?'

'His place was ransacked,' said Libby, 'so whoever did it was looking for something.'

'Cindy's papers?'

'It couldn't have been her,' said Libby, 'she only arrived in the country on Sunday, the police checked that straight away.' She suddenly sat up straight on the sofa. 'It couldn't be –' she looked at Fran '– Gerald Shepherd himself?'

Chapter Twenty-two

FRAN STARED AT LIBBY. 'If we're right about his Alzheimer's, no, it couldn't,' she said.

'But supposing we're not? Supposing he's still perfectly normal and Cindy's been feeding us a load of bollocks?'

Fran shook her head. 'Think about it. Why, in that case, did he give West power of attorney? And,' she added thoughtfully, 'when he disappeared, why didn't the police find out about it?'

'Were the police involved at that stage? It was only Kenneth who was looking for him.'

'No idea. I suppose they assumed it was a voluntary decision and didn't follow it up. That's the thinking with missing persons, isn't it? Unless it's a child.'

Libby shuddered. 'Horrible. But yes, I suppose it is. They think adults want to disappear. Especially if a pretty young woman is involved with a man.'

'I still want to know about the solicitor who drew up the power of attorney,' said Fran.

'The police will have been on to that, won't they? To find the will, as well.'

'The Office of the Public Guardian will have the details,' said Fran, 'but not of the will.'

'There's no way we can find out, then,' said Libby. 'Even if we were perfectly entitled to get in touch with them, I think there's something about only giving the information to a particular person or persons named.'

'So we only have hearsay and what Cindy Dale says about the whole affair,' said Fran.

'We do, but I bet the police have more. It's what we always say, isn't it?' Libby sighed. 'They always get there before we do.'

Fran laughed. 'And turn up to save our irritating bacon.'

'So it's nothing to do with us and we ought to stop worrying about it,' said Libby. 'That'll please the boys.'

Fran snorted. 'Boys!'

'Old men, then,' said Libby with a giggle, 'although I wouldn't say –'

'Don't want to know,' said Fran, sticking her fingers in her ears. 'Have another glass of wine.'

Thursday morning saw Libby in the conservatory wielding a determined paintbrush. She and Fran had more or less unanimously decided to leave the Creekmarsh investigation to the police and concentrate on other pursuits, the most important of which being Fran and Guy's forthcoming wedding. As summer was almost here and visitors to Nethergate would be increasing, Guy had gently suggested he might want more Sarjeant masterpieces for sale in the gallery. So here was Libby, trying to concentrate on a new view of Nethergate Bay and to dismiss Creekmarsh, Cindy Dale and Gerald Shepherd from her mind.

But, of course, this was almost impossible. However much one wished to concentrate on paint and paper, painting, to a degree, left the mind free to range wherever it wanted. And Libby's was certainly ranging.

The radio and television news that morning had only brief mentions of Cindy Dale being taken in for questioning and nothing at all about Gerald Shepherd, Kenneth or Tony West. Deliberately playing it down, wondered Libby, or simply no longer an urgent enquiry? No matter how hard she thought around all the corners, no startling light-bulb moments illuminated the story for her, and in the end she found herself making up stories to fit the facts. Enjoyable though this was, when she found herself imagining Cindy Dale as Gerald's daughter by Lewis's Katie, she decided she'd gone far enough and began to clean her brushes.

After a bowl of soup for lunch and putting a load of Adam's work clothes in the washing machine, she was about to curl up with a good book when her mobile rang.

'It's me,' said Fran. 'How would you like to come out and have a look at our venue with me? I've got to talk to the manager, apparently.'

'Now?'

'I'll leave now and collect you on the way. OK?'

'Great!' Libby bounced up from the sofa. 'I'll go and make myself presentable.'

By the time Fran arrived twenty minutes later, Libby was in a long dark skirt with a cotton tunic over the top. Stuffed inside her basket was a slightly moth-eaten shawl.

'Has that taken the place of the cape?' asked Fran, as Libby fastened her seatbelt.

'For summer, yes,' said Libby, 'although I suppose I ought to get myself a proper summer jacket.'

'And a proper winter coat,' said Fran. 'I can never understand how you can keep warm in that blue thing.'

'I can wear lots of jumpers underneath,' explained Libby. 'Where are we going?'

Pickering House was on the other side of Canterbury in a rather more affluent area than Steeple Martin and Nethergate. It sat at the end of a gravel drive, looking for all the world like a wisteria-covered farmhouse, but once inside, Libby could see what a fabulous venue it was for a small wedding. Nothing had been done to alter the interior, as far as she could see, except to add electric light and discreet central heating. The room where the ceremony would be conducted was, like most of the downstairs rooms, wood panelled, with what looked like old church pews set in rows. The reception room, too, was panelled, with long French windows leading on to a covered terrace. In a small library a bar had been introduced, and upstairs the bedrooms were equally delightful. The only modern touches were the bathrooms, which were reassuringly state-of-the-art.

When Fran had finished talking to the manager, they went to inspect the gardens.

'Will you stay here the night before?' asked Libby, dead-heading a straggly Queen Elizabeth rose.

'No, we're going to be traditional. Guy will be in his flat with Sophie and I'll be at Coastguard Cottage.'

'On your own? What about getting dressed?'

'I can use the room here to get ready. Guy will get ready at home and come with Sophie.'

'Who's bringing you?'

'I'll drive myself,' said Fran.

Libby was shocked. 'You can't do that on your wedding day! What about one of the children?'

'The farther away they stay the better I shall like it,' said Fran, grimly.

'Well, I shall come and fetch you, then,' said Libby, 'and we can get dressed together in your posh room. Ben will probably want to fetch Guy as well.'

'Yes, but if he did that we wouldn't have a car for the morning.'

'Where are you going?'

'I don't know, Guy won't tell me.' Fran giggled. 'I feel like a teenager again.'

Libby grinned at her and squeezed her arm. 'So you should. Now tell me about the terrible trio.'

Fran sighed. 'Not Jeremy, he's fine. It's the girls.'

'What have they been doing? Last I heard there'd been a stony silence.'

'Which they have now broken.' Fran sighed again. 'Honestly, those two have barely spoken in years, and now they're ganging up on me.'

'What about?'

'What I said before. I'm too old to be making such a fool of myself, and have I made sure that all my money is tied up safely for them to inherit.'

'And have you?'

'Oh, I've tied it up all right! They get a certain amount each, and a certain amount in trust for any of their offspring. I know there are only two at the moment, but Chrissie and Jeremy might both become parents, although I can't see Chrissie wanting children. She just dotes on that bloody Cassandra.'

'The Siamese you went to cat-sit when they moved? How is she? Have they kept any of her kittens?'

Fran shook her head scornfully. 'They were simply a money-making exercise. She's had at least one more litter since then. All the time Chrissie can say she's looking after the little cash cow – cat – she has an excuse for not going out to work.'

'Oh, well, perhaps we can hide them at the back of the room and not notice them,' said Libby. 'I suppose they are coming?'

'Oh, yes. Begrudgingly, but they are coming. Honestly, Libby, it upsets me so much. When I see you with any of yours, you're such a happy family.'

'I know.' Libby nodded. 'Even when they're driving me mad, I love them to bits. One of the reasons I wouldn't move in with Ben, or agree to marry him, was that I didn't want them to be unhappy. Now, of course, it turns out they've all been expecting the announcement for ages.'

'They know Ben. Mine don't know Guy. They've never met him.'

'Perhaps you ought to ask them down, or arrange to meet on neutral territory before the wedding.'

'They'd argue about where it should be,' sighed Fran. 'They've already complained about holding it here, so off the beaten track.'

Libby frowned. 'I don't know what to suggest,' she said, 'short of having Peter and Harry as bouncers to remove them if they start making a fuss.'

Fran brightened. 'I will, actually,' she said. 'And I'll ask Adam and Dominic, too.'

'Are you inviting my children?' Libby raised her eyebrows. 'That's very nice of you.'

'Of course, you're almost my family now. I shall invite cousin Charles, but I haven't got any other relatives, and I don't know any of my old London friends any more. I shall ask Dahlia from my old flat, but otherwise it's all the friends from Steeple Martin and Nethergate.'

'How lovely,' said Libby, and gave her a hug.

After a final look round inside the house, when the manager presented Fran with the typed-up itinerary of the day they had discussed earlier, the women left. They were almost into Canterbury when Libby's phone rang.

'Libby, it's Lewis. You'll never guess.'

Libby repressed a sigh. 'What's happened now?'

'They've let Cindy go.'

'Go? Why?'

'I don't know, Lib, they didn't confide in me.'

'Sorry,' said Libby, shooting a quick glance at an obviously interested Fran. 'Where is she?'

'Where do you think she is? Here of course. Bloody woman. I don't know what I'm going to do with her.'

'She can't stay, Lewis.' Libby put her hand over the mouthpiece. 'Cindy's been released and she's turned up at Creekmarsh.'

'So how do I get rid of her? She's a bit shaky. Will you come over?'

'No,' said Libby firmly. 'I'm in Fran's car just now, so I can't. Talk to Katie. She'll help, surely.'

'Katie won't even speak to her,' said Lewis miserably.

'Why on earth did the police send her back to you?'

'It was her choice. She said all her belongings were here, which they are, and they sent her off in a police car. I haven't dared ask her what happens next.'

'You're going to have to,' said Libby. 'Is Adam there? He'll back you up, surely?'

'She'd wonder what on earth he'd got to do with it,' said Lewis. 'And Mog's at home with Fiona and the baby, so he can't help.'

Libby sighed. 'You'll have to be brave,' she said.

'Are you sure you can't come over?'

Libby looked at Fran, who was nodding. 'Tell him we'll come,' she said. 'Half an hour.'

'We're coming over,' said Libby. 'Fran says so.'

'When?'

'On our way now,' said Libby. 'Half an hour, Fran says. Keep an eye on her until then.'

'Why? What's she going to do?'

'She came to Creekmarsh for a reason,' said Libby. 'Whatever that was, I don't think she's found what she was looking for. And I think that's why she's come back. She's going to cause trouble one way or another.'

Chapter Twenty-three

LEWIS WAS PACING UP and down in front of the house when they arrived.

'She's gone again,' he said, obviously exasperated. 'Bloody woman's a nightmare.'

'Gone?' Libby climbed out of Fran's car. 'Where? When?'

'I've no fucking idea!' roared Lewis. 'She went upstairs, I asked Katie to make her a cup of tea and called you. When I went and knocked on her door, she'd gone.'

'With her bags?' said Fran.

'Yes.'

'So what happened between her arriving and you going upstairs?'

'I don't know, do I? Katie took her a cup of tea.'

'Have you asked Katie?'

Lewis looked much struck. 'No,' he said. 'I've only just discovered it myself. Come on, let's ask her.' He turned on his heel and disappeared inside. Libby and Fran looked at each other and followed.

Katie was sitting at the kitchen table reading a magazine.

'I made the tea, yes,' she said, nodding towards the teapot beside the Aga. 'I thought she was coming down for it.' Her lips thinned. 'I've got enough to do without running after that little madam.'

Libby stifled a grin and Fran cleared her throat.

'Would you have seen her go past the window?' asked Fran.

'I wasn't looking.' Katie's eyes drifted down to her magazine.

'She could be here somewhere,' said Libby. 'Have you got a mobile number for her, Lewis?'

He shook his head. 'I suppose we could have a scout round.'

'How about the attic?' said Fran. Libby, Lewis and Katie all looked at her in surprise. 'I was thinking she might be up there looking for her passport if it had been hidden.'

'Hidden?' said Katie. 'Why should it have been hidden?'

'We – that is, the police – think Tony West hid her original documents when he gave her the false ones and they might be here,' said Fran.

'Why should they be?' Katie was looking belligerent now.

'He knew this place. And they obviously weren't at his London place,' said Libby.

'Why do you say that?'

'It had been ransacked when his body was found.'

Katie looked down at her magazine. 'So whoever killed him might have found them.'

'Well, yes,' said Libby, looking at Fran, startled.

'Could have been her, then.' Katie kept her eyes down.

'In that case, why was she here looking for something?' asked Fran reasonably.

'How do you know she was looking for something?'

'Because she said so,' said Lewis, who was becoming even more exasperated. 'Honestly, this is no bleedin' joke. I've had enough. Let's have a look round then I'm calling Big Bertha.'

They covered the same ground they had gone over a few days previously, but no trace of Cindy was found. Fran stood still, scenting the air like a bloodhound, Libby told her, but to no avail.

Back in the solar, Lewis called the police and informed them.

'And we've had a good look round,' he said. 'How she got past me I shall never know.' He switched off the phone. 'They'll be right out,' he said wearily. 'Gawd, why is this happening to me?'

'Is there anything we can do?' asked Libby, completely forgetting her vow to keep out of things.

'I don't know. Where would she have gone? And why did she want those documents so badly?'

'That puzzled me, too,' said Libby. 'After all, the minute she tried to use the passport she'd be stopped. Either passport, come to that.'

'It's the birth and marriage certificates, I think,' said Fran. 'Proof of who she is so she can claim the estate.'

'But could she claim the estate if she was accessory to murdering Kenneth? Anyway, Gerald's still alive, we think.'

'I'm not so sure about that,' said Lewis, shaking his head. 'If the poor old bugger was going loopy back then, he could be well dead by now.'

Libby grinned. 'Too true, but Fran doesn't think so.'

Lewis sent her a doubtful look. 'All right, so what does Fran think, then?'

Fran was silent for a moment, gazing out of the solar window towards the ha-ha. 'If Cindy didn't go out of the front door, where else might she have got out?'

'Kitchen door,' said Lewis.

'Not very likely with Katie the dragon sitting there,' said Libby.

'No. There's the old side door – well, back door, I suppose, at the end of the hall beyond the stairs. We've never used it.'

'Come on then,' said Fran, standing up. 'That's how she went out.'

Lewis and Libby looked at one another. Libby shrugged and went out of the room behind Fran.

Somehow, it wasn't surprising to find the small oak door swinging very slightly on its hinges.

'Where did she go from here?' said Lewis, and looked sharply round. 'That was a car, wasn't it? Reckon it's the police?'

'Probably,' said Libby. 'You go and see to them and we'll carry on here.'

'Down here,' said Fran, leading the way unhesitatingly towards the ha-ha. Libby puffed and kept up, and was unsurprised when Fran led them down to the sailing club.

'Well, she's not here,' said Libby, catching her breath and investigating the lock and bolt on the door. 'Do you think she got away from here?'

Fran was frowning. 'I'm not sure,' she said slowly. 'I'm certain she was here, though.'

'Had we better tell the police?'

Fran sighed. 'As if they'll believe me,' she said, 'but yes, I suppose we'd better.'

'You know,' said Libby, as she panted her way back up towards the house, 'I thought when I was down here before it would be a good way to get on or off the estate – from that little inlet. And it can't be seen from the house, so as long as you could keep out of sight on the way up or down it's a perfect secret way. Do you think she could have done that?'

'It seems so quick,' mused Fran. 'It couldn't have been more than twenty minutes between Lewis calling you and us arriving. She must have run like the wind.'

'With a heavy bag,' added Libby. 'I don't know. All seems very fishy to me.'

Outside the house they were met, to their surprise, by an irritated-looking DI Ian Connell.

'What are you doing here?' asked Libby, while Fran blushed and tried to blend into the background.

Connell sighed heavily. 'I could say the same to you, but I know you'll have a legitimate reason. Hello, Fran.'

'Hello,' said Fran in a muffled voice.

'As to what I'm doing here,' said Ian, 'we had a report that a Miss Cindy Dale –'

'Or Mrs Cindy Shepherd,' interjected Libby, smiling beatifically.

'Had disappeared very suddenly from here after being bailed by the police,' continued Ian, without pause.

'Bailed, hey?' said Libby. 'Lewis told us you'd let her go.'

'Hmm,' said Ian. 'Well, assuming you can't throw any light on the situation, I'll let you be on your way.'

'Oh, we weren't going,' said Libby blithely. 'We're just going back inside to find Lewis.'

Ian closed his eyes briefly and stood aside to give them access to the house. Fran paused before him.

'Actually, Ian,' she said, 'I think she might have gone to the boathouse.'

'Boathouse?' He frowned down at her.

'Sailing club,' said Libby, turning back and regarding the

two of them with interest. 'You can't see it from the house.'

'Where is it?'

'Would you like me to show you?' asked Fran diffidently.

Ian looked into the distance. 'Very kind,' he said, and Libby giggled. He shot her a look of pure evil and turned on his heel. Fran looked back at Libby, shrugged and followed him.

Lewis was in the kitchen with Katie, while upstairs could be heard the heavy sounds of investigating constables.

'Fran's gone to show Ian the sailing club,' said Libby, sitting down with them.

Katie looked up with a frown. 'Ian?' asked Lewis.

'Detective Inspector Ian Connell,' said Libby. 'We've worked with him before.'

'So he might be able to help us?'

'Oh, I doubt it,' said Libby. 'He thinks of me, in particular, as a nuisance. He does, however, believe in Fran's gift. She actually got asked in to help solve one murder.'

'He's the one you called to tell him about Fran's marriage,' said Lewis, enlightened.

'That's it. I don't know why he's suddenly been put on this case, he wasn't when I spoke to him before.'

'Well, perhaps it's lucky for us he has,' said Katie. Lewis and Libby looked at her in surprise. 'If he's a bit more pleasant than that Bertram woman. Perhaps we'll find out what happened to Tony. And Kenneth, of course,' she added hastily.

'But we know what happened to Kenneth,' said Libby. 'Gerald killed him.'

'Never on your life,' said Katie, a mulish expression on her face.

'Did you know him?' Libby was interested.

'I met him. With Mr West.'

'Was this when you were doing the outside catering?'

'You never told me,' said Lewis indignantly.

'You never asked.' Katie shrugged.

'Did you tell the police you knew him?'

'O' course I did,' said Katie, standing up.

'Didn't you say you didn't know Cindy?'

'I said she didn't,' said Lewis. 'Did you, Katie?'

'I met her.' Katie's mouth was like a rat trap.

'So you actually knew what the family was like before Gerald and Cindy disappeared?'

'Not to say know,' said Katie, moving towards the pantry. 'Met 'em.'

Lewis and Libby looked at each other. 'Oh, well, as long as you've told the police,' said Lewis. 'Do you want a cuppa, Lib?'

'No, I'd better go and find Fran.' Libby stood up. 'We didn't mean to be this long. Guy will wonder where his beloved has got to.'

Fran was walking back towards the house, with the two policemen running the other way towards the ha-ha.

'What's up?' asked Libby.

'Ian found some scratch marks or something.' Fran shrugged. 'Anyway, he's called for reinforcements. Apparently Big Bertha's having to stay deskbound for a bit and her team's been stretched to the limit, so Ian's been dragged in. I don't think he was that delighted to see us.'

'No, it struck me that way, too,' said Libby, with a smile. 'Nice to see him, though.'

'Do you think I ought to ask him to my wedding?'

Libby made a face. 'Difficult one,' she said. 'Ask Guy and Ben. They'll know what to do.'

Fran nodded. 'Have you said goodbye to Lewis? I ought to get going.'

'Yes, I told him.'

Fran was silent on the way back to Steeple Martin.

'Come up with anything?' asked Libby after a bit.

'Cindy. There's something altogether wrong about her.'

'I agree, but everything she says is logical.'

'Except, as we said earlier, why does she want those documents?'

'Perhaps it's not her own documents she's looking for?'

Fran nodded, carefully slowing down for the bend in the road that led into Steeple Martin's high street.

'Whose, then? Gerald's?' said Libby. 'To prove he's alive?'

'Could be,' said Fran. 'But did she ransack Tony West's house? And if so, did she do it after or before he was dead?'

'I told you, she couldn't have done,' said Libby. 'She didn't get in to the country until the Sunday when she arrived at Creekmarsh.'

'How did she get to Creekmarsh from the airport?' asked Fran.

'I don't know.' Libby looked bewildered. 'Taxi? Lewis didn't say.'

'We don't know everything,' said Fran, turning into Allhallow's Lane, 'by any means.'

'But we agreed yesterday we were going to leave it alone,' said Libby. 'We said it would be better, and Ben and Guy would be pleased.'

'And Lewis asked us over today.'

'Only to help him get rid of Cindy.' Libby shivered. 'And that turned out not to be necessary.'

'Hmm,' said Fran, and stopped the car.

Libby's mobile rang again.

'Lib, it's me again.'

'Lewis,' Libby said to Fran. 'What's up now?'

'I've just had another talk with Katie.'

'Yes? And?'

'So who do you think gave the police Gerald's DNA?'

Chapter Twenty-four

'*KATIE* DID?' SQUEAKED LIBBY.

'Unbelievable, ain't it?' Lewis was breathing heavily. 'Seems she knew Tony better than I thought. She come down here with him when he come to see German Shepherd and he – Shepherd – gave her some mem – mem – memory thing.'

'Memento?' suggested Libby.

'That's it. Anyway, that's what she gave the police.'

'Other people would have touched it, though,' said Libby dubiously. 'How did they isolate it?'

Lewis made an explosive sound. 'You ask the most fucking awful questions,' he said. 'How do I know, for fuck's sake?'

'All right, all right,' Libby soothed. 'Look, I'm sitting in Fran's car at the moment. I'll phone you back when I get indoors.'

She explained as she got out of the car. 'So, do you want to come in and hear what's going on?'

Fran looked torn. 'So much for non-involvement again,' she said. 'Oh, go on. You can make me some tea. I didn't get one at Lewis's.'

'No,' said Libby, 'I didn't fancy that stewed tea Katie made for Cindy.'

In the kitchen, she removed Sidney from the bread bin and put the kettle on the Rayburn. 'One day,' she said, 'I shall buy an electric kettle. So much quicker.'

'Only when you come in like we have now,' said Fran. 'When you're at home you keep it simmering just off the hotplate, don't you?'

'Mmm. S'pose.' Libby went in search of the phone and punched in Lewis's number. 'Lewis? Now, tell me the whole story.'

'I've told you,' said Lewis with a sigh. 'It turns out Katie knew Tony before I came on the scene. He helped her get in to the outside catering thing.'

'How did they meet?'

'I don't know.' Libby could almost see Lewis frowning. 'She didn't tell me that.'

'What did she actually say? Was it something like "he was a great help to me when I first started out"?'

'Could have been,' said Lewis slowly. 'Anyway she knew him then, and German Shepherd had a couple of dos down here and Tony brought her down to help out. So she met 'em all.'

'I'm surprised she's never told you.'

'She says she assumed I knew.'

'But what about when the skeleton turned up? Surely she would have said something then?'

'Well, she didn't know anything about Kenneth being killed, did she? If it is Kenneth.'

'I suppose not,' said Libby. 'But why did she give the police this memento, whatever it was?'

'They'd found out the house used to belong to Shepherd, and they wanted to find out if the body was him, didn't they? And when they interviewed her it all came out, so she gave them the – thing.'

'What is it? The thing?'

'A scarf of some sort, she said.'

'Well.' Libby looked over at Fran. 'What will you do now?'

'How do you mean? I don't do nothing. I just sit here until the police have finished with it all. Then maybe I can get back to real life.' He sighed again. 'Although I don't know whether I want to stay here, now.'

'I bet.' Libby nodded sympathetically.

'Anyway, I just thought you'd like to know.' He sounded wistful.

'Thanks, Lewis. Chin up. I'll call you tomorrow. Is Adam on his way home?'

'Dunno. I'll go and find out and give him a nudge.'

'He's fed up,' Libby told Fran, when she'd finished relating

Katie's story, 'and I don't wonder. I still think it's odd Katie didn't tell him all this when she first worked for him.'

'Sounds as though she was hiding something,' said Fran, accepting a mug of tea. 'And she definitely knew Cindy before.'

'That was why she was so mad at finding her there,' said Libby, sitting down at the table. 'I wondered why she was so anti.'

'Cindy *was* treating her like the help.'

'Which is explained by the fact that the last time they'd met, Katie *was* the help.' Libby frowned down at her mug. 'But it doesn't explain her loyalty to Shepherd.'

'How do we know about that?'

'She was so sure he didn't do it, wasn't she? When we were there earlier.'

'And she still wasn't admitting she'd known him.' Fran shook her head. 'Curiouser and curiouser.'

'She did say she'd *met* him.'

'Yes. And she had told the police. I suppose we shouldn't be surprised she hadn't told us. We're nothing to do with it, really.'

'Although when I first came over to talk to Lewis she was trying to convince me to come back and support him.'

'She probably didn't realise then how far it was going to go,' said Fran. 'And don't forget, West wasn't dead then.'

'Hadn't been found, anyway,' said Libby. 'No, you're right. I expect she's as annoyed as Lewis about getting involved. Perhaps they should both go back to London.'

'Does Lewis keep a home in London?'

'Oh – I don't know.' Libby looked up, surprised. 'Never thought to ask.'

'Well, if you speak to him tomorrow ask him and suggest he goes back to it for a bit. He was in London when the skeleton was first found, wasn't he? Adam told you.'

'Well, perhaps that means he's got somewhere to go back to,' said Libby, pushing her mug away. 'I suppose I'd better get on with feeding the hungry hordes.'

'And I'd better get back.' Fran stood up. 'I'm surprised Guy hasn't phoned to find out where I am.'

Later, over dinner, Libby told Adam and Ben about Pickering

House, and then about the latest episode in the Creekmarsh mystery.

'Yeah, I saw the police,' said Adam. 'They didn't come near me, though, which is odd, if you think about it.'

'Why?' asked Ben.

'Well, if they were looking for Cindy, who had skipped, by all accounts, then surely they would have searched the grounds and asked me – or anyone else working there – if they'd seen her.'

'Perhaps they found her, then,' said Libby.

'Lewis would have let you know,' said Adam with a grin. 'You're his mother confessor.'

'He's quite rude to his mother confessor, then,' said Libby.

'Well, you are a bit pushy,' said Adam.

'I'm not!' gasped Libby.

'Inquisitive, then,' said Ben, patting her hand. Libby scowled and went to fetch cheese and biscuits.

Lewis did call in the morning.

'Adam said the police didn't question him yesterday,' said Libby. 'We wondered why.'

'They didn't need to,' said Lewis. 'They know what happened.'

'What?' asked Libby, her stomach sinking in anticipation.

'It was what your mate said. The sailing club.'

'*I* suggested the sailing club in the first place,' said Libby, indignation momentarily overcoming apprehension.

'Whatever,' said Lewis. 'Anyway, they went to have a look.'

'We know that,' said Libby, exasperated. 'We were there.'

'They found something.'

'Oh, God, what?'

'A boat was missing.'

Relief whooshed through Libby and she sat down abruptly. 'I thought you were going to say they'd found her body.'

'That's what I thought. Anyway, they reckon she must have collected her bags, shot down there and taken off.'

'To where, though? Have they managed to trace her?'

'Not as far as I know. I don't understand any of it.'

'Wait a minute,' said Libby. 'How do they know she took the

166

boat?'

'They found something of hers, I think. Something she dropped?'

'Oh, please,' said Libby. 'Not a cigarette end, I suppose? With a distinctive lipstick colour on the end?'

'I don't know, do I?' Lewis sounded bewildered. 'Anyway, she didn't smoke.'

Libby sighed. 'It was a joke, Lewis,' she said. 'You know, like in detective stories.'

'Oh.'

'So you've got no idea what it was?'

'I've told you, no. Look, I gotta go. Katie and me are going shopping this morning, and I might pop back up to London for a few days. Ad and Mog can carry on here. They know what to do – at least Mog does.'

'Right,' said Libby. 'Will Katie go to London, too?'

'Yeah. She can go back to her flat and come to me during the days.'

'Have you got a flat in London, then?'

''Course I have! Only rented, see, I took it on when I first went on to *Housey Housey*, and I was going to buy something else when Creekmarsh came up.'

'Right. Well, keep your mobile on so we can ring you if anything comes up.'

'The police will let me know soon enough,' said Lewis gloomily.

'If anything *else* comes up, I meant,' said Libby.

'Ad'll let me know about the garden. They're going to plant up that little back bit next week so's it looks pretty.'

'Bit late in the year, isn't it?' said Libby.

'How would I know?' said Lewis. 'Mog says they can do it, and they did it loads of times on *Housey Housey*, didn't matter what time of year it was. And we've done it on my show, too.'

'Right. I'll talk to you soon, then, and see you when you come back,' said Libby.

'Yeah,' said Lewis, sounded unconvinced. Libby was rather afraid he'd had enough of the Sarjeant and Castle investigating team.

She reported all of this to Fran in another telephone call. 'What do you think?' she asked finally. 'Is it a con? Has she really disappeared on a rowing boat?'

'There was certainly the feeling that she'd been there, although I didn't see anything you might call evidence. It's a pity Lewis didn't know what they found.'

'Could you ask Ian?'

Fran snorted. 'Don't be daft, Lib. Of course I can't. Oh, and by the way, Guy invited him to the wedding. Seemed to think it was a good idea. And Jane and Terry are coming.'

'Great,' said Libby. 'So it's all organised, is it?'

'Not the outfits. How about you and me going shopping tomorrow?'

'It's Saturday tomorrow! It'll be horribly crowded.'

'Don't be a spoilsport,' said Fran. 'Go on. We could even go up to London.'

Libby thought about it, tempted. 'OK,' she said eventually. 'You're on. I'll get Ben to take me to Canterbury to catch the train.'

'I'll tell you which one I'm catching from Nethergate then,' said Fran. 'I'm really looking forward to it.'

'She sounded really excited,' Libby told Ben later. 'I didn't have the heart to tell her I hate shopping in London.'

'Well, I think it'll be good for you to get away from all the murder and mayhem,' said Ben, pouring her a whisky.

'I think it's got away from us,' said Libby with a sigh. 'We'd decided it wasn't any of our business before Lewis called us back in, but now I think he's had enough of it and has gone back to London. Apart from Ad still working over there, it would appear that our connection to it all has stopped.'

'We'll have to find you something else to keep you interested,' said Ben, coming to sit next to her on the sofa.

'There's Steeple Farm,' said Libby, 'if Lewis is still going to take it on, or I suppose I could project manage myself if it came to it.'

'There is,' said Ben, 'and there's also your painting. You've been neglecting that a bit lately, haven't you?'

'I took some in to Guy only a week or so ago,' said Libby,

'but yes. I need to get going again with those. Pity it feels like churning out a production line.'

'Just be grateful you can do it,' said Ben. 'It pays for all your little necessities.'

Libby raised her glass. 'Like this, you mean?'

'And those,' said Ben, retrieving the battered packet of cigarettes from the log basket.

Libby sighed. 'I will try and give them up,' she said, 'but I still feel resentful.'

'Don't do it for the government,' said Ben, patting her hand. 'Do it for me.'

She laughed. 'I'll see,' she said. 'And now I'd better get some supper. Adam's gone into Canterbury with Mog, so he won't be here.'

'House to ourselves, have we?' Ben leant over and blew on her neck. 'Ought to make the most of it, then, shouldn't we?'

So they did.

Chapter Twenty-five

Fʀᴀɴ ᴀɴᴅ Lɪʙʙʏ sᴘᴇɴᴛ a tiring but ultimately successful day in London. Libby's daughter Belinda met them for lunch, but Fran could not be persuaded to invite her own daughter Lucy.

'She'd whine about bringing the children and then try and insist I went out to Tulse Hill to see them instead,' she said. 'I can do without that.'

On Sunday the weather went back to being late spring-like and stayed like it for the next few days. Adam went back to work at Creekmarsh, Mog joined him for a few hours a day and Lewis and Katie apparently stayed in London. Adam reported that no police had been seen and everything seemed to have returned to normal. Ben and Libby had another look round Steeple Farm and decided that Lewis's interest had been fleeting and born of the circumstances at the time. They would have to go it alone. Luckily, Mog had contacts with reliable local builders, one of whom was a qualified lime plasterer and had been employed by English Heritage on restoration work in the area. He was able to make a start on the odd bits of refurbishment that would be needed, but before that Libby and Ben had to decide what extremities of bad taste would have to be ripped out.

Libby regularly pushed down the uncomfortable feeling that she was doing the wrong thing, and found herself going round her cottage talking to it. She kept reminding herself that she wasn't selling it, and only moving into Steeple Farm as a sort of caretaker, but it didn't make any difference.

Ben, usually sensitive to her moods, had happily accepted what he saw as the new situation and spent the evenings talking renovations. He had also thrown himself into the role of Guy's best man, and was helping move some of Guy's belongings and furniture into Fran's still sparsely furnished Coastguard Cottage.

'Don't you mind?' asked Libby curiously. 'You so wanted to be on your own at first.'

'That was at first,' said Fran. 'And I had a lot to work through, didn't I? All those memories and discoveries from the past.'

'And Ian didn't help, did he?'

'It wasn't Ian's fault,' sighed Fran. 'It was me. It was the novelty of having a younger man fancying me. It confused me for a bit.'

'And he is very attractive,' said Libby slyly.

'Yes, he is.' There was a short silence. 'But not as attractive as Guy,' Fran said eventually, and Libby smiled.

The Skeleton in the Garden case, as the media referred to it, slipped to the inside pages of the newspapers and wasn't mentioned at all on the television news. Neither was Tony West's murder, although the press hadn't been told of the link between the two cases. If they had been, thought Libby, it might still have been at least page two news.

On Thursday, two weeks before Fran and Guy's wedding and two weeks since Libby first met Lewis, Fran called Libby.

'I know this sounds silly,' she said, 'but I had a dream last night.'

'Oh?'

'Yes. And I'm pretty sure it meant Cindy was in England before Sunday.'

'Oh, Fran, that doesn't seem very –'

'I know what you're going to say, Lib,' interrupted Fran, 'but it is based on something concrete.'

'Her reaction when she found out he was dead, though. Lewis said she was hysterical.'

'Yet she didn't say anything about going to see him when she arrived at Creekmarsh, did she? Wouldn't you have thought she would have asked if she could at least call him after Lewis told her the whole story?'

'I suppose so,' said Libby slowly. 'And she didn't, did she? You would have thought she would want to know where the money was, as it was due to be hers eventually. And the other thing was, she actually told Lewis all about knowing Tony, and him covering up the murder.'

'Why didn't Lewis mention it to her then?'

'I think he thought he had, or that she already knew.'

'Her behaviour doesn't ring true. I'm going to try and find out a bit more.'

'Fran! We're out of it,' said Libby. 'Why do you want to do this?'

'Because I can't get it out of my mind. I'm going to see if I can track down any historical references to Creekmarsh.'

'What good will that do?' asked Libby, bewildered.

'Hiding places,' said Fran crisply. 'I'll let you know if I find anything.'

'I'm going to look too,' said Libby, and switching off the phone went straight to the computer.

At first, it looked as though there was little on the Internet about Creekmarsh, but by dint of following seemingly insignificant clues, she eventually chanced on a local website about villages in the area with a whole page about the village, the church and the house.

Creekmarsh Place had been built towards the end of the sixteenth century, and most of the history concerned the families through whose hands it had passed. Part of the house had been destroyed by fire in the eighteenth century and there were rumours of passages running between the church, the house and the inn, although none of these had been found, and both the church and the inn had been rebuilt during the nineteenth century, so it was unlikely that, if they ever had existed, they continued to do so now.

After an hour of following up promising-looking clues and cross-referencing with historical documents, Libby was ready to give up, when something caught her eye. There was a tunnel at Creekmarsh. Leading to an ice-house. Her heart gave a great thump in her chest just as the phone began to ring.

'Lib?' Fran's voice sounded muffled.

'Where are you?'

'Just outside the library,' said Fran. 'Trying to keep my voice down. I've found something.'

'So have I.'

'Oh?' Now Fran sounded put out.

'On the computer. What did you find?'

'There's an ice-house.'

'Joined to Creekmarsh by a tunnel.'

'Oh, bugger,' said Fran, who never swore. 'I never should have taught you how to use a computer.'

Libby laughed. 'I'm so pleased you did,' she said, 'although I do waste time on it. Anyway, did you find anything else?'

'Yes. Did you?'

'No, that was it, except bits and pieces about the history.'

'Well, in the library they've actually got archives of all sorts of things, how much people were paid, what was ordered for the kitchen, that sort of thing.'

'And?'

'There's mention of a "strong room". Where do you think that was?'

'I don't know. What date was this?'

'Mid eighteen hundreds. About 1848, I think.'

'Hmm,' said Libby. 'That was when the church was rebuilt.'

'Has that got anything to do with it?'

'I don't know. I'm thinking.'

'Be careful,' said Fran.

'Can you take any notes about that strong room? Or copy the pages? And would there be anything about the pub?'

'The pub?'

'The Fox, opposite the turning towards the house. On the history site I found, it said it used to be connected to the church and the house before it was rebuilt.'

'I'll go and try. You carry on playing with the Internet. I'll call you when I've finished.'

Libby laughed. 'What are we like?' she said. 'We're not supposed to be doing this.'

'I know.' Fran sighed. 'I just can't seem to help it.'

Libby returned to the computer and searched for The Fox. Luckily, it had its own website, with a good sprinkling of interior photographs and a history page, which actually mentioned the "secret passage". The writer had indulged his or her love of romance by embroidering the story with tales of reckless smugglers, which wasn't altogether unlikely, thought Libby, given that Creekmarsh had such excellent masked access from the river via the inlet. Which brought her back to Cindy and the reason Fran had embarked on this search.

However, The Fox claimed to have no knowledge of the continued existence of the passage, and although there was a very limited website for the little church, it made no reference to anything secret: passage, tunnel or otherwise.

Fran phoned a little late and said she'd been allowed to make copies of relevant pages, but there was nothing else in the library except a small poster advertising The Fox.

'Shall we go and have a look?' asked Libby. 'We could go to The Fox for lunch.'

'OK, I'll meet you there in – what? Half an hour?'

'You're keen,' said Libby, and switching off, went upstairs to put on something respectable before calling Ben to ask once more for the loan of the Land Rover.

The Fox, on the bend of the road opposite the lane to Creekmarsh and the church, was a two-storey, cream-washed building under a red-tiled roof, with two single-storey additions, one at each end. Window boxes planted with pelargoniums and petunias hung under the windows and a chalkboard apparently held aloft by a beaming chef announced daily specials. Libby parked the Land Rover next to Fran's little car in the car park behind the pub, and found Fran in the garden.

'Have you ordered?'

'No,' said Fran, squinting up into the sun. 'I thought I'd wait for you.' She stood up and led the way inside.

There hadn't been too much tarting up, thought Libby; no glittering horse brasses or tables with beaten brass tops, and at the end of the bar were copies of several daily papers. They ordered two mineral waters and two ham salads and Libby smiled confidingly at the woman behind the counter.

'We hear there's a secret passage here?' she said.

The woman shook her head and laughed. 'Oh, that's just on the website and in the brochure,' she said. 'My Frank got a bit overexcited about that.'

'Oh?' Libby hitched herself onto a bar stool. 'He didn't make it up?'

'Oh, no,' said the woman. 'There was a tunnel, apparently, went to the church and then on to the big house, but it was blocked off when this place was rebuilt.'

'What a pity,' said Libby. 'When was that? It looks old.'

'Same time as the church, we think. 1849, '50. Something like that.'

'Smugglers?' asked Fran.

'Yeah, definitely. 'Course, by that time there weren't many left, it was all through those old wars it went on.'

'Brandy for the Parson,' said Libby.

'Baccy for the Clerk,' added Fran.

'Laces for a lady, letters for a spy,' they chanted together. The landlady stared at them in surprise.

'Rudyard Kipling's 'Smuggler's Song',' said Libby. 'I bet your Frank's heard of it. Very famous. Otherwise known as Watch The Wall My Darling, While The Gentlemen Go By.'

'Right.' The landlady looked doubtful. 'I'll ask him.'

'So he doesn't know where the tunnel might have come out?' asked Fran.

'In the cellars, I suppose. Makes sense, doesn't it?'

Libby and Fran looked at each other.

'Cellars?' said Libby.

'Are they still there?' said Fran.

'Well, of course they are!' The landlady laughed. 'All pubs have cellars. Don't suppose they're the same as they were a coupla hundred years ago, though.'

'No,' said Libby, disappointed.

'Why are you so interested?' The landlady turned and leant through a hatch, bringing back two plates of ham salad with a brief thanks to a disembodied voice from beyond.

'We read about it on the Internet,' said Fran, shooting Libby a warning glance.

'You're not tourists?' The woman frowned.

'No, I'm from Steeple Martin and Fran lives in Nethergate,' said Libby, unwrapping her knife and fork.

The landlady's brow cleared. 'Hang on,' she said, 'I know you! You're the lady who does the murders!'

Libby made a face and Fran blushed.

'You're the psychic lady, aren't you?' The landlady now looked delighted. 'Is this passage something to do with – ooh!' She put her hand over her mouth and her eyes widened. In the corner a group of locals looked over their shoulders with interest. 'That skeleton they found?' she continued in a whisper.

Fran sighed. 'No, I'm afraid it isn't,' she said. The landlady looked disappointed. 'It is for the owner of Creekmarsh, though,' Fran continued, lowering her voice. 'He thought he might be able to trace the passage.'

'Fantastic!' The landlady's eyes were shining. 'I'll tell Frank the minute he gets back.'

'Is he away?' asked Libby, wondering what Fran was up to.

'Oh, he's just visiting an old mate of his who's in a home, bless him.'

'Oh, dear, I'm sorry,' said Libby.

'Yeah, it's a shame,' said the landlady. 'I never knew him, but he wasn't all that old. Alzheimer's, you know.'

Chapter Twenty-six

IF THE LANDLADY NOTICED the frozen expressions on the faces in front of her, she gave no sign of it. Libby was the first to recover.

'Alzheimer's? That's terrible. An old friend, was he?'

'Yeah. Frank knew him before we met.' The landlady nodded at them cheerfully. 'I'll leave you to your salads. I'll tell Frank as soon as he gets back.'

'It couldn't be, could it?' whispered Libby, as they carried their plates back into the garden.

'I don't see how,' said Fran. 'It's just one of those coincidences that crop up all the time. After all, if this Frank knew where Gerald Shepherd was all the time when the hunt was on for him, and especially now with the discovery of the skeleton, he would have spoken up, wouldn't he?'

Libby nodded. 'And the wife isn't in the first flush of youth,' she said, through a mouthful of ham, 'so they must have been married for some time.'

'Which means the friend must date from years ago,' said Fran.

'But,' said Libby, pointing her fork, 'that doesn't mean it isn't Shepherd. Frank might have known him years ago, but only started to visit him when he got Alzheimer's.'

'I think we're making too much of it,' said Fran, squirting mayonnaise from a sachet onto her lettuce. 'It's coincidence, like I said.'

They finished their meals and loitered for as long as they decently could, but Frank declined to put in an appearance, and they were forced to leave, promising the landlady ('Call me Bren, everyone does') they would return.

Fran drove down the lane and parked next to the church.

'Will it be open, do you think?' asked Libby as they climbed out.

'I think they lock them these days, don't they?' said Fran. 'Vandalism.'

Libby went up to the door and checked. 'Yup,' she said. 'Locked.' They stood together in the porch and read the few notices; times of services, a couple of appeals and a poster advertising meetings of a local branch of the WI.

'Churchwarden's number, look,' said Fran. 'Perhaps we should ring him.'

'And perhaps we shouldn't,' said Libby. 'Come on, we can't go that far.'

'Shall we go down and see Adam, then?' Fran walked out of the porch and began to go round the church, peering at the bottom of the walls.

'We can if you like.' Libby watched her friend with amusement. 'You're not going to find anything here, you know,' she said.

'I know, I know.' Fran straightened up and pushed a lock of her hair behind her ear. 'Shall we walk across to the house?'

'What are you actually looking for?' asked Libby, as they crossed the lane to the Creekmarsh drive.

'The opening of a passage,' said Fran.

'But they will all have been closed up,' said Libby.

'What about the ice-house?' said Fran. 'I bet the tunnel to that will be somewhere in the kitchen area.'

'And the strong room? Did you find any more references to that?'

Fran shook her head. 'What would you keep in a strong room?'

'The dictionary says jewellery and valuables.'

'So it would be an ideal place for Tony West to hide any of Cindy's and Gerald's documents.'

'Well, yes,' said Libby doubtfully, 'but we've searched the house and so have the police. They'd have found a secret room or a hidden passage even if we didn't.'

'What about the unrestored part of the house?'

'The police would have searched that, too,' said Libby.

They continued towards the house in silence and found the big oak door open. Following sounds of clattering crockery, they went into the kitchen and found Mog and Adam making tea.

'Tea break,' said Adam cheerfully. 'Want some?'

'No thanks,' said Libby, pulling out a chair and sitting down. 'We've just had lunch at The Fox over the road.'

'Oh?' Mog looked interested. 'What's it like?'

'Average pub food. We had salads, so you can't really tell,' said Libby.

'But the ham was good,' said Fran, sitting beside Libby.

'Anyway, what are you doing here?' asked Adam. 'Lewis still isn't back.'

'I know,' said Libby, looking at Fran.

'I'm still interested,' she said, looking down at her hands clasped before her on the table.

'Even if the police aren't,' said Libby.

'Oh, they are,' said Adam. 'They've been here on and off all week. I think they're still looking for clues about Cindy.'

'So am I,' said Fran. 'They've found no trace of her, then?'

'Nothing except the boat down at the sailing club. That turned up just round the corner of the inlet where it goes into the river, jammed into the bank.'

'So was it a red herring?' asked Fran.

Adam looked dubious. 'I think she did go off in it, but how it got back here I've no idea. I don't think they have, either.'

'So what do you think happened?' Libby asked Fran.

'I think she's been running rings round everybody,' said Fran slowly. 'I'm sure she was back in the country before Sunday, and knew Tony West was dead. Otherwise why would she turn up?'

Mog was looking bewildered. Adam grinned at him. 'I'll explain it all later,' he said.

'You mean if Tony West was still alive she wouldn't have dared come back?' said Libby.

Fran nodded.

'So what are you saying? She went to his house and found him dead?'

'Or –' said Fran.

'She killed him?' gasped Libby. 'But why?'

'Don't you think her story of being packed out of the way after Gerald killed his son was a bit thin?'

Libby frowned. 'Well – yes, I suppose it was.'

'Wouldn't it make more sense if she went off because *she* killed him?'

Libby stared blankly. 'But what about Gerald? Why was he packed off?'

'Not being reliable enough to stick to a story?'

'Yes, but –' began Libby.

'Why did Tony help her in the first place?'

'Yes.'

'I don't know.' Fran shrugged. 'I'd got that far, because it gives her a motive for killing West before coming to try and claim her inheritance.'

'Or what she thought of as her inheritance,' said Libby. 'Is that why she killed Kenneth?'

'We don't know that she did kill Kenneth,' said Fran. 'As I said, I'm only theorizing.'

'So why has she run away now?' asked Adam suddenly.

'Perhaps she thought she wasn't going to get away with it.'

'So she found her passports and skedaddled?'

Libby shook her head. 'She couldn't use either of the passports. The false one would have been retained by the police, and if she tried to use her real one she'd be stopped straight away.'

'So where's she gone?' asked Adam.

'Does she know where Gerald is, do you think?' said Libby, turning to Fran.

'You think she'd go after him?' Fran said. 'I suppose she might, if she did know.'

'Then we need to find out where he is first,' said Libby.

'Oh, come on, Lib!' Fran laughed. 'I expect the police have been looking for him for the last two weeks.'

'You don't suppose you're barking up the wrong tree after all?' Mog put in diffidently. 'Couldn't it have been this West guy who killed the skeleton, whoever it is?'

'In that case who killed him?' asked Libby.

'Someone who wanted revenge?'

'It's all just speculation,' said Fran, standing up. 'Whatever the police thought, they must have changed their minds after Cindy's story, so now they'll be trying to prove or disprove it.'

'While looking for Cindy again. She's disappeared once in her life, so she must be good at it,' said Libby.

'According to her, she had help from West the last time,' said Fran.

'Are you saying we still don't really know about that, too?' said Libby.

'We already knew Cindy and Gerald had disappeared. And a skeleton with matching DNA to Gerald has been found. The police haven't confirmed that it's Kenneth – perhaps they don't know, either. I think that's about all we *do* know for certain,' said Fran. 'Anyway, I want to see if we can find the entrance to any of these passages.'

'Passages?' Adam looked up. Libby explained. 'The police were poking around in the other part of the house yesterday,' he said. 'Do you reckon that's what they were looking for?'

'Could be,' said Fran. 'As I said before, when we found the photographs, I'm just thinking that if Tony West knew this house well he would have known where to hide stuff. Not sure whether the police would have found out about the passages.'

'We can always tell them if we find anything,' said Libby. 'If we try and tell them before, they won't take any notice of us.'

'You can't blame them,' said Adam with a grin.

'We're usually right,' said Libby indignantly. 'Come on, Fran. Let's start looking.' She turned to Adam. 'Lewis won't mind, will he?'

Adam shrugged. 'I doubt it. He's let you run tame so far.'

'Yes, but when he left he'd had enough. Not just of the whole case but of us, too,' said Libby.

'Well, he's not here now, so carry on.' Adam stood up. 'We'll get back to work.'

Mog, who looked as though he would rather help with the search, followed Adam outside and Fran went towards the door Katie always used to leave the kitchen.

This led into a small inner hall with two more doors. Fran opened the first one, peered in, then shut it again.

'Katie's rooms,' she said, and opened the other door. This led to another passage which looked in far worse repair and ended at the bottom of a staircase. This was definitely the unrestored part of the house. Cobwebs festooned the curving banisters, and rubble and possibly unmentionable detritus covered most of the floor. There were no other doors.

'What about the strong room being up there?' said Libby, peering up the staircase.

'Do you think those stairs are safe?' asked Fran.

'They're stone,' said Libby, testing the first step, 'so they should be.'

Cautiously, they set off up the stairs, keeping close to the wall, but as they rounded the curve halfway up they discovered a fall of plaster that cut off further ascent.

'That's that, then,' said Fran as they made their way down. 'Unless we can get through from Lewis's part of the house.'

'He wouldn't let us before,' said Libby.

'That was because we were only thinking about Gerald leaving something behind, not Tony West hiding something. Shall we try?'

'I'm not sure,' said Libby, feeling uncomfortable. 'How about we go out that little back door and have a look round the walls and see if we can find anything?'

They retraced their steps back along the passage and through the kitchen to the hall. The little oak door was bolted. Fran looked round. 'No other doors,' she said.

Libby looked at the floor. 'Heavy stone flags,' she said, 'nothing under there.'

Fran drew the bolts on the door and pushed it open. 'Where do you think the passages would have run?' she said.

'If there really is one linking here, the church and the pub, I would have thought it came from the river,' said Libby. 'But that doesn't matter, it's the entrance that's important.'

'Yes,' said Fran, 'but if the entrances have all been blocked up this end, there might still be an entrance somewhere else.'

'After all this time? I shouldn't think so,' said Libby. 'I think this is a wild goose chase, Fran.'

'I know you do,' said Fran, 'but those documents have got to be somewhere, and I think that's here. And you said yourself, Gerald needs to be found.'

'Do you really think Cindy would go for him?'

'If he's the only one left alive to witness her murdering Kenneth, yes,' said Fran, 'but if she isn't the killer – I don't know. I think he needs to be found in any case.'

Libby started inspecting the old brick walls to the right of the little door, going towards the unrestored part of the house. 'If there is anything it's going to be this side,' she said.

But the brickwork and the bleached timber framing were in a bad state of repair and no openings were apparent. 'It wouldn't be here on the outside anyway,' said Fran, straightening up. 'I bet it's under the floor somewhere inside.'

'The ice-house passage might still be there,' said Libby. 'And the strong room.'

'Ice houses were usually some distance from the house,' said Fran.

'And I didn't know they had internal passages to go to them,' said Libby. 'I thought they were miles out in the grounds and the poor servants had to trudge out in all weathers.'

'Most of them were underground, though, or had the ground built up round them.' Fran turned to peer down towards the river. 'And they were often near water, so ice could be collected easily.'

'Why would it have had a passage?'

'Part of the ventilation and cooling system, I expect,' said Fran. 'And if that was the only way in there won't be any external entrance.'

'What about loading the ice?'

'That's a point,' said Fran. 'I wonder if the police have searched the grounds thoroughly?'

'Adam said he didn't see them when they were first looking for Cindy.'

'Do you think he might know where the ice-house is?'

'I suppose Mog might, but only if Lewis did, and surely he would have mentioned it as a possible hiding place earlier.'

Fran nodded. 'What I want to know now is how much of a search was made at the time Gerald and Cindy disappeared.'

'Yes, because it couldn't have been Kenneth looking for them as it said on those websites,' said Libby. 'Not if he was already dead.'

'So were the police involved?' Fran turned and went back inside the house. 'How do we find out?'

'Google it again?' suggested Libby.

'It was mainly newspaper articles, wasn't it? They would say if there was a police investigation.'

'Let's go home and do that,' said Libby, who was beginning to feel like a trespasser. 'We're not going to find anything here.'

'I might call in at the pub again,' mused Fran, as they went back through the kitchen. 'See if Frank's back.'

'You be careful,' warned Libby. 'Don't go asking him about his friend with Alzheimer's.'

'No, I shall just ask him about his cellars. I bet he knows more than his wife –'

'Bren,' put in Libby.

'Than Bren does.' Fran smiled. 'He's probably got smuggled beer and cigarettes down there!'

'Not much call for cigarettes in a pub these days,' said Libby gloomily.

'Plenty of people still smoking at home, though,' said Fran. 'Look at you.'

'Yeah, look at me,' said Libby. 'What a sad case.' She put a hand to cup her mouth and shouted for Adam. An answering call came from the direction of the parterre, and he soon appeared in the doorway. 'We're off. See you later.'

Libby collected the Land Rover from The Fox car park and Fran disappeared inside. Libby sighed, put the big vehicle in gear, and set off back towards Nethergate. Somehow, not concentrating on her journey, she found herself driving along Pedlar's Row past March Cottage. She slowed down and came to a stop outside The Red Lion. What prompted her to get out and go into the pub she couldn't have said, but here she was, in the empty afternoon bar, and there was George sitting at the end of the bar with his newspaper.

'Hello, hello!' he said, beaming with pleasure and sliding off his bar stool. 'And how are you? And your friend?'

Libby assured him she and Fran were both well and that Fran was getting married in two weeks.

'And the cat?' he asked, over the noise of a brand new coffee machine. He presented Libby with a foaming cup and sprinkled chocolate on top. 'Latest thing,' he said.

'Yes,' said Libby, eyeing it doubtfully. 'Thank you.' She put it on the bar. 'The cat? Balzac? Oh, he's fine. Living with Fran and spoilt rotten.' Balzac had been adopted by Fran when his previous owner died.

'And what about –' George lowered his voice and nodded significantly towards the door. 'Her?'

'Bella? As well as she can be, you know.' Libby tried the coffee and got a foam moustache. 'You still keeping an eye on the cottage?'

'Go in once a month or so,' said George. 'More if the weather's bad. Will she …?'

'Come back to it? No idea,' said Libby, feeling uncomfortable talking about her friend who had such a bad time eighteen months ago. 'Anyway, George, I wondered if you knew anything about a couple called Frank and Bren who run The Fox over at Creekmarsh?'

'Cor, bless you, love! Known old Frank since we first came into the trade. Here,' he leant forward confidentially. 'You're not on the trail again, are you?'

'No,' said Libby, feeling the telltale colour creeping up her face. 'Just Fran and I had lunch there today, and we were wondering about the old smuggling passages in his cellar.'

'Oh, there's always been talk about them,' said George. 'I'm supposed to have them, too.'

'Are you?' said Libby in surprise.

'Any pub not far from the sea along this coast was supposed to have been involved in the trade. Don't know much about Frank's.'

'So he's been there some time?' said Libby, sipping her coffee.

'Good few years,' said George. 'Good friends round there, he has.'

'There don't seem to be many houses,' said Libby.

'Ah, no, but that didn't matter, see. His best mate was the bloke who owned the big house.'

Chapter Twenty-seven

'GERALD SHEPHERD?' MANAGED LIBBY, after spluttering on a mouthful of cappuccino.

'That's him. Went off with his daughter-in-law a few years back, didn't he?' George leant back and stared at Libby. ''Course, that's what it is, isn't it? That skeleton. They reckon it's the son, don't they? You're on that, aren't you?'

'Um,' said Libby.

'Well, I don't mind telling you what I know. Old Frank used to know him, see, the actor bloke, from London. In fact, it was because he – what's-'is-name–'

'Gerald Shepherd.'

'Yeah – come down to visit Frank he found the big house. So he bought it.'

'How long ago was that?' asked Libby.

'Years and years. The son was still at home, then.'

'And when Shepherd vanished, did the police look for him?'

'Cor, bless you, no! It was obvious what had happened, wasn't it? While the son was in that telly thing, his dad and his missus went off together. Not been seen since, have they?'

'Er –' said Libby.

'Oh, 'course, they must be looking for 'em now.' George rubbed at a spot on the bar with a tea towel. 'They could always ask old Frank,' he said diffidently. 'I always reckoned he knew a bit more about it than he said. But he was a loyal bloke, even if he did think they was doing wrong.'

'You really think he might know where Gerald went? The police have been searching for him for weeks now,' said Libby.

'Couldn't say for certain,' said George, 'but it'd be worth a try, wouldn't it? Not that I reckon he did it or anything, but –

well, best be sure, eh?'

Libby thanked him effusively, drained her coffee and fished for her mobile. Outside she punched in Fran's number.

'Fran? Are you still at The Fox?'

A crackly voice answered her. Then there was a pause.

'Fran? Are you there?'

'Yes,' said the voice more clearly. 'I was in the cellar. I'm in the bar now. What did you want?'

'You're still there, then. I'm coming back. Have you found anything?'

'Yes, Frank's shown me where he thinks the tunnel used to come out, but what's the matter?'

'I'll tell you when I get there. I'm at The Red Lion – I've been talking to George.'

'What? What are you doing there?'

'I'll see you in five minutes,' said Libby. 'Keep him talking.'

Libby turned the Land Rover round with difficulty and set off back to Creekmarsh. It was just over five minutes later when she pulled up in The Fox car park and Fran came out to meet her.

'What did you say to him?' asked Libby, locking the car.

'I said you wanted to see the tunnel entrance,' said Fran, frowning. 'What on earth's up?'

Libby repeated her conversation with George, while Fran's eyes got wider and wider.

'Come on, then,' she said, 'we'll go and ask him.'

'Hang on a minute,' said Libby. 'He knows the police have been looking for Gerald Shepherd. If this friend of his really is him, he must have a good reason for keeping quiet. He may clam up.'

'Then we tell him what we know,' said Fran grimly. 'The general public don't know any of that. Did you say George didn't know Cindy was back?'

'It seemed that way,' said Libby, following Fran into the pub.

'Let me do the talking then,' said Fran. 'And don't put your foot in it.'

Libby opened her mouth for an indignant reply, but was forestalled by the appearance of a large man in a short-sleeved checked shirt, with broad shoulders and an even broader grin.

'This your mate, then?' he said to Fran, and stuck out a large hand.

'Libby Sarjeant,' said Libby, smiling nervously back.

'You want to see where the tunnel was, too?' said Frank, standing back from the open bar. 'Come on, then.'

Fran nodded to Libby, and they went behind the bar. Libby peered at a trapdoor from which led a steep stepladder.

'I'll go first, shall I?' said Frank, and with surprising agility he lowered himself through the hole and down the steps. Libby followed and Fran brought up the rear.

The cellar was brightly lit, smelt slightly damp and was crowded with crates and crates of bottles and barrels of beer, positioned under another trapdoor which Libby guessed led up to the outside of the pub for the draymen.

'Here you are then,' said Frank, going right to the end of the cellar, where the stone ceiling began to slope downwards. She could just about make out the shape of a low, arched doorway, which had obviously been painted over many times.

'That's where it was, right enough,' said Frank.

'Bren didn't seem to know,' said Libby. Fran frowned at her.

'Oh, Bren takes no notice of things like this. Lives in the moment, you might say.' Frank let his hand wander over the outline of the door. 'I'd love to open this up, but I think the whole place might come down if I tried.'

'Where do you think it goes?' said Libby. Fran sighed and rolled her eyes.

'To the Place and the church,' said Frank. 'I got a coupla old maps upstairs they say was drawn by an old parson at the church. I was just telling your mate. Want to see 'em?'

Libby could hardly contain her excitement, and Fran had to keep digging her in the ribs to remind her to keep calm. In the bar, Frank told Bren he was taking them upstairs, prompting some ribald comments from the regulars who still sat at a corner table.

'Don't mind them,' said Bren. 'You go and enjoy yourselves.'

Upstairs, Frank took them into a pleasant living room with views to the back of the pub. From a glass-fronted bookcase, he took a large leather folder, which he opened on a coffee table.

'There,' he said, pointing. 'See, it looks a bit like one of those old treasure maps, don't it? Bloke I took it to reckons it's genuine because it's a bit rough, like, and could be a plan for when they dug the tunnel.'

'Why do you think it was the parson who drew it?' asked Fran.

'Bloke says because he was the only educated one. This would be in the mid 1700s, he says.'

'When the smuggling was at its height,' nodded Libby, 'and the revenue men were being posted all round the coast. Lots of churches were involved, weren't they?'

'Some even had their towers raised,' said Frank, 'so they could be seen from the sea, and they reckon ours was, so they could get into the inlet.'

'But if the big house and the church and the inn were all involved,' frowned Libby, 'why did they need tunnels? There wasn't anyone else around.'

'Ah, yeah, but it was them dragoons, you see,' said Frank with delight. 'This little bit, almost an island –'

'Peninsula,' suggested Fran.

'Yeah, well, it was all on its own, see, so the dragoons, or revenue men, were always sniffing around. There's an old diary they've got in the county library that talks about it.'

'So, wouldn't the squire, or whoever owned the Place, have drawn this map?' asked Libby.

'Squire couldn't read or write properly,' said Frank. 'Parson was his sort of secretary.'

'The Clerk!' said Libby, delightedly.

'Ah.' Frank beamed at her. 'Rudyard Kipling.'

'So can we tell where the tunnels came out the other end?' asked Fran.

Frank pulled the map round. 'See this? That's the old church. Burnt down about a hundred years later. Some say because of the smugglers.'

'They were getting much hotter on the enforcement by then,' said Libby. 'The French had been using the smuggling routes to escape, and the Napoleonic spies had got in through the same

189

routes.'

Frank gave Libby an approving nod. 'That's right. So the original church was destroyed and they reckoned the passage and whatever was down there went with it.'

'What about Creekmarsh Place?' asked Fran. 'Where did the tunnel come out there?'

'Same place as here,' said Frank. 'In the cellars.'

Fran and Libby looked at one another. 'I didn't know Creekmarsh had cellars,' said Libby.

''Course it has,' said Frank. 'Hasn't your mate been down there, yet?'

'You mean Lewis?' said Fran. 'I don't think he knows they exist, either.'

'Where do they go?' asked Libby.

'What, the other end? The ice-house,' said Frank. 'You know what an ice-house is?'

'Yes,' sighed Fran and Libby together.

'We were trying to find out where the tunnel to that was, too,' said Libby.

'One and the same,' said Frank. 'The ice-house was down by the river, somewhere, so they could get ice from boats and cut it from the river in the winter, so it made sense to have that as the smugglers' tunnel.'

'Might have known,' muttered Libby.

Fran sat back in her chair. 'And do you mean to say the police haven't been here asking you questions about the house?' she said to Frank.

'Why should they? No one's told 'em I know anything about it.'

'But when the skeleton turned up and they started asking questions –' began Fran.

'Only came and asked me some general questions, like,' said Frank.

'And you didn't tell them you knew Gerald Shepherd.'

There was complete silence while Frank stared at Fran as though mesmerized.

'Or,' Fran continued with her fingers crossed, 'that you still visited him in a home because he has Alzheimer's disease.'

'How do you know?' Frank's voice was almost a whisper and he leant forward so that Libby could see the veins standing out on his neck. She pushed herself back in her chair.

'I'm right, aren't I?' said Fran. 'And you've been doing it to protect him, haven't you?'

'He was my mate,' said Frank truculently.

'Still is, obviously,' said Fran. 'But don't you see you could have helped the police find out the truth? They thought that skeleton was him at first.'

'I could have told them it wasn't,' said Frank scornfully.

'Then why on earth didn't you?'

He looked awkward. 'I promised.'

'Promised who?' Libby said in surprise.

'Gerry. Him and me was mates years ago, see, in London, and when he went into this home he didn't want everyone to know. He wasn't that far gone, then, see.'

'So you knew all about him going missing, supposedly?' Fran looked astonished.

'Oh, yeah. It fitted with Ken's wife going off and the papers put two and two together. That's when I promised, see. Ken said he'd look for her –'

'*Ken* said?' echoed Libby.

'Yeah. It was Tony who organised the home, see, while Ken was in that telly thing.'

'Tony West?' said Libby faintly. Why on earth hadn't the police been to see this man?

'Yeah. Another old mate, he was. Can't believe he's gone.' Frank shook his head. 'Anyway, when Ken come out, he went straight down to see Gerald, and when he got back to the house Cindy was gone.'

'So he started looking for her?'

'He made a show of it,' said Frank. 'He couldn't have cared less, really, she was a grasping little bitch. Anyway, then he goes off, and that was it. Didn't think any more about it. I just kept visiting Gerry. I asked Tony why Ken didn't come any more and he said he didn't know where he was.'

'So when they put out that the skeleton was probably Kenneth, and Tony West had been murdered, you didn't come

191

forward?'

Frank's cheeks became pink. 'I didn't want to get involved,' he said. 'Poor old Gerry. Don't know what's going on these days.'

'What about the people who look after him?' asked Fran. 'Why haven't they said anything?'

'They don't know who he is,' said Frank.

'But they'd need all his medical records,' said Libby, 'how can they not? You can't go into a home under a false name.'

'He didn't,' said Frank, surprisingly. 'We just said it was the same name as the actor and they believed us. 'Course, poor bugger was looking old then, not even like he was in that *Collateral Damage*.'

'Well.' Fran sat back. 'You're going to have to talk to the police now, Frank.'

'Why?' The truculent manner was back.

'Because Cindy Dale came back.'

'That cow?' Frank's fists bunched. 'You wait till I see her.'

'But now she's gone again.'

'Gone?' Frank looked bewildered.

'They questioned her about Kenneth's murder – or supposed murder – then let her go and she vanished. We don't know where she's gone.'

Frank pulled at his lower lip. 'I reckon I'll have to think about this,' he said.

Libby leant forward. 'Frank,' she said, 'Cindy told them Gerry killed Kenneth.'

'What?' Frank looked, eyes blazing. 'Fuck's sake. I'll soon put that right.' He stood up. 'All right, ladies. I don't know how you managed to get on to me when no one else has, but you're right. I'll go to the police. Who should I speak to?'

'Superintendent Bertram,' said Libby, with a grin, 'and don't forget to tell her we sent you!'

Chapter Twenty-eight

THE FOLLOWING MORNING LIBBY remembered she hadn't asked Frank where Gerald Shepherd was. He answered the phone on the first ring.

'Oh, it's you,' he said.

'Who were you expecting?' asked Libby.

'The police,' said Frank. 'I phoned 'em this morning. Yes, I know I said I'd get on to them straight away, but I didn't think one more day would hurt, and I wanted to talk it over with Bren. So I phoned this morning.'

'And they said they'd phone you back?'

'I asked for that Bertram, and they said she was in London. So I left a message that it was about Gerald Shepherd and they said someone would call me back straight away.'

'So I'd better get off the line,' said Libby, 'but before I do, where's the home Gerald's in?'

'Why should I tell you that?' Frank was cautious. 'You're not to go and see him, now.'

'I just wondered how far away it was,' said Libby.

'Not far. He used to be in a place called The Laurels, but they had a murder there a coupla years ago, so we moved him.'

'Hmm,' said Libby. She knew all about The Laurels. 'So where is he now?'

'What do you want to know for?'

'I wondered if Cindy would go after him,' said Libby.

'Why? She wouldn't know where he was, anyway.'

'Oh, I think she might,' said Libby, with a sigh.

'I'll tell the police. He'll be safe enough.'

Libby had to give in. Frank was probably right to keep the secret for that bit longer, although how the police were going to see it was another matter. She hoped they didn't charge him with obstruction. Then she called Adam.

'Any news from Lewis?'

'Not sure,' said Adam, sounding puzzled. 'We had the police round here again this morning, although they didn't talk to us. They were going over the inside of the house again. Then Mog got a text from Lewis saying he's delayed.'

'By what?' said Libby.

'Didn't say. The message just said "Delayed". Mog texted back and so did I, but nothing else and now his phone's switched off.'

'Have you tried Katie?'

'Haven't got her number,' said Adam. 'We thought of that, and we were going to go and look for it in the house, but the police were there.'

'Were you expecting him back today?'

'No, which is even funnier. He hadn't said anything about coming back.'

'Looks like some kind of message,' said Libby slowly.

Adam snorted. 'Yeah, Ma – a text message.'

'You know what I mean. Something must have happened and he wanted to let you know – or warn you, perhaps – and that was all he had time to do.'

'You think something's happened to him?' Adam sounded alarmed.

'I was wondering about the police, actually.'

'The police? Why?'

'Because Big Bertha's gone to London.'

'How do you know that?'

'I have my sources,' grinned Libby. 'Let me know if you hear anything.'

Next she called Fran and told her what she had learned so far.

'West's murder,' said Fran. 'Oh, dear.'

'You think that's what it is? But Lewis said they weren't interested in him for that.'

'They must have found some new evidence.' Fran was silent for a moment. 'Libby, I'm sure there's a weapon involved.'

'A weapon?'

'It looks like an outsized darning mushroom.'

'You can see it?'

'I think so,' said Fran, sounding doubtful. 'It popped into my head as soon as you told me about Lewis's message. I should think he's being questioned by the police about it.'

'Heavens,' said Libby. 'I wonder what they'll do next.'

'Send someone to see Frank, I expect,' said Fran. 'I wonder who it'll be?'

'I bet I know,' said Libby.

Ian Connell called Fran at lunchtime.

'Not that I expect you to tell me,' he said in a weary voice, 'but just how did you get on to Frank Cole?'

'At The Fox?' said Fran warily.

'Of course at The Fox.'

'It's a long story,' said Fran.

'I bet it is,' said Ian. 'Are you lunching with your fiancé?'

'Er – no,' said Fran, waggling her eyebrows at Guy, who was poring over seating plans.

'May I take you to lunch then?'

'Yes, OK. Where? It isn't going to be an inquisition, is it?'

'The Sloop,' said Ian, 'and of course it'll be an inquisition.'

'Do you want me to come with you?' asked Guy, when she explained.

'No,' sighed Fran. 'It'll be awkward enough as it is, without you firing up in my defence all the time.'

'That's what I get for being the protective male,' said Guy, dropping a kiss on her head. 'Go on, go and tart yourself up and make him see what he's missing.'

Ian was already in the bar at The Sloop when Fran walked in. He stood up and held a chair for her.

'Drink?' he said.

'Orange juice, please,' said Fran, much though she would have loved a gin and tonic.

'So tell me what you and the inestimable Mrs Sarjeant have been up to this time,' he said, after they had ordered. Fran sat back in her chair and looked at him.

'You'll only be angry,' she said. 'And we came across Frank completely by accident. We were looking for tunnels.'

'Tunnels? You found him in a tunnel?'

'Not quite.' Fran giggled at the thought. She explained about the ice-house and smuggling tunnels, and the coincidence of Libby talking to George at The Red Lion.

'I expect the police have been looking for tunnels, too, haven't they?' she said innocently. 'They were there again this morning.'

'Tunnels, no.' Ian looked thoughtful. 'Was this something to do with your – er – thoughts?'

'Not really,' said Fran, 'although there was something else.' She looked down at the table and played with her glass. 'I saw a sort of, um, implement when I heard Lewis had been delayed in London.'

'Delayed? How did you hear that?' Ian's voice was sharp.

'He texted Mog. Libby's son's boss.' Fran looked up at him anxiously. 'Is there something wrong?'

Ian's mouth twisted. 'You could say that,' he said.

'Well, tell me, then,' said Fran.

The waitress arrived with their food and smiled fetchingly at Ian, who scowled.

'All I can say is that he is helping with enquiries,' he said, cutting savagely into a sausage.

'New evidence,' said Fran, spearing a lettuce leaf. 'The weapon?'

Ian glared at her. 'All right, yes, but don't you dare tell anyone.'

'Not even Libby?' said Fran sweetly.

Ian cast his eyes to heaven. 'I would like to say especially not Libby, but there would be no point.'

Fran nodded and chewed thoughtfully. 'Did Frank tell you Shepherd used to be at The Laurels?'

'He did. I was charmed at the coincidence.'

Fran laughed. 'Poor Ian,' she said. 'I'm sorry we're such a nuisance. We do try not to get involved.'

'Not hard enough,' said Ian with a reluctant smile. 'Come on, tell me what else you've been thinking about this business.'

So Fran told him everything she and Libby had thought and done since Adam first told his mother about the skeleton.

'And I began to wonder about Cindy,' she concluded, 'because I think she saw Tony West before she claimed to have arrived on Sunday.'

'She didn't claim to, she *did* arrive on Sunday,' said Ian. 'That's proven.'

'Then she came over before. Have you checked that?'

'Why are you so sure?' asked Ian. 'Or is that a silly question?'

'She said nothing about West when she first arrived at Creekmarsh, then flew into hysterics when she first heard he was dead. None of it rang true. I was sure I could see her at West's. In fact, I was almost certain she was his killer.'

Ian stared. 'I wish I could tell them all this in London,' he said. 'They're questioning Osbourne-Walker about it now.'

'Don't you think that's a coincidence too far? The current owner of Creekmarsh killing the man who had power of attorney to sell it to him just after the body –'

'All right, all right,' said Ian, 'don't get so complicated. But the evidence is incontrovertible.'

'So what is it?' asked Fran, pushing her plate away.

'The murder weapon. It belongs to Osbourne-Walker.'

'They found it?'

'Oh, yes.'

'Where?'

'Come on, Fran, I've already told you more than I should. What was this weapon you – er – saw?'

'It was like a sort of enlarged darning mushroom,' said Fran, sketching with her hands.

Ian's eyes widened. 'It's a handmade carver's mallet, a really unusual one,' he said. 'And that's just what it looks like. It's an antique.'

Fran nodded. 'And Tony West gave it to him, didn't he?'

Ian's mouth fell open. 'I give up,' he said. 'I'll call London and ask them to look for Dale's fingerprints. There were a few there that they couldn't match.'

'Suppose you could prove Dale had been there. Could you prove whether or not she killed West?' asked Fran.

'We'd have a damn good try.' Ian pushed his chair back. 'I

don't want to hurry you, but I think I ought to get on to this straight away.'

Fran stood up. 'So do I,' she said.

'Oh, and Fran, thank you,' he said as they left The Sloop, 'but if you ever breathe a word that I'm gullible enough to listen to you, I'll clap you in jail.'

'You've listened before,' said Fran, 'it even got into the papers. If I'm right it won't matter, but if I'm not, I'll keep quiet as long as you do.'

Ian kissed her cheek. 'Deal,' he said. 'I'm a very bad policeman.'

'How did it go?' asked Guy when Fran went into the gallery to report.

'All right, I suppose,' she said, perching on the table he used as a desk. 'He's going to follow up a suggestion I made. But I mustn't talk about it.'

'Not even to me?'

'Not even to Libby, according to Ian,' said Fran.

'But you will,' laughed Guy.

'Of course,' said Fran, 'and I'll tell you, too.'

Later, she called Libby and told her everything Ian had said, including the warning about spreading the glad tidings.

'Cheek!' said Libby indignantly. 'After all we've done for him.'

'Not that much, actually, Lib, but I convinced him with my description of the murder weapon, so he was willing to give it a go. He'll take a lot of flack if they don't find any evidence of Cindy being in that house.'

'Will he let you know if they do?'

'I don't know whether he'll be able to, but I expect he'll try.' Fran paused. 'He's really very sweet, you know.'

'Hey!' said Libby warningly. 'Wedding day two weeks away, remember.'

'He's still sweet,' said Fran. 'So what do we do now?'

'Have they seen Gerald Shepherd yet?'

'He didn't say,' said Fran. 'They'll probably need specially trained officers, won't they?'

'Well, I suppose we'll find out all about it soon,' said Libby with a sigh. 'If Lewis comes back it means they no longer suspect him. Oh, and you didn't tell me Tony West gave him the mallet.'

'It only came to me while I was talking to Ian,' said Fran. 'I expect we'll hear the whole story if Lewis comes back.'

'And if he isn't still fed up with us.'

'If what I told Ian means he's been released, he'll be too grateful to ignore us,' said Fran. 'Let me know as soon as you hear anything.'

'And you,' said Libby, and disconnected. Almost as soon as she had done so, the phone rang again.

'Hello, Ma, it's me,' said Adam unnecessarily. 'Lewis is on his way back. He wanted to know what everybody was doing this evening.'

Chapter Twenty-nine

Harry MANAGED TO FIT them all in at The Pink Geranium: Libby and Ben, Fran and Guy, Adam and Lewis. Mog said wistfully he would love to come but thought he might be needed at home.

'I'm surprised Fiona's let you come back to work so soon,' said Libby.

'So'm I,' said Mog. 'But I get under her feet, and her mother's there almost every day.'

'Ah,' said Libby. 'I see. Better go back home now, then.'

Lewis, looking drawn but relieved, arrived a little after the appointed time of nine o'clock, bearing a large bouquet, which he handed straight to Fran.

'I don't know what to say, and I don't know how you did it, but thanks to you I'm off the hook,' he said, then leant over to kiss Libby. 'And you, of course, Lib.'

'It was nothing to do with me,' said Libby, 'only marginally, anyway, so sit down and tell us what's been going on.'

Donna came over to take their orders and Harry sent out a bottle of champagne on the house.

'Shame I don't drink,' said Lewis, 'but lovely thought. He's a dish, isn't he?'

'Hands off,' said Adam.

'Yeah, I know he's spoken for, but a fella can look, can't he?' Lewis gave a tired grin. 'Well, here goes. I was up at the London flat, see, and Katie was at hers. I been talking to my producer, and they want to firm up ideas for the next series. It's been a bit delayed, so they're keen to get on with it. Anyway, this morning these coppers turn up on my doorstep with a warrant for my arrest.' He paused, looking down at the table. 'It was … well, I dunno how to describe it.' He looked up. 'I wanted to tell you, but I didn't have a chance.'

'That was when you sent the text to Mog?' asked Adam.

'Yeah. His was the first memory button, and I thought he'd tell you.' He grinned at Libby. 'And you. And I knew you'd make a guess at what was going on.'

'And Fran saw your carver's mallet,' said Libby. Fran went pink.

'You what?' Lewis gaped.

Libby explained. 'Then she told Ian Connell, the inspector down here, and he relayed the info to London.'

'What, that she'd seen it?'

'No, that Cindy Dale's prints might be on it,' said Fran.

There was an astonished silence round the table. Lewis and Adam looked at each other, stupefied, and Guy and Ben looked bewildered. Fran told them what she had suspected.

'So Ian must have persuaded them to check for the prints and look into the possibility that Cindy was in the country before Sunday,' said Libby. 'Brilliant, Fran.'

'They must have found the prints,' said Fran, 'or they'd never have let Lewis go.'

'They were quick about it, then,' said Lewis. 'They let me go late afternoon.'

'I asked Ian if he'd tell me what happened, but I doubt if he will,' said Fran. 'He opened up to me more than he should have at lunchtime.'

'I wonder why?' said Guy.

'Oh, shut up,' said Fran, giving him an affectionate nudge.

'Well, congratulations, Lewis,' said Ben, raising his glass. 'I'm really pleased. That means you can get on with the next series as soon as possible, I suppose?'

'Yeah,' said Lewis, 'and guess what, Ad? We're going to do a whole programme on the garden at Creekmarsh, with updates through the rest of the series.'

'Blimey!' said Adam. 'Have you told Mog?'

'Not yet. And we can't do it until the police say we can, so I guess we need to clear all this up quick.'

'We?' said Libby, amused.

'Well, you and the cops,' said Lewis, looking from her to Fran. 'So what do you think the whole story is, then?'

Libby and Fran looked at each other.

'I'll start,' said Fran, 'and you butt in if I miss anything.' She sipped her wine and put the glass back on the table. 'Here goes. We think, based on our own assumptions and information received, that Cindy Dale killed her husband Kenneth, and Tony West helped her disappear and got Gerald Shepherd into a nursing home as he was already going downhill with Alzheimer's disease.'

'Why?' asked Ben.

'Why what? Why did he help her disappear, or why did she kill Kenneth?'

'Both.'

'Not sure about why she killed Kenneth, except she does seem to have wanted to inherit Creekmarsh, or Gerald's estate, in any case, and as to why Tony helped her, we don't know. Coming up to date, once she'd heard about the skeleton being discovered, she was scared that the whole thing would come out. She didn't at this stage, remember, know that Lewis had bought Creekmarsh. Anyway, she came into the country somehow – I expect the police have found out when by now – went straight to Tony's house and killed him with the carver's mallet he gave Lewis.'

'What was it doing at Tony's house?' asked Adam.

'I was over there a few weeks ago doing a little job for him and I'd taken it with the rest of me tools. I left it there by accident.' Lewis shook his head. 'Teach me to be more careful, won't it.'

'So she didn't use it to implicate you on purpose?' said Guy.

'I don't think she knew of Lewis's existence at that time,' said Fran. 'All she was keen to do was shut Tony up. She then decided to reappear as the grieving widow and daughter-in-law, to reclaim the estate.'

'Did she think Gerald was dead?' asked Libby.

'I think she would have known if Gerald was dead, wouldn't she?' said Fran.

'Maybe, but she didn't know Lewis owned the property, so

Tony hadn't kept her up to date with events at all, had he?' said Adam.

'No, and that's why we're concerned that Cindy might go after Gerald,' said Libby.

'And what's all this you've found out about him?' asked Ben. 'And smugglers' tunnels?'

Fran and Libby told them of their discoveries with the two landlords.

'Trust my mother to be on those sorts of terms with pub landlords,' said Adam with a snort.

'So will the police confirm all these theories?' said Guy.

'Well, one seems to be confirmed,' said Libby. 'They've let Lewis go. Let joy be unconfined.'

At the end of the meal, Lewis gave a little speech and became slightly emotional, to Fran and Libby's delight and Ben and Guy's embarrassment. He then sat down, blew his nose and drank a whole glass of water.

'Hope Katie's come back to look after you,' said Adam, patting him on the arm.

'Tomorrow,' said Lewis. 'She had a few things to clear up, she said, because I'd told her we were going to be in London for weeks. She'll be down in the morning.'

'She won't lose any sleep over Cindy's fate,' said Libby. 'She couldn't stand her, could she?'

'Hated her,' said Lewis. 'I should have realised they'd met before, you know. There was such a – oh, I dunno, a *feeling* between them. Why didn't she tell me before, though?'

'Perhaps she didn't think she had to?' said Fran. 'Did you know she'd known Tony and Gerald that far back?'

'I didn't know she knew Gerald at all,' said Lewis, 'and I didn't realise she knew Tony as well as she did, either.'

'I can see why that was,' said Libby. 'She was probably scared you'd think she'd got the job with you through undue influence or something.'

'We've already talked about whose idea it was that she came to work for you, haven't we?' said Fran. 'It was Tony's, wasn't it?'

'Think so,' said Lewis. He stood up. 'Listen. Thanks for

being such a support, everybody, but I gotta go. I promised me mum I'd phone her this evening. I talked to her earlier, but she's a bit jumpy. I've asked Katie to drive her down here tomorrow, so she needs to start packing.'

'Typical male,' said Libby, watching Lewis leave the restaurant. 'Not bothering to tell his mum until eleven o'clock at night that someone's picking her up tomorrow morning.'

'Perhaps she'll say no,' said Fran.

'That'll larn him,' said Libby.

The next morning Lewis rang Libby to invite her and Fran to lunch at Creekmarsh to meet his mother, who would be arriving with Katie around eleven.

'She said yes, then?' said Libby.

''Course,' said Lewis in surprise. 'Why shouldn't she?'

Fran and Libby arrived in their separate vehicles just before one. They were greeted at the door by a beaming Katie, who led them into the kitchen, where a small brown-haired woman sat at the table in front of a large mug of tea.

'This is Edith,' said Katie, 'Lewis's mum. Edie, this is Mrs Sarjeant and Mrs Castle who've been helping Lewis.'

Edie pushed back the chair and stood up unsteadily, holding out a hand to Libby.

'Pleased to meet you, I'm sure,' she said. 'You done a lot for my boy.'

'Nothing really,' said Libby, 'just stood by. Fran – Mrs Castle – is the clever one.'

'Never had no truck with all that nonsense before,' said Edie, gripping Fran's hand with both of hers, 'but blessed if it weren't right as rain this time.'

'I'm really glad for you,' said Fran, looking uncomfortable. 'How is Lewis this morning?'

'Full of plans, he is,' said Katie. 'Down talking to that Mog and Adam about his show. Police have been and gone, and you wouldn't believe how they've changed.'

'How do you mean?' said Libby, pulling out a chair.

'That nice detective inspector, the dark one –'

'Connell?' said Libby, with a sideways look at Fran, who ignored her.

'That's the one. So polite, he was. They were here when Edie and I arrived, and he couldn't have been nicer. Looks like they'll have finished here, unless that Cindy turns up again.' Her face darkened. 'Which she won't, if she's got any sense. I always knew she was a bad'n.'

'You knew her when Gerald lived here, didn't you?' said Libby.

'Not to say knew,' said Katie. 'Met her. She was a little – well. I'd best not say. Glad she's gone, that's all. Now, anyone for tea? Shall I freshen that, Edie?'

Lewis came in a little while later, during which time Fran and Libby had heard all about Lewis as a little boy, Lewis as a tearaway teenager, Lewis as an apprentice chippy and Lewis as a joiner, before going on to the great heights of Lewis as a TV personality.

'I liked that *Housey Housey*,' said Edie. 'Better than his own show.'

'Really? Why?' said Fran.

'Because she don't like watching a half hour of me without the other presenters,' said Lewis, giving his mother a kiss. 'Everyone all right this morning?'

'Yes, thanks, and Katie tells us the police are going to be leaving you alone soon,' said Libby.

'They certainly are,' said Lewis, looking his bright and perky self. 'And we can start filming as soon as we can set it up. Have to get on to it quick, though, or we'll lose the best of the season.'

'Right,' said Libby, raising questioning eyebrows. ''Course you will.'

They had lunch in the kitchen, as usual, and Adam and Mog joined them. By the end of the meal Adam was complaining that he'd always assumed he had one mother, but now it seemed he had three.

'Not counting me, eh, Ad?' smiled Fran.

'You don't mother me,' said Adam. 'I don't think you're the motherly sort.'

'Out of the mouths of babes,' said Fran with a wry smile at Libby.

'Anyone who's a friend to my boy's like a son to me,' said

Edie, complacently. 'Aren't you going to eat up that spinach, boy?'

Libby snorted and Lewis roared. 'Now you see what I had to put up with,' he said.

Later, he saw Libby and Fran to their cars.

'That it, then?' he said. 'Have we finished with the mystery of Creekmarsh?'

'As far as you're concerned,' said Fran, 'but there's still the mystery of Cindy Dale and Gerald Shepherd.'

'But it's nothing to do with me any more, or Creekmarsh, so we can relax, can't we?' Lewis put an arm round each of their shoulders and gave them a squeeze. 'And you can get on with your wedding. Not long now, eh? Am I still coming to the evening do?'

'Of course you are,' said Fran. 'You're welcome to come to the whole day, if you like.'

'I'll hitch a lift with Inspector Connell, shall I?' he said with a wink. 'Go on. I'll see you both then, if not before.'

Chapter Thirty

THE SUN NOW SEEMED to shine in earnest every day. For Fran, it was a time of anticipation and joy, only slightly marred by the occasional phone calls from her children, still complaining. In the end Guy took the receiver from her in mid-conversation with Lucy.

'Lucy, I'm very sorry both your mother's and your first marriages went wrong, but they're both over now and I'm going to make sure that your mother, at least, spends the rest of her life happy and secure. She does not need your constant whining that things are not fair. It's quite true that neither you nor your sister are being fair to *her*, but she hasn't complained. So I suggest you leave her alone, or you'll find you're cut off from her altogether. I'll make sure of that. And you can pass that on to your sister.'

There was a confused spluttering at the other end of the line. 'You can't do that!' gasped Lucy.

'Oh, I can, and I will. I don't want to, because it would upset your mother,' said Guy, 'but *you're* upsetting her now, so it would be the lesser of two evils. We'll look forward to seeing you at the wedding. We've booked you into a little hotel a mile away where several of the other guests are staying and if you wish you can stay there the night before as well.'

'I can't afford that!' snapped Lucy.

'I didn't say you had to, did I?' said Guy wearily. 'It's your mother's treat.'

He switched off the phone and handed it back to Fran. 'And that's the end of that,' he said. 'Presumably she'll phone Chrissie and they'll tear me to pieces, but it may give them pause.'

'You wouldn't really cut me off from them, would you?' said Fran.

'If they were upsetting you, yes,' said Guy. 'I can be ruthless, you know.' And he twirled imaginary moustaches.

While Fran had plenty to keep her occupied, Libby was bored. Lewis had asked to be excused from the Steeple Farm project as he was so busy with his new series, in which Adam and Mog were heavily involved, to Adam's delight, and Ben was waiting for a builder friend of his to come over and give them a quote. So there was nothing to do on that front. Early summer kept Ben at The Manor for longer than usual and Fran was unavailable for long chats or girlie evenings.

Twice she went to The Pink Geranium for lunch and hovered around the kitchen getting in Harry's way, once she went to visit old Jim Butler and his dog Lady, who lived on the outskirts of Nethergate, and once she went to see Flo and Lenny in their sheltered accommodation down by the church.

Eventually she realised she was putting off finishing the paintings Guy had requested and made a determined effort. However, this kept her inside and the weather was beautiful, so the Friday of the week before Fran's wedding, she borrowed the Land Rover and drove to Creekmarsh.

A large lorry was parked on the drive, with several attendant cars. Libby left the Land Rover near the gates and walked up to the front door, which was open.

'Hello, dear.' Edie came out of the kitchen. 'Did you want Adam?'

'I was bored, Edie,' confessed Libby, 'so I came over to see how things were going. Are they filming?'

'Not sure, dear. I go down and have a look now and then, but I don't understand what's going on, so I leave 'em to it. They'll be down by that there party garden, I think.'

'Thanks, Edie. I'll take a wander down there,' said Libby. 'See you before I leave.'

Sure enough, there was a crowd of people round the parterre garden, where Lewis was on his haunches with Adam's string in his hand, while Mog and Adam stood at the back looking bored.

'Hi, Ma,' said Adam, his face brightening. 'Come to have a

look?'

'Yes, but it doesn't look as though much is happening.'

'Nothing is,' said Mog. 'They're planning everything out and holding us up into the bargain.'

'Ah, but that means it'll take you longer and *that* means more money,' said Libby.

'Hmph,' said Mog, scowling at a young woman with tied-back hair and collapsing trousers.

'Will you appear in the show?' Libby asked Adam.

'In the background doing the heavy work,' said Adam. 'The peasants, you know.'

'No more police?'

'I haven't seen any,' said Adam. 'I would have told you if I had.'

'Did they investigate the ice-house?'

'Ice house?' Adam wrinkled his brow. 'N-no. Where is it?'

'Don't know,' said Libby cheerfully. 'Perhaps I'll go and look for it if I won't get in the way.'

'Where do you think it is?'

'Somewhere down by the river,' said Libby. 'Do you know where they found that little boat?'

'Just round from the sailing club, I think,' said Adam. 'Do you think it's there? What is it exactly, anyway?'

Libby explained, then set off, circling the walled parterre garden and setting off towards the ha-ha. She passed the bench where she had sat with Lewis, and branched off to the right without going down to the sailing club and the pontoon. The inlet reached like a hand from the river into the Creekmarsh estate, the thumb towards the sailing club and the other fingers just round a bend. Libby went towards these, but discovered a mass of brambles and vegetation that made it almost impossible to reach, especially for a slightly overweight, vertically challenged person in sandals.

Trees overhung the sloping ground and police tape fluttered in the breeze. No boat was thrust into the bank now, but Libby could see where it had been. Above it, roots from the overhanging trees formed an archway, almost an entrance …

Libby's heart thumped. An entrance. She tried leaning

forward to see if there was, indeed, a tunnel, but from her vantage point she couldn't. Besides, she thought, if there was a tunnel, the police would have found it, surely. From down there, where the boat had been, they would have been able to see. Nevertheless, she started up the slope to see if she couldn't work her way round and come out above the inlet.

It was a scramble, and after five minutes Libby was red in the face, with bits of vegetation in her hair, feeling very glad she was wearing jeans. Suddenly, to her surprise, she came up against what appeared to be wire netting. She sat back on her heels and looked at it. It ran uphill through the bushes and downhill to disappear over a slight mound.

'Must be the boundary of the estate,' thought Libby. 'And still no sign of a tunnel.'

Dispirited, she hauled herself to her feet and struck off to her left, which, if her sense of direction was intact, would take her back to the meadow below the ha-ha. Sure enough, through the trees, she could see the artificial trench with its retaining wall, which must start, she thought, looking round, about here. And then her feet went out from under her and she slid inelegantly forward into darkness.

When she'd recovered enough to know (a) she wasn't dead and (b) she could still see daylight behind her, she sat up.

'This is it,' she whispered to herself as she got tentatively to her feet. The ceiling of the opening was the same height as the ha-ha, so it looked as though it ran under the meadow and must have been created at the same time. She looked left and right, and ahead, but could see nothing. 'And this,' she continued to herself, 'is where the heroine of the film naturally goes forward into impenetrable darkness without anyone knowing where she is.' She grinned at herself and began to look round the floor near her feet, lit slightly by the daylight behind, which seemed mainly to consist of rotting leaves. And then, just behind her, almost out of sight, something that looked slightly different.

Gingerly, she got down on her knees and pulled at a corner, which revealed the object as a leather document case. With shaking fingers, Libby unzipped it, although the zip was both old and slightly rusty. Inside, she could see what looked like a birth certificate, and closed it again hastily. There was no reason why she shouldn't look, but she felt instinctively that it was none of her business and that the police should see it first.

She scrambled shakily out of the hole and stood looking at it. If it was an entrance to a tunnel, somebody else would have to investigate, but she had seen no evidence of bricks, only packed earth, so it looked as though it possibly wasn't the ice-house. She turned and made her way along the bottom of the ha-ha until she got to the place where she could climb up to the meadow. Then, deciding not to take her find to the house, she made for the lane and from there to the Land Rover at the bottom of the drive. Once inside, she called Ian Connell, thanking her lucky stars that she still had his mobile number in her phone memory.

It took some time for him to answer, and when he did he didn't sound too pleased to hear from her.

'No, Ian, listen,' she said urgently. 'I've just fallen into some kind of tunnel at Creekmarsh and found this case. I think it's got a birth certificate in it.'

'A what?'

'Well, you know we thought Cindy Dale must be looking for documents? Couldn't this be it?'

There was a short silence. 'Does anyone else know you've found this?'

'No. I came straight to the Land Rover and called you. What shall I do? Shall I bring it in?'

'No,' said Ian, slowly. 'We'd better have a look at this place where you found it. Can you wait there for us?'

'Yes,' said Libby doubtfully. 'They've got television people here, so it won't be easy for you to get down there without people seeing. Shall I tell anyone?'

'You'd better tell Mrs North and Osbourne-Walker we're coming.'

'If I can detach him from the television people,' said Libby.

'We'll be there as quickly as we can,' said Ian and rang off. Libby climbed down from the Land Rover and plodded up the drive.

Katie was in the kitchen with Edie. Libby had worked out what to say and hoped there wouldn't be too many questions.

'Just to tell you,' she said, 'the police are coming back shortly to have a look at the area down by the river.'

Katie and Edie looked at her blankly.

'Are they?' said Katie. 'What for?'

'I don't really know,' said Libby. 'Had I better tell Lewis?'

'Well –' said Katie.

'See you in a bit, then,' said Libby, and vanished.

She made quickly for the parterre, where she beckoned to Adam and whispered her news to him before jogging back to the Land Rover just in time, as Ian's car drew up in the lane, followed by a police car.

'You have your uses, I suppose,' said Ian, shaking Libby's hand.

'Here you are,' she said. 'I only had a quick look. I haven't taken anything out.' She handed over the case. Ian looked inside and drew out some documents. He nodded.

'Cindy's marriage certificate,' he said. 'And her original passport. This is what she was looking for all right.'

'Is there anything else?'

'Yes, but I haven't time to look at them now.' He grinned at her. 'Don't worry, I'll let you know what they are, even if I shouldn't. Where's this hole?'

Libby led them down the lane to avoid the company in the parterre, and along the trench.

'This isn't the first time you've fallen into a hole, is it?' said Ian, with another grin.

'No, but I don't know how you know about the first time,' said Libby.

'Word gets around.' Ian bent his head and went into the opening carefully, motioning his minions to do the same. Libby watched from a safe distance. Eventually, Ian came out looking grubby and beckoned her over.

'There seem to be passages leading both ways from here,' he said.

'Down to the river and an ice house,' said Libby.

'How do you know that?' Ian frowned.

'An educated guess,' said Libby. 'And the other way will lead to the house with some kind of offshoot tunnels to the pub and the church.'

'Fran told me about the tunnels, but as we didn't find any sign of them inside the house we didn't pursue it,' said Ian, still frowning. 'You think there's an ice-house near the river?'

'That's where they were always built, for easy access,' said Libby, 'and of course it helped the smugglers.'

'Where we found the boat?'

'Probably. It looked to me as though there could be an entrance up on the bank.'

'When were you there, or is that a silly question?'

'This morning. I was on my way back when I fell into the hole under the ha-ha.'

'Show me,' said Ian, and motioned her to take the lead.

'Shouldn't you tell your mates to try the left-hand tunnel and see if we meet up?' asked Libby. Ian scowled at her.

'I'll do that when I've had a look from this end,' he said.

He was more adept at crawling through the vegetation than Libby, and soon confirmed that there was what looked like an opening, shielded by brambles, above the still fluttering police tape.

'I don't know why we didn't notice it before,' he said, as he slithered back down to join Libby.

'You weren't looking for it,' said Libby.

'Did Cindy come this way? Instead of across the field?' Ian pulled at his lower lip. 'Was that a blind? Leaving the boat where it was?'

'Or perhaps she came down, took the boat, sailed it or rowed it round into the inlet and escaped through the tunnel,' suggested Libby.

'How did she know about the tunnel?'

'She was living here when she disappeared, wasn't she? And was supposedly looking after Gerald, who we now know was already suffering from Alzheimer's. He could have told her without realising.'

Ian nodded. 'Possible,' he said. 'Probable, even.' He gave Libby a quick smile and she could see what Fran had seen in him. 'Thanks, Libby. You and Fran between you might be a bloody nuisance sometimes, but as I said before, you have your uses.'

Libby grinned. 'I know,' she said.

They returned to the entrance under the ha-ha and Ian went in after his officers. Libby sat on the ground with her back against the retaining wall and squinted in the sunlight. Muffled sounds and voices came from behind her, but she was unable to distinguish anything other than the odd call of 'Sir!' She wondered who was in charge of the search of the passage towards the house, and whether it would be open, or if all the theories would go tumbling down in the face of a rockfall or an extended root system.

Her thoughts were disturbed by a much louder scuffling and confusion and Ian, followed by a constable with a mobile to his ear and a green look about his face, stumbled out into the open.

'What?' said Libby.

'I shouldn't really tell you,' he said and held out a hand to help her up. 'But you've a right to know.'

Libby scrambled upright. 'Know what?'

'Cindy Dale. She didn't go anywhere. We've just found her body.'

Chapter Thirty-one

'IN THE ICE-HOUSE,' Libby told Fran over the phone. She was sitting in the Land Rover feeling distinctly shaky. 'It was where we thought, by the river. And there is a tunnel right through to the house. They're trying to find out where it comes out at the moment.'

'What about the tunnels to the pub and the church?' asked Fran.

'I haven't asked. Ian was too busy. I was lucky he told me what he did. Trouble is, I'm now a witness, because I told him where I thought the entrance from the river was and showed him the opening where I fell in. I've got to make a statement.'

'You've done that before,' said Fran, 'don't worry about it.'

'I'm not, but I want to go home.' Libby shivered. 'I'm beginning to hate this place.'

'Can't you go home? They can always come out and see you.'

'Not unless Ian says I can, and he's a bit tied up at the moment. He told me to wait here.'

'Then I don't suppose he'll be long,' said Fran soothingly. 'You'll soon be back to normal and revising all our theories.'

'That's true,' said Libby, thinking. 'If Cindy didn't kill Tony –'

'Ah, but she still might have.'

'But someone killed Cindy. Why?'

'Good question,' said Fran. 'I'll have a think about it. Call me when you get home.'

After another ten minutes, Libby was getting edgy. She climbed out of the Land Rover, locked it and walked up the drive to the house. In the kitchen she found Lewis, Edie and

Katie, all looking scared, with the police presence evident from the sounds of boots from all directions.

'Have they found the entrance yet?' asked Libby.

Lewis shook his head. 'They can't open it from the tunnel, and we can't hear anything from inside the house, so they haven't got a clue where it is.'

'They'll bring in all sorts of sophisticated equipment, you'll see,' said Libby, 'and pinpoint it with absolute accuracy.'

'How did Cindy know it was there?' asked Katie. 'I could have sworn she wasn't that familiar with the house.'

'Perhaps she didn't go into it from the house,' said Libby. 'Before they found the – er – her, I thought she'd taken the boat and left it as a sort of red herring and escaped through the tunnel from the other end, so perhaps she did that, but someone caught her.'

'Someone who'd come from the house?' asked Lewis dubiously.

'Or someone who was waiting for her down there.'

'Like who?'

'How do I know?' Libby shrugged and turned to Katie. 'How long was it since you saw her till we discovered she'd gone?'

'Not long. I made a pot of tea. You came in and asked me if I'd taken her a cup.' Katie looked up at Lewis. Edie still hadn't said anything, but clasped Lewis's arm tightly.

'Couldn't have been longer than twenty minutes,' said Lewis. 'How did she get down to the river in that time without being seen?'

'That's always been the question,' said Libby, 'but if she went through the tunnel, that explains it.'

'What was the tunnel like?' asked Katie. 'I mean, was it clear?'

'I didn't go into the tunnels, just the bit where there's the opening I fell into. But that was full of leaves and stuff. I see what you mean, though. If the tunnels hadn't been used for a long time they could be blocked up. I thought that myself while I was waiting down – um – there.'

'She wouldn't be able to go fast, would she?' said Katie. 'And didn't she take a bag with her?'

'That's what I said at the time,' said Libby. 'If she ran down to the boathouse after getting out through that little side door we found open, she must have gone like the wind. And no one saw her.'

'But she couldn't run along a tunnel in the dark with a heavy bag, either,' said Katie.

'Unless she had a torch. I wonder if they found one?' said Libby.

'It would make sense, though,' said Katie, getting up to move the kettle onto the Aga. 'That's why none of us saw her.'

'Why *you* didn't see her,' said Lewis. 'We weren't here. You were the only one in the kitchen.'

'Well, I didn't see her. I told you,' said Katie, warming the brown teapot. 'And why was that little door open?'

'A ruse,' said Libby. 'She opened it to look as though she went that way.'

'We still don't know how she got to the tunnel if she did go that way, though,' said Lewis. 'It must be somewhere near that door.'

'There isn't anything near it – just a passage,' said Libby. 'And Fran and I looked round the outside and there's no sign of any concealed doors or whatever.'

Katie poured water into the teapot. 'They'll find it, don't worry,' she said comfortably. 'Trust the police.'

'They wouldn't have found her body without me poking my nose in,' said Libby. 'They'd have gone on looking for her for the murder of Tony West and the suspected murder of Kenneth.'

'Hmm,' said Katie, setting out mugs. 'At least she won't be going after Gerald now. If he really is alive.'

'Oh, he's alive all right,' said Libby. 'Ian just won't tell us where, but I'm pretty sure he's already been to see him.'

'Has he?' Katie looked up.

'He hasn't said so, but Frank at the pub will have told him the name of the home, so he must have been by now.'

'And not got very far if he's got Alzheimer's,' said Lewis gloomily. 'What a bugger. I wish I'd never seen this place.'

'Well, you have,' said Katie, 'and you're going to get a good series out of it, so stop moaning. C'mon, Edie, have a biscuit with your tea.'

Ian appeared at the door, his habitual scowl much in evidence.

'I thought I said to wait for me,' he said to Libby.

'I have,' she said. 'I didn't see why I shouldn't wait in here in comfort rather than sitting in a stifling car.' She smiled at Katie, who pushed a full mug towards her.

'Could you come outside for a moment.' It wasn't a question. Libby sighed, got up and followed him out into the hall.

'I need to take a formal statement,' he said stiffly. 'I can hardly do that with them in there.'

'I know,' said Libby. 'But wouldn't it be better if someone came round to see me at home? You can't do it here, and I'm blowed if I'm trailing in to the police station.'

Ian sighed. 'All right, all right,' he said. 'Are you in this evening?'

'I can be,' said Libby and batted her eyelashes at him. His scowl deepened.

'I'll come with one of the DCs,' he said, 'if that's all right. As soon as I can get away.'

'Don't rush,' said Libby, with a grin. 'I'll wait.'

'He's coming to take my statement tonight,' she said, returning to the kitchen, 'so I can go when I've finished my tea.'

'Did he tell you anything?' asked Lewis.

'No, he wouldn't. If I can get Fran to come over this evening she might be able to get something out of him. He's still got a soft spot for her.'

'Nice looking, he is,' said Katie with a nod. 'You couldn't do better than him, lovey.'

'I'm spoken for, Katie, but thanks for the thought. Anyone got anything they'd like to ask him if we get him in a mellow mood?'

'When can I get back to normal,' said Lewis, looking gloomier than ever. 'Never-ending, this bloody business.'

Katie put her hands on the table and pushed herself upright. 'You just ask him to get it all cleared up nice and quick,' she said. 'Edie, you look like you need a lie down. Not nice, murder, is it?' And she shepherded Lewis's mother out of the room towards her little sitting room.

'Is your mum all right?' asked Libby.

'Just a bit shaky,' said Lewis. 'All a bit much for her, I reckon.'

'A bit much for you, too,' said Libby, patting his shoulder. 'I'll get out of your way. Tell Ad I've gone home, will you?'

'OK, and thanks, Libby.' Lewis gave her a kiss.

'What for? Finding a body and making life more complicated?' Libby shook her head. 'Not a good move.'

''Course it was,' said Lewis, walking beside her down the drive. 'They're that much nearer clearing it all up because you went nosing around. You ought to get a medal, that's what.'

'So should Fran,' said Libby.

'For getting me out of clink,' said Lewis. 'So she should.'

Ian and the fresh-faced Constable Maiden, he of the bright blue eyes and red hair, arrived at number 17 Allhallow's Lane only minutes after Fran and Guy that evening. Guy promptly dragged Adam and Ben out for a drink, winking at Fran over Ian's shoulder. She made a face.

'Hello, Mr Maiden,' said Libby. 'Would you like tea?'

'It's DS Maiden, now,' said Ian, smiling at his junior officer. Maiden blushed.

'Congratulations,' said Fran. 'To think I've known you since you were in uniform!'

'This is a formal interview,' warned Ian, 'so Mrs Castle should really not be in the room.'

'Oh, rubbish. If we were at the police station, yes, but not here,' said Fran briskly.

Ian looked sideways at his sergeant, who grinned back innocently.

'Very good,' he said. 'No tea for me.'

Maiden's face fell. Fran patted him on the shoulder. 'I'll make you some,' she said. 'Is that all right, Libby?'

'Of course it is. Pour us a glass of wine while you're there.' Libby turned back to Ian who was looking even more disapproving. 'Carry on.'

The interview was little more than a reiteration of the information Ian had already received from both Fran and Libby.

He listened to their theories while DS Maiden got more and more interested and forgot to take notes.

'So aren't you going to satisfy our curiosity now?' asked Libby, returning from the kitchen with the bottle of wine. 'Did you find the entrance to the tunnel from the house?'

'No,' said Ian. 'In fact, we don't think there is an entrance there any more. The end of the tunnel is simply packed earth with no suggestion of a door.'

'Have you tried to get through the earth?' asked Fran.

'Even if we did, Dale couldn't have done, whether she was coming or going.'

'No,' said Libby, 'so what about the other tunnels?'

'Other tunnels?'

'The ones to the pub and the church.'

'They wouldn't be any use to someone escaping the house, would they?' said Ian, finally accepting a cup of tea from Fran.

'But if she was coming from the river,' said Libby. 'Maybe she knew how to get out at the church. Or even the pub. Frank showed us where they thought the tunnel had come out in his cellars.'

'With someone waiting for her who would then lug her body all the way back to the ice-house?' Ian shook his head. 'I don't think so.'

'Oh.' Libby looked crestfallen. 'I didn't think of that.'

'She needn't have been killed then,' said Fran slowly. 'Suppose she just ran away and hid – say in the tunnel where Libby fell in. Or in the ice-house – she could have climbed up into it. Libby and I didn't get down to the sailing club until some time after she'd gone. Perhaps she was waiting until the fuss had died down.'

'But you showed Ian where you thought she'd been and the police were swarming all over the area. She wouldn't have been able to get out for ages,' Libby said.

'Or until someone came and found her.'

'It would have to be someone who knew the ice-house was there, and who was agile enough to climb up to it,' said Ian. 'No, I'm afraid we're stymied at the moment. Not,' he added hastily, 'that that's for publication.'

'No, of course not,' they reassured him. 'But what about Cindy killing Tony West?' asked Fran. 'Did you find her prints?'

Ian sighed. 'Yes. She was extremely careless. And they were the prints we hadn't identified previously.'

'Why did you pull Lewis in?' asked Libby.

'It was the discovery of the carver's mallet. At first, if you remember, the cases weren't officially linked, so the prints weren't identified. Dale's prints didn't get into the system until later.'

'And did you find out when she'd come into the country?' asked Fran.

'Oh, yes. She wasn't exactly subtle about it. Landed at Gatwick on her false passport as bright as a button. Went back and reappeared on Sunday.'

'But why did she kill West?' said Libby. 'He was on her side if he helped her get away.'

'There's one thing we haven't thought of,' said Fran, 'although you probably have, Ian. Libby and I haven't.'

'What's that?' asked Libby.

'We only have Cindy's word for it that he helped her get away.'

'Oh.' Libby looked nonplussed. 'Have we?'

'She said Gerald killed Kenneth. We believed her at first.'

'We can't be sure that he didn't,' said Ian.

'Have you spoken to him?' asked Fran.

'Oh, yes.' Ian shook his head. 'A whole team of professionals got permission to try and talk to him, but it was hopeless. He has no idea about anything – even who he is – now. We showed him photographs, but it was hopeless.'

'So what did the solicitor say? West's solicitor?'

'And Gerald Shepherd's, as it happens,' said DS Maiden, speaking for the first time.

'Really?' Libby and Fran looked at each other. Maiden looked at Ian, who nodded.

'West sold Creekmarsh to fund Shepherd's nursing home. He was given power of attorney about a year before Shepherd "disappeared". West said nothing about the fact that Shepherd hadn't run off with Miss Dale, even though there was speculation in the press. Kenneth never asked the police to find him, there was only a statement purporting to come from him through West.'

'So West was mixed up in it all right from the start,' said Libby. 'But why?'

'That we don't know either,' said Ian.

'What about Shepherd's will?' asked Fran.

'As he's still alive there's a legal complication about our access. How we get round that I've no idea.' Ian looked glum.

'And have you decided the skeleton is Kenneth?' said Libby.

'Oh, yes, definitely.' Ian looked at them in surprise. 'Didn't you know?'

'We were working on that assumption, but no one had confirmed it,' said Fran. 'Funnily enough, we didn't have access to the DNA.'

Ian laughed. 'You seemed to manage fairly well without official access.'

'Intelligent guesswork,' said Libby smugly.

'And an extremely helpful policeman,' added Ian. 'Who shouldn't really talk to you about anything.' He turned to his sergeant. 'Should he, Maiden?'

Maiden's ears turned pink. 'No, sir,' he said.

'Another thing,' said Fran. 'Why was Superintendent Bertram on the spot so much? Surely she should have been back at the office superintending.'

'New promotion,' said Ian.

'Ah,' said Libby. 'Making her mark. We thought it might be because the case was higher profile than we thought.'

Ian and Maiden exchanged looks.

'Shepherd was a famous actor,' said Ian. 'And we did think it was his body at first.'

'That puzzles me,' said Libby with a frown. 'Because the first reports said it was a male between thirty and fifty, and Shepherd was well over sixty when he disappeared. And you didn't know it had been Shepherd's house then, did you?'

'Libby! Of course we did. Just because Osbourne-Walker hadn't seen fit to tell us about his slightly unorthodox purchase of Creekmarsh didn't mean to say we didn't immediately do a search and discover who was the previous owner. And that West was his power of attorney.'

'So you linked the murders straight away?' said Libby.

'I wasn't on the case then,' said Ian, 'but yes, of course they were linked. We're not as dumb as all that, you know. And we do have access to all sorts of information the public don't.' He sent Libby a significant glance.

'See,' said Libby to Fran, 'we always say the police get there before we do.'

'But we're always grateful for certain unorthodox help,' said Ian with a grin.

'When you can bring yourselves to accept it,' said Fran.

'Well, we did this time,' said Ian, 'and it let Osbourne-Walker off the hook.'

'Didn't save Cindy's life, though, did it?' said Libby. 'Why do you think she was killed?'

'Well, it wasn't for the documents in that briefcase. Her passport was there and her marriage certificate, but that was all. There were no documents relating to Kenneth or Gerald Shepherd and no details of the home he was in.'

'So if we hadn't found Frank for you, you might never have found Gerald?' said Libby.

'I'm afraid that's true,' said Ian.

'Yay!' said Libby.

'Did Cindy kill Kenneth?' asked Fran.

Ian and Maiden both looked startled. 'I can't tell you that,' said Ian. 'There's no evidence to suggest it. We're not even sure how he died.'

'How did Cindy die?' asked Libby suddenly. Everyone froze.

'I can't tell you that, either,' said Ian eventually, looking uncomfortable.

'And have you found the cellars?' asked Fran.

Ian sighed. 'As I said before, I don't think any entrances exist to tunnels or passages anywhere.'

'Frank showed us his map and said that there were cellars at Creekmarsh,' said Libby. 'They must still be there.'

'Have you proved whether Cindy got into the ice-house from

the water or the land? Or through the tunnel?' asked Fran.

'Oh, really!' Ian stood up. 'I've been extremely forbearing, but this is too much. You know I can't tell you anything more. And don't go poking around any more, either,' he added, 'or I'll lock you both up.'

'He wasn't that mad,' said Libby, as she shut the door behind the two men, 'or he'd never have said that.'

'And he is grateful for our information,' agreed Fran, 'he had to admit that.'

'Right,' said Libby, fetching the wine bottle, 'what do we do now?'

Chapter Thirty-two

OVER THE WEEKEND FRAN and Guy had pre-wedding things to do and Ben and Libby began to make lists of what needed to be done at Steeple Farm. The sitting room and the kitchen were the most obvious rooms needing resurrection, and although Libby had fairly firm ideas about interior decoration, or the lack of it, the job before them was beginning to look insuperable.

'I wish Lewis would project manage it after all,' said Libby with a sigh, picking at a piece of unsuitable wallpaper on the wide chimney breast. 'We don't know this other chap, do we?'

'He's a friend of Mog's,' said Ben, 'and comes with excellent credentials.'

'It's more telling him what to do than his ability to do it,' said Libby.

'It's easy in this room,' said Ben. 'Strip everything.'

'I know,' said Libby, 'but what about the kitchen?'

She continued to worry about it all through Sunday until Ben told her he'd change his mind about going to live there if this was what she was going to be like.

'Sorry,' she said, sinking down on the sofa and gathering Sidney onto her lap. 'I know I'm being a pain.'

'You don't really want to move, that's what it's really about, isn't it?' said Ben, coming to sit beside her.

'No, it isn't,' said Libby. 'I would love to live there, but I still love this cottage. I can't have both.'

'Perhaps you could sign this over to the children?'

'Adam would be the only one to use it,' said Libby. 'Mind you, he'd probably be delighted.'

'Let's leave it on the back burner for a while,' said Ben. 'It's the wedding of the year on Friday, after all. Fran might have things she'd like help with.'

'Nothing,' said Libby. 'She's so organised. All we've got to do is take the bride and groom to the venue.'

'Separately,' said Ben. 'They won't have a car the next day, then.'

'I think Guy's got a taxi booked to the airport. He's giving her a traditional surprise honeymoon.'

'Great! Where?'

'Wouldn't be a surprise then, would it?'

But Libby's real problem was that the Creekmarsh mystery was still churning away in the back of her mind. She wanted to know what Cindy was after, why she'd killed Tony West and if she'd killed Kenneth.

After Ben had left for The Manor on Monday morning, she rang Fran and asked in which library it was she'd located the documents relating to Creekmarsh.

'Here in Nethergate,' said Fran. 'Why?'

'I'd just like to have a look at them,' said Libby. 'I know you've seen them and there isn't anything useful, but I was curious. I thought I might ask Frank for a look at those maps he's got, too.'

She could almost hear Fran shrugging. 'Go on, then,' she said, 'but I don't know what you hope to find.'

'Nothing probably,' said Libby.

Once again, she trudged up to The Manor to borrow the Land Rover. Neither Hetty nor Greg were to be seen, but Ben waved from the stable yard, now used as a machinery store.

On an impulse, she drove up to Steeple Farm and walked right round the house before making a circuit of the paddock and the garden. It was a beautiful place, no doubt about it, but was it really *her*? Niggling away in the back of her mind was Fran's assurance that she could not see Libby living there, even though Fran had tried to say she was probably losing her grip. Libby sighed, went back to the Land Rover and climbed in.

The Nethergate library was in part of the old civic hall and the reference section was right at the back in a modern extension. The librarian, intrigued that she'd been asked for the same documents twice in a short time, fetched them immediately.

'Do I have to wear white gloves?' asked Libby.

'Oh, no,' said the librarian earnestly. 'They aren't very valuable.'

Libby raised her eyebrows but said nothing.

Sure enough the only pages of interest were the same ones Fran had been allowed to copy, but Libby was soon immersed in the day-to-day minutiae of Creekmarsh in the mid-nineteenth century, marvelling at the amounts of food, servants and animals recorded. It was while reading the faded writing detailing expenditure in July 1843 that she came across an item that caused an adrenalin-fuelled tingle up the back of her neck.

It seemed to be payment to a blacksmith for the creation of an iron door, locks and keys.

'The strong room,' whispered Libby. 'Now where did Fran find mention of it in the papers she copied?'

But in those papers, it was merely a passing reference to buildings as part of the estate, including 'an ice-house and a strong room'. Libby sat back and looked at the two references. Why had the ice-house and the strong room been coupled together? Was it because they'd been created at the same time? Was the strong room outside the house as the ice-house was? She began to look backwards through the accounts books to see if she could find anything else, but there was nothing. The library held no original architectural drawings, but the librarian did volunteer that the original garden designs were kept at the central library in Maidstone as they were thought to be very old and valuable.

Libby rushed outside and rang Lewis. His phone went straight to voicemail, so she tried Adam.

'Has Mog had sight of the original garden designs?' she said breathlessly.

'The – what? Whose designs?' said Adam sharply.

'Old ones. Very old.' She heard him call Mog and ask him the same question.

'No, he didn't know there were any. Where are they?'

Libby explained and asked if he knew where Lewis was.

'Closeted with his TV people in the house,' said Adam. 'Is it important?'

'Well,' said Libby, thinking quickly, 'if the garden there is going to feature in the series, what better than to have the original designs to work from?'

Excitedly, Adam relayed this to Mog, who then grabbed the phone.

'Libby? I'm going to interrupt Lewis right now. Where are these drawings?'

'Maidstone Central Library,' said Libby. 'I don't know whether we need permission to see them. The librarian at Nethergate didn't think so. I suppose technically they belong to Lewis now, anyway.'

'Unless they were donated to the library by a former owner,' said Mog. 'I've known that to happen. Anyway, I'll go and interrupt Lewis and call you back.'

Would the original designs show the strong room, though, wondered Libby, as she sat on a low wall near the library and waited for Mog's call. Probably not, if the work was being paid for in 1843. The designs for the garden would date back much further than that. On the other hand, it might show the ice-house, and maybe the strong room without its sophisticated iron door.

Libby was sure in some way that the strong room, like the ice-house, had a role in the Creekmarsh mystery. Was Cindy hidden there before she was killed? Is that where she ran to when she disappeared?

Her phone rang.

'Libby? Lewis said he didn't know anything about them, but that we should go and have a look. Do you think we should phone them first?'

'The library? Perhaps we should. When do you want to go?'

'Now?'

'Don't be daft. We'd not get there in time to have a good look. Tomorrow morning.'

'Oh.' Mog sounded deflated. 'OK. Will you and Ad meet me there?'

'Yes,' said Libby, sliding off the wall. 'I'll call them when I get home, then I'll let you know what time.'

Fran rang when Libby reached home.

'Have we ever seen a photograph of Tony West?' she asked.

'Don't think so,' said Libby, dumping her basket on the table. 'Why?'

'Just a thought,' said Fran. 'Would Lewis have one?'

'Maybe. I know he's busy at the moment.' She explained what had happened about the garden design.

'That's odd,' said Fran. 'That sort of thing's usually held at the house, isn't it?'

'That's what I thought, but it seems as though either Gerald or someone else cleared it of everything historical.'

'It was almost derelict when Gerald bought it, wasn't it? Hadn't it been used by the military or something during the war?'

'Yes, so maybe it was cleared of relevant documents then,' said Libby. 'What we need is an old portrait or something, like we found at Anderson Place.'

'There would hardly be portraits of the people we want to find out about,' said Fran. 'Will you ask Lewis about a photo of West?'

'Later on, I will. When I'm sure he's free. Why won't you tell me why you want it?'

'I'd prejudice you,' said Fran. 'This is only a thought.'

As it happened, Libby didn't have to call Lewis, as he called her about the original garden designs. She explained her theory about the strong room, but he was more interested in the garden.

'But I thought you must have had the original designs,' she said, 'because Adam and Mog are restoring the parterre.'

'Mog unearthed the layout of that,' said Lewis, 'and the whatjer-call-'em fruit trees in the walled garden. Them ones up against a wall.'

'Espalier?' suggested Libby.

'That's them. All sorts he found, although some are too far gone, but they're replacing them.'

'Good,' said Libby. 'Now, Lewis, Fran wants to know if you've got any pictures of Tony West.'

'Pictures? Photos? No, 'course I haven't. What for?'

'I don't know, she won't tell me. Oh, well, I'll see if I come up with one on the Internet. What did we do without it?'

229

'Dunno. Can't see how anyone can live without it these days. Though I'm not much good at it, but it ain't half useful.'

'Certainly is,' said Libby. 'Right. Mog and Ad are coming with me tomorrow morning to Maidstone to look at the designs. We'll find out whether they belong to the library or you. If they belong to you, I expect you'll have to go and collect them, but at least we'll be able to have a look tomorrow. Mog's very excited.'

After Lewis had rung off, Libby made herself a cup of tea and sat down at the computer. Once again she searched for Tony West and came up with the sites she'd found before, augmented by many news sites reporting his murder. She checked all of these to see how much had been released to the public, but apart from mention of Gerald Shepherd and Cindy Dale allegedly running off together, there was no further news of them. Even more odd, thought Libby, there was no mention of Lewis being called in for questioning. It was all being kept very dark.

She found three photographs of West, all taken at media events where he smiled toothily at the camera above a black tie. She emailed Fran the results and then called her to tell her.

'Do you think Frank would take us to see Gerald?' asked Fran, after looking at the pictures.

'What on earth for?' said Libby. 'If the police can't get anything out of him with trained officers what chance would we stand?'

'I've got a theory,' said Fran stubbornly. 'I'm going to call Frank.'

'Fran, you can't!' wailed Libby. 'You're getting married in a few days' time. You've got things to do.'

'It's all done,' said Fran. 'If I can organise it, will you come with me?'

'Well, OK,' said Libby unwillingly, 'but not tomorrow morning. I'm going to Maidstone Library to see these garden designs.'

'Right. I'll call you when I've made arrangements,' said Fran.

'You're quite sure you can, then?' said Libby.

'Trust me,' said Fran and rang off.

By the time Libby and Adam met Mog at Maidstone Central Library she hadn't heard from Fran, who was now merely days away from her wedding. They were directed to the County Archives section and finally given the fragile plans. Libby asked how the library had got hold of them, which seemed to be an impossible question to answer, judging by the bewildered look on the librarian's face, but when Mog explained that the current owner of the property would like them back, the expression changed to outrage. He was, however, allowed to copy them and told to write to the archives department for further information.

Libby left them to enthuse over the plans and went outside to wait, punching in Fran's number on speed dial as she went.

'Hi, it's me,' she said. 'How did you get on with Frank?'

'I'm still waiting for an answer,' said Fran. 'I left a message with Bren yesterday, but he hasn't got back to me.'

'Shall I pop in there after I've finished here?'

'I don't see what good it would do, but you might as well. I'll meet you there unless I hear in the meantime. Then I'll ring you.'

'OK. Is Guy all right with you galloping around sleuthing?'

'As long as I'm there on Saturday I don't think he cares,' said Fran with a laugh.

Adam came out of the library with large folders and an excited expression.

'Something that'll interest you, Ma,' said Adam. 'Look.' He spread one of the plans out on the bonnet of Mog's van.

Sure enough, once Libby had worked out which way was up, she could see the ice-house and one passage leading from the house. She frowned at it.

'Only one passage,' she said. 'Nothing towards the church or the inn.'

'Well, there wouldn't be, would there?' said Adam reasonably. 'They would be secret smuggling passages. This one would be official, like.'

'Hmm.' Libby peered at the faint markings. 'No sign of a strong room, either.'

'Too early, according to what you saw in Nethergate library,' said Adam.

'Yes,' sighed Libby. 'I just thought there might be something marked that might have been turned into a strong room later – you know with the addition of that iron door, or whatever it was.'

'Where does the passage to the ice-house come out?' asked Mog, turning the plan towards him.

'Under the house,' said Adam.

'But it wouldn't have been under the house, would it? It was a legitimate passage, so needn't have been hidden.'

'Is the ha-ha marked?' said Libby suddenly.

'No,' said Mog, peering. 'No, it isn't. Why?'

'Do we know when that was created?'

'After these designs, presumably,' said Mog, looking puzzled.

'Well, the passage was created at this time, and once the ha-ha was formed it would have been exposed, wouldn't it?' said Libby. 'It runs along the edge of the ha-ha where I fell in.'

'So?' said Adam, frowning.

'Actually, I don't know,' said Libby, sighing. 'I wish we could find out where it entered the house, though.'

'It would have been the kitchens, wouldn't it?' said Mog, carefully gathering up the plan.

'The kitchen's been checked thoroughly,' Adam said.

'But that's the modern kitchen,' said Mog. 'Edwardian, by the look of it.'

'That's what I thought,' said Libby, turning a look of undisguised admiration on him.

'There must be cellars where the kitchens were. There are signs of built-up ground round the outside walls.' He turned to Adam. 'You remember where it looked as though there was the shape of a lintel on the side facing the wood?'

'F – blimey, yes!' said Adam. 'Have the police looked there?'

'No, I bet they haven't,' said Libby, excited. 'They've been looking in the inhabited part of the house.'

'We'll have a look when we get back,' said Mog. 'Coming, Mrs S?'

'I've got to meet Fran at The Fox,' said Libby, 'but let me

know if you find anything.'

Adam went back in the van with Mog and Libby followed slowly in Romeo the Renault. She hadn't thought of old kitchens, and of course she should have done. The house had been there for centuries and had probably been subject to subsidence, which would mean there were quite likely to be rooms below the present ground floor. In which case, there should be an entrance to them.

Round and round the garden, thought Libby. They'd been here before.

There had been no phone call from Fran by the time she reached The Fox, but the Roller Skate was in the car park. Libby locked the Renault and went in through the back door.

Fran was standing by the bar facing a red-faced and truculent Frank.

'Libby,' she said with relief, turning towards her friend. 'I've been trying to tell Frank –'

'And I'm saying he's had enough.'

Libby looked from one to another. 'Have you told him what you want to ask Gerald?' she said.

'No,' said Fran, looking surprised. 'Sorry, Frank. I just want to show him some photographs. See if it jogs his memory.'

Frank looked suspicious. 'What photographs?'

'Some we found at Creekmarsh and a couple from the Internet.'

'Show me,' said Frank.

'I don't think –'

'Or I won't even think about taking you,' he said.

Reluctantly, Fran took a buff manila folder from her bag and opened it. 'There,' she said, handing over a few pictures. Libby recognised some from the collection at Creekmarsh, and the others as printouts from the Internet. Surprised, she peered over Fran's shoulder at two pictures of Kenneth, both looking sullen. Cindy Dale was in one of them as a blurred and shadowy figure behind Kenneth's left shoulder.

'Can't see as how he'll remember any of them,' said Frank, pushing the photographs about on the bar, 'but I suppose it can't hurt, neither.' He heaved a huge sigh. 'It's been a bugger these last years, keeping him quiet.'

'Keeping *him* quiet?' asked Libby.

'Not him,' said Frank. 'Keeping quiet *about* him.'

'Why did you?'

'Not my place to go spilling the beans, is it?'

'Do you recognise anyone in these pictures?' asked Fran.

Frank pulled them towards him. 'Gerald, Tony West and Ken, And that'll be that little cow Cindy, I s'pose.' He pointed. 'Don't know any of these. Looks like the seventies, doesn't it? I didn't know him that far back.'

'So will you take us to see him?' Fran gathered up the pictures. Frank looked uneasily towards the kitchen hatch. 'Bren,' he called.

Brenda appeared and stuck her head through the hatch with a friendly grin at Fran and Libby.

'Could you cope without me for an hour?' Frank reached out a hand to pat her on the arm. She covered his hand with her own.

''Course I can,' she said. 'Hardly a rush on, is there? Going to take the ladies to see Gerald, are you?'

Frank, Libby and Fran all showed varying degrees of astonishment.

'Good idea. You never know – it might bring him out of himself a bit,' said Brenda.

'Well,' said Libby, as they climbed into Frank's huge SUV five minutes later, 'I hope it doesn't do any harm, but suppose we don't get anything from him and only succeed in upsetting him?'

'We'll get something from him,' said Fran. 'I only hope it's what I want.'

Chapter Thirty-three

BROOKMEAD HOUSE, LIKE SO many other houses in their present incarnations, sat at the end of a gravelled drive surrounded by manicured lawns and well tended flowerbeds. No discreet sign gave any indication of the nature of its inhabitants, although there were metal hand-rails on both sides of the shallow steps to the front door. A ramp led up separately, for wheelchairs, Libby supposed and, she thought with a shudder, stretchers.

Frank led the way into the hall which contained a row of uncomfortable looking plastic chairs and a long, high desk, behind which sat a woman with grey hair and an intimidating expression.

'Hi, Sal,' said Frank. Blimey, thought Libby.

Sal's expression changed to coy. Libby blinked.

'Frank! You back again?'

Libby looked at Fran and made a face.

'Brought some more visitors, if that's OK,' said Frank. 'Do you need to give them badges or anything?'

'If you'd just sign in,' said Sal. 'Health and Safety, you know.'

'Huh?' said Libby.

'So that they know who's in the building in case of a fire,' said Fran.

'Oh.' Libby took the proffered pen and signed the book Sal pushed towards her. Fran followed suit.

'Come on then,' said Frank and turned to a corridor on his left leading to an open French window, where a white voile curtain fluttered like a bridal veil. Libby and Fran followed him to the end, where he knocked briefly on a door and, without waiting for a reply, opened it.

Gerald Shepherd sat in the inevitable high backed hospital armchair gazing at nothing in particular. The room, with its window too high to gaze from, contained a high bed, a plethora of small tables and what looked like a door to an en-suite bathroom. There were no photographs. He didn't look up as his three visitors entered.

'Hey, mate.' Frank sat down on an upright chair opposite Gerald and motioned Fran and Libby to pull up similar chairs which stood against the wall. Gerald looked at him vaguely and put out a tentative hand. Libby felt a lump in her throat. Fran cleared hers and handed Frank the folder.

'Gerry, these ladies have come to see you.' Frank waited for a response, then opened the folder. 'They've brought you pictures to look at.'

Gerald's eyes dropped to the folder. He understood that much, Libby realised.

'Look, here.' Frank pointed out the picture of Kenneth. 'Who's that?'

'Kenny.' The voice was a whisper. Frank beamed.

'That's it! That's Kenny. And who's this?'

Gerald took all the photographs with a shaking hand and dropped most of them. Fran dropped to her knees and helped to pick them up. Gerald snatched one from her, the one of young people on a beach.

'Amanda,' he whispered. Libby and Fran looked enquiringly at Frank.

'His wife,' he said in a low voice. 'Ken's mother. Died years ago.'

'Kenny,' said Gerald again, with a frown, looking at the photograph with a blurred Cindy Dale behind him.

'Who's that?' asked Fran, pointing to Cindy.

'Amanda,' said Gerald.

'He's muddled,' said Frank, stating the obvious. Fran shuffled the photographs and showed one of Tony West.

'Tony,' said Gerald in a firmer voice. Then he pulled out the one taken in the seventies and pointed to the young man with the moustache. 'My son,' he said.

236

The other three looked at each other.

'No, that's your son, Kenny,' said Frank, showing the one of Kenneth. Gerald shook his head and pointed again. 'My son,' he said, and, shockingly, smiled. He picked up the one of Tony West. 'My son,' he said again.

'Tony?' said Libby. 'Tony's your son?'

'Where's Tony?' Gerald looked up at Frank. 'Where's Tony?'

Frank was looking stunned. Libby gave him a nudge. 'Don't tell him,' she whispered. He shook his head slightly and leant forward.

'Away, Gerry,' he said. 'Tony's away.'

'Look after Kenny,' said Gerald, and turned his head to the window.

Nothing more could be got from him, but he held on to the photograph of himself and the moustachioed young man, stroking it gently. Eventually, Frank jerked his head and stood up. He gripped Gerald's shoulder, and with a soft 'Bye, mate,' to which he received no answer, left the room. Libby and Fran followed him. Outside, he leant against the wall and pulled out a large handkerchief to wipe his face.

'Bloody hell,' he said.

'You never knew?' asked Fran. He shook his head.

'Did Kenneth know?' said Libby.

'No idea,' said Frank. 'I'd say no. I was as close to Gerry as anyone, and if I didn't know, no one knew.'

'But Kenneth was his son. Wouldn't Gerald have told him if Tony was his older brother?' said Libby.

'Gawd knows,' said Frank, pushing himself away from the wall and starting back down the corridor. 'You going to tell the police?'

'I expect so,' said Fran. 'It gives someone the motive for murdering West.'

'But we know Cindy did it,' said Libby.

'Yes, but now we know he was Gerald's son, which was why, presumably, he was given power of attorney –'

'Of course!' breathed Libby. 'I never could work out why that was.'

'As I was saying,' said Fran, 'as he was Gerald's son, perhaps Cindy thought he stood in the way of her inheritance.'

'Hang on, though,' said Libby, scurrying to catch up with Frank, who had reached the entrance hall, 'how could it be her inheritance? Kenneth was dead. So whatever happened the money, or the estate, whatever, wouldn't go to her as Kenneth's widow. He pre-deceased his father.'

'Hmm.' Fran frowned at Frank's back, where he was bending over the high counter to speak to Sally, who looked shocked.

'You shouldn't have said anything to her,' said Fran, when he rejoined them.

'She's got a right to know,' he said, striding down the steps to the SUV. 'Tony paid her.'

'Paid the fees, you mean?' said Libby.

'And paid her a bit extra to keep shtum.' He looked back up the steps. 'Good rottweiler, that one. She's the only one on the staff there that knows who he was.'

'So where did you come into the picture, then?' asked Libby, clambering up into the high vehicle.

'Told you. I knew Gerry in London. He come down to visit, saw old Creekmarsh and bought it. Tony was part of the crowd. Told you that, an' all.'

'Yes, you did.' Fran settled herself comfortably. 'So his mother can't have been Amanda?'

Frank frowned over the steering wheel. 'We-ell,' he said. 'See, I don't know. Bit funny, ain't it? Both of them keeping quiet about it if it was all legal like.'

'I suppose so,' said Libby. 'So do you think he fathered Tony before he was married to Amanda?'

'Must have done,' said Fran. 'It looks as though he was very young when Tony was born. Perhaps he didn't know about Tony until he was grown up.'

'You mean Tony traced his real father, sort of thing?' said Libby.

'Maybe,' said Fran. 'In which case it might have been bad publicity if it came out. Things weren't quite as enlightened as they are now.'

They arrived back at the pub and thanked Frank for taking

them. He shook hands with them both, still looking stunned.

'I'm going to tell them about this,' said Libby. 'Coming?'

'No, I'd better get back and play at being a bride-to-be,' said Fran.

'You'd guessed, hadn't you?' said Libby, watching her friend unlock her car.

Fran nodded.

'That was why you kept asking how old Tony was?'

'Yes,' said Fran. 'Just one of those things.'

'Oh, right.' Libby frowned at her. 'But I still don't quite see what difference it makes.'

'Tony is probably Gerald's heir. If the police have got to the will by now they'll know that.'

'So Cindy killed him to remove the obstacle to her inheritance? I said before, that doesn't make sense. Gerald was still alive and she thought he still owned the house.'

'Yes,' said Fran, 'Gerald was still alive. I think she had expected to come home and find Gerald dead, so would walk into Creekmarsh as Kenneth's wife – or widow. I don't suppose she thought much further than that. Then she found out about Tony.'

'How? She went and killed him after she heard about the skeleton. She must have known already that he was Gerald's son.'

'I expect she went to see him to ask what she should do before she turned up officially. Then he would have told her Creekmarsh had been sold and, anyway, it was all his. I don't suppose she thought about what she was doing. Probably just lashed out.'

'With Lewis's mallet.' Libby nodded. 'But then, who killed her?'

Fran shivered. 'That's the worrying part, isn't it?'

Libby let herself into the kitchen and called out. Katie appeared and went straight to the kettle.

'Tea, lovey?' she asked.

'Oh, yes please, Katie,' said Libby. 'Do you know where Lewis is?'

'Out there with his telly mates somewhere,' said Katie. 'Did you want him for anything?'

'No, not really,' lied Libby. 'What about Adam? I've got to give him a lift home tonight. I mean, I know he won't be ready yet, but I thought I'd let him know I'm here.'

'Him and that Mog were over towards the wood last time I saw them,' said Katie.

'How's Edie?' asked Libby. 'Is she still here?'

'Having a lie down,' said Katie, pouring tea. 'She's bit frail, poor thing. Seemed really shook up when that Cindy died.'

'Well, it can't be very nice knowing someone's been found dead in your son's garden,' said Libby, taking her mug.

'No, and she was already worried about him.' Katie tutted. 'I don't know what the world's coming to, I really don't. Murders and skeletons. I'm not so sure I want to stay down here, meself, now.'

'Oh, Katie, you can't leave him,' said Libby. 'He really needs you.'

Katie looked doubtful. 'I dunno,' she said. 'He can get other staff if he needs them. I'm getting on a bit, after all. I should think about retiring. I'm not as strong as I was.'

'But he relies on you,' said Libby.

'Hmm,' said Katie, and sat down with her mug looking thoughtful.

'I'm going to find Adam and Mog,' said Libby after a moment. 'Can I take my mug with me?'

'Long as you bring it back,' said Katie with a smile. 'Those boys are always leaving them places.'

'I'll tell them off,' said Libby and went out into the grounds.

Adam and Mog weren't far away. In fact, they were at the back of the house, very carefully loosening turf away from the wall.

'What's going on?' said Libby.

'Told you, didn't we?' said Adam. 'Look!'

And sure enough, a curved row of bricks was showing in the wall just above the ground.

'That's what Fran and I were looking for the other day,' said Libby.

'Where?' asked Mog.

'At the church and on the other side of the house. Near that little side door no one uses.'

Mog looked dubious. 'Newer part of the house,' he said.

'Well, you won't be able to break in from here,' said Libby, bending down to get a closer look. 'Can you work out where it is on the garden plan?'

'It doesn't show the interior of the house, Ma,' said Adam scornfully.

'All right, all right,' said Libby. 'But I bet I know where it is.' She straightened up and looked up at the building. 'See that window? The tall one?'

Mog and Adam looked up.

'Yes,' said Adam.

'That's over the staircase in the other part of the house. What's the betting that there's a staircase *down* as well?'

Mog nodded slowly. 'But how would you find it? It's almost derelict in there isn't it?'

'There was loads of rubble at the foot of the staircase, yes,' said Libby.

'In which case, Mother, Cindy wouldn't have been able to get down there, let alone you.' Adam was triumphant. Libby gave him a look.

'If we could get down there we could find out where tunnel came out. Where *else* the tunnel came out,' she insisted.

'We'll have to tell Lewis,' said Mog. 'And it's getting a bit late to do it today.'

'OK. I'll see if I can find him and have a quick chat,' said Libby. 'By the time I've done that you'll be ready to leave, won't you, Ad?'

Adam and Mog agreed and returned to their self-imposed task, although Libby wasn't quite sure why, if they weren't going to be able to knock it through. Just boys' curiosity, she supposed.

She met Lewis on the drive waving off a car load of "telly people".

'Got a minute?' she asked him.

He looked nervous. 'What for?' he said.

'Oh, Lewis, what's the matter?' Libby tucked her arm

through his and turned him back towards the house. 'Come on. It's almost over, all this, and you've got your new series on the way, *and* the original garden designs. What's the problem?'

'You,' said Lewis. 'I'm beginning to get nervous about you. Something always seems to happen around you.'

'That's not true,' said Libby, shocked. 'And you asked me into it in the first place, after all.'

'I know,' sighed Lewis, 'but that was before Tony was killed and I was worried.'

'And you're not worried now?'

''Course I bloody am. I don't understand any of it. What did you want, anyway?'

'Can Adam and Mog and I do a bit of excavating in the old part of the house tomorrow?' Libby led the way into the kitchen and put her mug on the table with a wink at Katie.

'Excavating? What d'you mean?'

'Where the old staircase is, you know? There's a lot of rubble there. We thought there may be an entrance to the cellars of the tunnels there. Mog and Adam have found signs of an old window bricked up below ground level.'

'Have they?' Lewis's expression brightened. 'Where's that then? Are they there now?'

'Yes, or they were. They'll be finished soon. Do you want to go and see?'

'Yeah.' Lewis grabbed her arm. 'Come on, nuisance. You always get your way, don't you?'

Libby looked back at Katie and raised her eyebrows. Katie shook her head and picked up her magazine.

Adam was carefully rolling the turf they'd removed while Mog watered it thoroughly. They showed Lewis the window and the indications that there were others along the same wall.

'Do you think they are cellars?' Lewis asked.

'Sure of it. We'll probably find stashes of brandy and baccy down there,' said Libby with a grin.

'What?' Lewis looked puzzled.

'Don't take any notice of her,' said Adam. 'Can we look in the house tomorrow, Lewis?'

'Yeah, I'll come with you.' He straightened up and gave

242

Libby a squeeze. 'Sorry I called you a nuisance.'

'Why are you sorry?' asked Adam. 'She is!'

'Come back to the house while they finish up,' said Libby, 'I've got something else to tell you. I think Fran will have told the police by now, but don't mention it to anyone else.'

Adam and Mog looked interested, but Libby pulled a puzzled Lewis away towards the house.

'Now,' she said. 'You're never going to believe this, but –'

Chapter Thirty-four

'I DIDN'T TELL THE police,' Fran said on the phone. 'I'll talk it over with Frank first, I think. He seems to be the only one left who cares about Gerald, and he might not want him bothered.'

'But we've got to tell the police! You said yourself it gives a motive for Tony's murder.'

'But you said it's a pretty shaky one,' said Fran.

'I know, but it explains such a lot, doesn't it? You'll have to tell them.'

'All right, all right. So what did they say up at the house?'

'I only told Lewis. I didn't think it was right to tell the others. But they've found windows to what could be cellars. We're going exploring tomorrow. Want to come?'

'I'd love to,' said Fran wistfully, 'but I really can't. I'm picking up the dress tomorrow – yours as well, I might add – and doing all sorts of last-minute things. You'll have to ring me later.'

'OK. I'll have the others there, so I won't do anything stupid,' said Libby crossing her fingers.

The following morning Libby drove Adam to Creekmarsh in the Renault and left him to find Mog while she went in search of Lewis.

'He had to pop out, lovey,' said Katie, when Libby put her head round the kitchen door after looking in the solar. 'Don't know where he's gone. Said he wouldn't be long though.'

'OK, thanks,' said Libby, and wandered off to find Mog and Adam, who now seemed to have disappeared. They weren't standing over the pile of turf near the uncovered window, nor were they at the parterre. Libby scowled and began to walk towards the ha-ha. But the view down to the little sailing club's boathouse was clear – no one was down there either. Heaving an irritated sigh, she retraced her steps and went back into the house. This time even Katie wasn't there, so, with a shrug, she went through to the uninhabited part of the house and came to the blocked staircase.

She wandered round the hallway aimlessly for a while, then decided she might as well make a start and began moving the smaller of the pieces of fallen masonry that blocked the stairwell. After a few minutes, she stepped back wiping the back of her hand across her forehead. And heard a sound.

It was little more than a rumble, a bowling ball thrown down a gulley. Then it stopped. Libby took another step backwards and, as if the movement had started an avalanche, the pile of masonry began to fall away.

She stepped even further backwards and pressed her back against the wall as suddenly the whole staircase began to fall.

She crouched down and covered her head with her arms, feeling the dust settle on her head and arms, terrified that the whole floor would give way. Eventually the noise stopped, and, after waiting a minute, Libby stood up.

In front of her lay an open stairwell. The remains of the upper staircase hung melodramatically in the air.

'Now this,' she said out loud, 'is where the stupid heroine goes down those stairs and meets the murderer. Only I'm not going to. Except…'

She took a step nearer and managed to peer down into the hole. As far as she could see it was indeed a tunnel which led both ways away from the broken steps. She turned round and began to make her way shakily back to the kitchen, where she hoped Katie would offer her a restorative cup of tea before she set off once more to find Adam and Mog.

But when she got to the kitchen Katie was still nowhere to be seen.

'Bloody Marie Celeste,' muttered Libby and went to Katie's private door and knocked.

There was no answer, but the door swung slightly open. Libby looked inside. No one was there.

Feeling even more rattled and definitely worried, Libby went back outside and called. No one answered.

'Phone,' she said to herself and took out her mobile.

'Ad?' she said when he answered. 'Where are you?'

'Nethergate,' he said. 'Why, where are you?'

'Nethergate? What are you doing there? I'm at Creekmarsh. You went off to find Mog and after that I couldn't find *you*. I've just caused a landslide inside the house and I can't even find Katie, now. What shall I do?'

'A landslide? What are you talking about, Ma? Look we'll be back when we've picked up this stuff. Katie gave Mog a message from Lewis when he arrived. Don't know where Lewis has gone, but he wanted to look into the cellars with us, didn't he?'

'Yes, and I think I've found them,' said Libby. 'But I don't want to go down there on my own. I'll go back inside and make myself some tea.'

However, after she'd rung off, she changed her mind. Fetching her torch from the glove compartment of the Renault, she set off down to the ha-ha and made her way to the opening of the tunnel where she'd found the document case.

'This isn't stupid,' she told herself. 'This tunnel is perfectly safe. The police have checked it out.' She flashed the torch to the left and right and saw large well-rounded tunnel roofs that looked solid. 'Towards the house,' she said loudly, in case there was anyone around, and set off.

The tunnel was much lighter than she had anticipated, running fairly straight, slightly uphill towards the house, the opening under the ha-ha still visible if she looked back. It wasn't until she was a good way along that she realised there was also light coming from ahead.

'Odd,' she muttered. 'The police said there was no opening at all this end.' And her heart gave a leap.

'The stairwell,' she gasped, 'it must be.'

As she drew nearer she could see that it was the set of steps she had discovered only half an hour earlier. And that there was another door just beyond the steps. And it was open.

Libby froze. Now what? What would she find beyond that door? Nothing, she thought, because she wasn't going to look.

She just wished she was back in the kitchen with Katie making her a cup of tea. Why hadn't she stayed there? Katie wouldn't have been long. Or even Edie. She must be around somewhere.

She began to walk stealthily backwards, cursing herself for being a fool. 'I said don't be a stupid heroine,' she whispered to herself. 'Now look what's happened.'

Not daring to turn her back on the open door, she continued to walk backwards until the opening under the ha-ha was only feet away, when she turned and ran. Out in the open, she made for the bench where she'd sat with Lewis, collapsed on to it and rang Adam again. Between panting breaths she told him what had happened.

'OK, Ma, just stay put. We're coming back right now,' said Adam firmly. 'Has Lewis turned up yet?'

'I don't know,' said Libby, her stomach doing a rather nasty swoop. 'Do I have to look?'

'Have you tried ringing him?'

'No, have you?'

'Yes, we did, but his phone was off,' said Adam, sounding rather more perturbed. 'You just stay there, and we'll be right over. Ten minutes tops.'

'OK,' said Libby and turned back to the house. She shivered involuntarily and wondered whether to go and risk making herself a cup of tea, or to go and sit in the car. The car won, partly because she was fairly convinced there was a rogue packet of cigarettes lurking in the door pocket.

However, as she got to the drive she saw Katie waving from the house.

'Where did you get to?' she asked. 'I thought something had happened to you. I heard this crashing noise and when I came down to look you'd gone. I thought you were underneath all that rubble.' She put a hand to her chest and Libby saw how pale she was.

'I'm sorry to worry you,' she said. 'I came looking for you, too. How did we miss each other?'

Katie shook her head. 'I've put the kettle on,' she said. 'Come and have a cuppa.'

'I phoned the boys,' said Libby, hovering by the door.

'They're coming right away. They said you gave them a message.'

'Yes, Lewis wanted them to pick something up from Nethergate.' Katie put out mugs.

'Did you see him this morning?' asked Libby.

'No, he left me a note.' Katie looked up, alarm in her face. 'Why? Do you think something's happened to him now?'

Libby wasn't sure what she thought, but she gave Katie a wobbly smile and said she was sure nothing had.

'I'm going to ring him now,' said Katie and went to the house phone on the wall. He won't answer, thought Libby, and sure enough, after a few minutes Katie tutted and put the phone back on its rest.

'He's got his blasted phone turned off,' she said, going to pour boiling water into the teapot. 'Where's the perishing boy got to?'

Libby's mind was racing like a hamster in a wheel. If only Fran was there.

'Katie,' she said carefully, 'where's Edie?'

'Upstairs,' said Katie, stirring the pot. 'I was with her when we heard your crash. I'll take her a cup of this.'

'I would,' said Libby, thinking, with a sinking feeling, of the small woman who adored her son.

'Or do you want to take it up to her? Make a change from me?' said Katie pouring tea into three mugs.

'No, thanks, she knows you better,' said Libby. Katie gave her an odd look, shrugged and picked up a mug. 'Won't be a mo,' she said. 'Help yourself to biscuits.' She waved at the plate on the table and disappeared towards the main stairs.

Libby sat very still, wondering if she should call Fran, or the police, or even Adam again. She realised with some surprise she hadn't once thought of calling Ben.

The house was very quiet. She wondered what would happen about the ruined staircase and whether it would be worth restoring it. And of course, the cellars below. If they were intact. Her mind began to wander to the other putative tunnels and the business of smuggling. Had Gerald known about the tunnels? And what if he had? Had Tony? Had he told Lewis?

Libby shivered again and sat up straighter, clasping both hands round her mug and wishing Katie would come back. Then, to her relief, the sound of a car on the gravelled drive. Mog and Adam had arrived.

But there were no voices. Only footsteps on the gravel, coming towards the door. They paused, and Libby bit her lip. Perspiration sprung out on along her hairline and her upper lip and her heart was beating so fast she thought she might faint. And then the footstep behind her and the hand on her shoulder.

'Hello, Lib,' said Lewis.

Chapter Thirty-five

'LEWIS,' SAID LIBBY FROM a dry mouth. 'Where have you been?'

He raised his eyebrows. 'Didn't Katie tell you?'

Libby shook her head, afraid she would never be able to speak again. She remembered Ben telling Lewis about how much trouble she'd been in during other investigations and how horrified he'd seemed. And how fond of him she'd become. She closed her eyes for a moment to try and calm her brain, but it was no good. The hamster wheel was back.

'Libby, you look awful.' Lewis moved round the table and sat down in Katie's chair, feeling the teapot. 'Still warm. Where's Katie?'

No point in not telling him, thought Libby. 'With your mum,' she said.

'Right. Well, I'll pop up and see them,' he said, 'unless I can do anything for you? You look buggered, girl. What've you been doing?'

'Nothing,' croaked Libby, hoping against hope to hear the sounds of another car on the drive.

'OK.' Lewis shrugged. 'I'll just pop upstairs, then.' And he was gone.

Libby realised she was covered in cold perspiration and that she'd been holding her breath. Even her shoulders ached with tension. She tried to relax and attempted a sip of her rapidly cooling tea. She spilt it. Then she heard footsteps on the stairs. Swallowing hard, she turned towards the door, repeating in her head like a mantra "Adam and Mog will be here soon, Adam and Mog will be here soon."

Her shoulders sagged with relief as Katie came back into the kitchen.

'You all right?' Libby asked through still dry lips.

Katie sat down and shook her head.

'No,' she said.

'Lewis?' whispered Libby.

'He's back,' said Katie. She stood up again. 'Come with me. I've got something to show you.'

Libby stood up. 'Will he – he's with his mum?'

'They're fine,' said Katie wearily. 'Come on. You might as well see this.'

Libby followed her out of the kitchen and across to the door, still slightly ajar as Libby had seen it earlier.

'Sit down,' said Katie, going to a cupboard by the side of the small fireplace, which held an equally small gas fire. She took out a large scrapbook and what looked like a photograph album. 'I hoped no one would ever have to see these,' she said, 'but there's no hope for it now.'

Libby watched as Katie pulled up a small table and sat down beside it. 'There,' she said. 'Now you'll know all about it.'

'About Lewis?' asked Libby.

'Lewis?' Katie frowned. 'Why should it be about Lewis?'

'Because –' Libby stopped as her heart once again performed a somersault. 'Who, then?'

'Who? Gerald, of course,' said Katie.

Libby looked down at the album and tried to sort out her thoughts. She was staring at a family group: a young man, hardly more than a boy, a girl of the same age and a baby, about six months old. They were a happy, laughing group, the baby wearing a brimmed hat which could have denoted either sex. Not wanting to comment, she turned the page. And now the picture was similar to the group of young people on a beach Fran had found in the solar. Libby kept her eyes on the page and tried to think of something to say.

A movement from Katie made her look up. As she did so, Katie's hand came up to cover her mouth, while her eyes stared over Libby's shoulder.

'That's where it was after all, then, Katie,' said Lewis. Libby didn't turn round but heard him come round the table. He looked down at Katie. 'Look, Lib,' he said. 'Just look.'

'At what?' said Libby.

'Behind you.'

Libby half turned in her chair and found herself staring into a black void where a section of panelling had swung open revealing stout locks on the inside. Libby turned back to Katie, bewildered.

'What is it?' she asked. She looked up at Lewis. 'Is it the strong room?'

'Looks like it,' he said, still looking at Katie. 'It is, isn't it, Katie?'

Katie took her hands from her mouth and nodded.

'And this?' Libby turned the page back to the photograph of the little family. 'Is this you?'

Katie nodded again.

'With Gerald,' said Libby.

'And our son,' said Katie. 'Tony.'

Silence fell in the little room. Both Lewis and Libby watched as Katie took the album and began turning the pages. Eventually she looked up.

'You guessed, didn't you?' she said to Lewis. 'Just now, upstairs with your mum.'

Lewis nodded. 'And then I had a message on my phone from Adam,' he said, 'telling me that there was an opening at the end of the tunnel that Libby had found. If I got here before he did I should check if you were all right. So I came along the tunnel and here I am.'

'Cindy?' Libby's voice cracked.

'I don't know.' He turned back to Katie. 'Tell us, Katie.'

'I was going to tell Libby. That's why I got these out.' She gestured towards the album and scrapbook.

'I was only seventeen,' she said, addressing Libby. 'Gerry was twenty and still at his acting school.'

'RADA,' put in Lewis.

'Yes. Well, these things happen, and I had a little boy. Anthony we called him. But we talked about it and decided it wouldn't be good for Gerry to saddle himself with a wife and family then. It was at the beginning of the sixties, see, and there were all sorts of opportunities, he felt.'

'What about you, though? It was really hard for an unmarried mother in those days,' said Libby.

'Oh, I was all right. My old mum was a good sort and my dad had long since gone, so we all stayed together and faced down the neighbours. Gerry sent what money he could and I trained to be a shorthand typist. Tony grew up with me and my mum and I don't think he wanted for nothing. Gerry stayed in touch but didn't come to see us.' She paused, looking again at the photographs. 'Then one day he phones and says would Tony like to meet him. Tony's about twenty himself now. So off he goes and from then on Gerry introduces him to people – not as his son, of course – who can help him in his career.'

She shrugged. 'Well, you know the rest. Tony made himself into a businessman and he helped me get into the outside catering business, Gerry helped me get into the OB business and then – well, then young Kenneth married that little tart.'

'She didn't look like a tart,' ventured Libby.

'Huh! You should have seen her a few years ago. Showed everything she'd got and that much make-up you wouldn't believe. This time, she comes round looking like butter wouldn't melt. I could hardly believe it myself.' Katie stopped, a brooding expression on her face.

'When did you first see her?' asked Libby.

'This time? When I got back here and she was in the kitchen. Gawd, I was livid.'

'Why were you so livid?'

'Because I knew what had happened three years ago, and I'd kept quiet for Gerry and Tony. And here she was going to stir it all up again.'

'But they'd already dug up the skeleton,' said Lewis. 'It was already stirred up.'

'And I'd said nothing, had I? Nothing to be gained, I thought. Then I gave the police Gerry's scarf. I thought it would just prove the skeleton wasn't him, I didn't realise it would prove it was Kenneth.'

'So what really happened when Kenneth was killed?' asked Libby gently. 'And why did Tony help cover it up?'

'It was when Kenny went into that *Dungeon Trial*. Gerry was beginning to show signs of dementia, so he came down here and signed for Tony to have power of attorney. And he made his will. Then down comes Miss Glamour Puss to "look after him" she says. Huh.' Katie paused and pushed a hand through her short hair. 'Making up to him she was, really. So Kenny comes out of the show and Tony drives him down here. With me.'

'With you?' gasped Libby.

'Oh, yes,' said Katie. 'Miss Cindy Dale wasn't pleased to see me last week, I can tell you.'

'So then what?' asked Lewis, leaning forward.

'We find Cindy trying to – well – get into bed with Gerald. At least Kenny did. He went a bit mental, I think; well, you would, wouldn't you? And she lashed out and killed him. Tony and me came in and Tony tried to calm things down. Cindy was hysterical and Gerry was upset. He didn't really understand what was going on.'

'So Tony arranged to get Cindy and Gerry away and bury Kenneth in the grounds?' said Libby.

'It seemed best all round,' said Katie. 'Then we could forget it ever happened. Trouble was it was expensive to keep Gerry in those homes, especially with extra security.'

Sally, thought Libby.

'So Tony sold Creekmarsh to me?' said Lewis.

Katie looked slightly ashamed. 'Yes. He said you wouldn't ask questions.'

'Bloody idiot, I was, wasn't I?' Lewis snorted.

'And then the skeleton turned up,' said Libby. 'And after that, Cindy. When did she tell you she'd killed Tony?'

Katie's eyes flew to Libby's face. 'You knew?'

'Well, the police found evidence,' said Libby.

'After they'd had her in for questioning, when she came back here. Lewis had gone to call you and she came down here wanting this tea Lewis had asked me to make. She told me then. She and Kenneth hadn't known Tony was my son before. So I told her then and I think she was a bit well – shocked. She said she'd found out Tony was Gerry's son and mentioned in the will.'

'Was he?'

Katie nodded. 'Divided between me and Tony, Gerry's estate. Me now, for all the good it'll do me.'

'Are you actually saying you killed her? But how? She completely disappeared.' Libby frowned.

Katie nodded towards the strong room. 'Gerry, Tony and me always knew that was there and where it led to. I told Cindy to hide down there and I'd put everyone off the scent.'

'So she was in here while we were searching and you were sitting at the kitchen table?' said Lewis.

'Yes.'

'But why? She'd just been released by the police,' said Libby.

'I told her they'd got new evidence. And of course, they had, although I didn't know it. She believed me. Then I went down the passage and left a little ring on the landing stage for them to find, and set a dinghy loose. The police thought she'd done a runner.'

'So did we,' said Libby. 'It was very clever.'

'Libby!' Lewis gave her a disgusted look.

'Then I went back and said to go down to the ice-house, I'd see her later.' Katie looked down at her hands. 'And I did.'

'And the dinghy?' asked Libby.

'Oh, it drifted in on its own.' Katie laughed humourlessly. 'Funny that.'

'Why have you told us now?' said Libby.

'You were getting so close.' Katie sighed. 'And I'm so tired.'

'What were you going to do in the end?' asked Libby.

Katie sighed. 'Wait for it to go away. I was going to give notice,' she nodded at Lewis, 'and go back to London. Maybe retire. Go travelling.' She shook her head. 'Somehow I didn't believe it.' She put her hands on the little table and pushed herself to her feet. 'Come on then. Time to go for the police.'

Lewis looked shamefaced. 'I think they might be here,' he said. Libby looked a question. 'Adam said you sounded frightened, so I called them.'

'What were you frightened of?' asked Katie, who by this time was putting on an outdoor coat.

'I wasn't sure,' said Libby, avoiding Lewis's eye.

'Not me?' His voice rose several notches. 'Why, for Gawd's sake?'

'I'm really not sure,' said Libby. 'Can we talk about it later?'

They followed Katie into the kitchen where, to Libby's astonishment, Adam, Mog, Ian Connell, Sergeant Maiden and Ben were grouped round the kitchen table. Adam rushed at Libby, while Ian gently took Katie's arm and escorted her outside, murmuring the official warning to her as he did so. Libby saw her nodding as she left the house, and suddenly burst into tears.

'My mum!' said Lewis, and shot upstairs, while Ben and Adam offered hugs and handkerchiefs to the weeping woman at the table.

Five minutes later Edie appeared in the kitchen with Lewis, her eyes suspiciously bright, but looking upright and determined. She came over to Libby and gave her shoulder a pat.

'You bin a help to my boy,' she said. 'Now I'm goin' to look after him. You pop off home, like, and we'll see you soon.'

'Thank you, Edie,' said Libby, 'but I think the police will want to speak to us before we go.'

Ian, having returned to the kitchen, nodded apologetically and asked if there was somewhere comfortable they could go. Lewis said they could use the solar and led the way back upstairs.

'Funny,' he said, standing and looking out of the large window down to the river and the sea. 'I remember sitting here right at the beginning of all this and being scared.' He turned and smiled sadly at Libby. 'I didn't know what I was scared of then, did I?'

She came to his side and put an arm round him. 'You had nothing to be scared of,' she said. 'Katie loved you.'

'That was the trouble,' said Ian from behind them. 'She loved so many people, particularly her own son. Frightening thing, mother love.'

Epilogue

AND SO FRAN AND Guy were married a few days later. Libby once again found herself in the role of first attendant, and Ben was a proud and handsome best man. Adam and Dominic appointed themselves groomsmen and kept an eye on Fran's unpredictable children, the fretful Lucy and her unruly offspring, the social-climbing Chrissie and her husband Bruce, who looked as though they'd sucked lemons, and placid Jeremy, charming American girlfriend in tow, both still suffering from jet lag.

Later, in the marquee, where an extremely good jazz quartet were playing, Libby and Fran sat together with glasses of champagne while Libby brought Fran up to date on the unhappy finale to the Creekmarsh mystery.

'So we were almost right,' said Fran, sipping thoughtfully. 'Cindy really did kill Tony because of Gerald's will.'

'Yes, but she can't have thought she had any way of getting back into it,' said Libby. 'I think the crunch came when Katie told her she'd done it for nothing because *she* was now the only beneficiary. Then she would have panicked.'

'And Katie pretended to help her.' Fran twirled her new wedding ring round her finger and held it up to admire it. 'Why on earth did the silly girl believe that?'

'Because she realised she would have left traces and because Katie said they'd found new evidence. She just wanted to get away.'

'So she walked into her own death.' Fran shook her head and looked across to where Guy was attempting to charm her daughters.

Libby nodded and looked for her own children in another corner of the marquee, laughing and talking with Harry and Peter, and then Ben, sitting quietly with Lewis and Edie, watching her.

'As Ian said,' she whispered, 'a terrible thing, mother love.'

First Chapter of *Murder in the Green*

OUT OF THE DARKNESS they came, bells silenced, boots muffled on dead leaves. The whites of their eyes caught the torchlight and reflected an ancient excitement. Above them, budding branches whispered, ahead of them the need-fire was already burning.

The path wound down the shallow hillside among the trees. Two figures broke away, feathers nodding above black faces. Neither of them returned.

'Please, Libby. Just come and talk to them.'

Libby Sarjeant frowned at the phone. 'Gemma, I can't.'

'Why not? You've been involved in murders before.'

Libby squirmed. 'Not intentionally.'

'But you have. You're like – like – oh, I don't know, bloody Miss Marple or something.'

Libby closed her eyes and squirmed some more. 'No, I'm not, Gemma. Let me tell you, the police always get there either ahead or at the same time as the amateur in these cases. Let well alone. They'll find out what happened.'

'It's nearly two months now. How can they find out now?'

'Just think of all the cold case reviews they do these days,' said Libby. 'They solve those, don't they?'

'They do on telly,' grumbled Gemma.

'Anyway,' said Libby, hastily returning to the point. 'I can't see your lot welcoming a batty old woman asking a lot of impertinent questions, can you? Be sensible.'

There was silence at the other end of line. Eventually Libby said, 'Are you still there, Gemma?'

'Yes. I was thinking,' said Gemma. 'Couldn't you at least

come along? See the celebrations?'

'On the longest day?'

'Yes. We start at sunrise.'

'What? You must be joking!'

'It's traditional.' Gemma sounded defensive. 'Even the Mayor comes out to watch.'

'Good for him,' muttered Libby.

'Well, if you can't come then, you could come to one of the public displays during the day. Or even,' Gemma was disparaging, 'to the Saturday parade.'

'What's wrong with that?' asked Libby. 'I seem to remember that being good fun. I used to go with the kids.'

'Oh, yes, how are they?'

'Adam's working with a garden designer locally, and Belinda and Dominic are both working in London. How are yours?'

'Still at home,' said Gemma gloomily. 'Anyway, will you come?'

Libby sighed. 'Possibly to the Saturday parade,' she said. 'Where does it finish up?'

'Same as we always do – on the mount.'

'What time?'

'Two-ish. But you won't get a chance to talk to anybody then.'

'I didn't say I'd talk to anyone,' said Libby.

'But I want you to talk to them,' wailed Gemma. 'You don't understand!'

'Oh, yes, I do, Gemma. Believe me.'

Libby put the phone down and frowned at her sitting room. Sidney the silver tabby twitched an ear in her direction and buried his nose more firmly under his tail. Libby sighed again, picked up the phone and sat down on the cane sofa.

'Fran? It's me.'

'Hi. What's up?'

'I'm fed up.'

'You sound it. Been missing me?'

'As it happens, I did, but I've seen you twice since you've been back, so I think I've recovered.'

'From the shock of my marriage, or my enforced absence on

260

honeymoon?'

Libby laughed. 'Both. No, I'm fed up about lots of things.'

'Lots of things? Good lord!'

'Two anyway,' said Libby. 'One is Steeple Farm, which is turning into a monster, and the second is – well, someone's asked me to Look Into Something.'

Fran sighed. 'I don't believe it. A murder?'

'Yes. Have you ever met my old friend Gemma Baverstock?'

'No. Should I have?'

'No, I just wondered. She's a member of the Cranston Morris, if you've heard of them.'

'No, I haven't, but don't forget I've only been in Kent for a few years. And aren't Morris sides supposed to be men only?'

'Used to be, yes, and purists still argue about it, but there are loads of female sides now. Cranston have a male side, a female side and a mixed side, but still uphold the old traditions.'

'Well, I don't know anything about that,' said Fran, 'except that they dance at May Day.'

'Hmmm,' said Libby. 'Well, on May Day their Green Man was killed.'

'Sorry, you'll have to explain,' said Fran. 'I thought that was a sort of gargoyle.'

'Can be,' said Libby. 'Often carved up high in churches and cathedrals. But in this case it's a bloke inside a sort of conical wire frame covered with vegetation.'

'And this bloke was killed?'

'Stabbed inside the cage. No one knew until he didn't start to move when everyone else did.'

'People would have seen blood, surely.'

'I didn't think of that. Anyway, it's got nothing to do with me. I don't ever want to get mixed up with murder again. It's quite ridiculous.'

'Oh, I agree,' said Fran with a laugh in her voice. 'I bet Ben does, too.'

'Mmm.'

'Come on, Lib. There's something else, isn't there? You said Steeple Farm. And Ben?'

'Yes. I know I'm being silly, but –'

'Do you want to talk about it? Guy's at the shop and won't be home until at least half five.'

'Do you mind? I'll bring lunch with me.'

'Don't be daft,' said Fran. 'You can bring a bottle of wine, if you like. You'll be allowed one glass, won't you?'

'OK.' Libby brightened. 'I'll leave as soon as I can.'

Leaving a note in case anyone appeared and wondered where she was, she collected a bottle of wine from the kitchen, gave Sidney a perfunctory stroke, and left the cottage. The sky was grey, but as there was very little wind the air felt muggy, and much warmer than it had indoors. Romeo the Renault, now freed from servitude with Libby's son Adam, sat under the trees on the other side of the little green and started at the first turn of the key.

'I suppose I shall have to upgrade you sooner or later,' Libby told the car, as she turned round to drive out of Allhallow's Lane, 'but while you behave yourself, I shall keep you.'

The drive from Steeple Martin, the village where Libby lived, to Nethergate, the seaside town where Fran's cottage looked out over the sea, was quiet and pleasant, through undulating Kentish countryside and the occasional remaining hop gardens, but today Libby was too immersed in her thoughts to admire her surroundings.

Reaching the sign which announced itself as "Nethergate, Seaside Heritage town, twinned with Bayeau St Pierre", she drove past the entrance to the new estate and dropped down the hill to the high street, past Luigi's, the Italian restaurant favoured by Fran and her husband, Guy, and finally along Harbour Street, past Lizzie's ice cream shop and Guy's gallery until she reached Coastguard Cottage.

The heavy oak door stood open, and Libby found Fran leaning on the deep windowsill gazing out at the small harbour, the yellow printed curtains billowing round her. She turned and smiled.

'I still can't believe how lucky I am,' she said.

Libby gave her a hug. 'All this and a husband too, eh?'

Fran blushed. 'I can't get used to it,' she said. 'I'm Fran Wolfe now. How strange is that? I've been Castle for the last thirty years.'

'I bet people will still call you Castle,' said Libby, hauling the wine bottle out of her basket.

'I expect so,' said Fran, 'and I don't really mind, as long as it isn't the children.'

'No change there, then?' Libby followed Fran into the kitchen.

'No. I sent them all postcards from the honeymoon and while Jeremy was staying here until we got back he says Chrissie and Lucy never stopped badgering him. He was very rude to them eventually, and I haven't heard a word from them since he went.'

'He phoned me at one point,' said Libby. 'He was so sick of them, and they were being so selfish. Not that I could do anything, but by that time his lovely girlfriend had gone back to the States and I think he wanted to let off steam.'

'He said you had him over to dinner twice. He thought you were lovely.'

'Good.' Libby grinned. 'Adam was there too, so he had someone of his own age.'

'I thought Adam wasn't living with you now?' Fran handed over a glass of wine.

'He isn't. You know where he is, don't you?'

Fran shook her head. 'I've only been back a week, I haven't caught up.'

'In your old flat!' Libby announced triumphantly.

'Over the Pink Geranium?'

'And giving Harry a hand in the restaurant in the evenings if necessary. It seems to be working really well.'

'And Lewis?'

'Oh, Adam and Mog are still working on his gardens. They're going to be beautiful. And Lewis has got a new firm in to re-do the interiors. I don't think he wants to live there any more –'

'Not surprised,' said Fran, remembering the unpleasant events that had taken place at Lewis's house, Creekmarsh Place, only a few weeks before her wedding.

'– but he still wants to run it as a venue. He's going to get someone in as an events manager.'

Supplied with glasses of wine, they went back into the sitting room and sat either side of the empty fireplace.

'Still liking married life?' asked Libby.

'Yes.' Fran leant back and sipped her wine. 'It feels so good after all these years.' She fixed her eyes on Libby. 'And in that direction things are still not going well with you?'

Libby shook her head. 'Oh, we came to a sort of accommodation before your wedding, you know we did. But even though he's stopped pushing to get married, he's still banging on about Steeple Farm.'

Fran eyed her friend thoughtfully. 'Last I heard,' she said, 'he was going to do it up while you stayed at number 17 and then think again.'

'I know,' Libby nodded. 'But he's so enthusiastic about it. He keeps dragging me off to have a look at what's being done – which isn't much yet, to be frank.'

'And don't you like it?'

'It's still Aunt Millie's house to me, even if I've stopped thinking of those dormer windows as eyes.'

'But you said –'

'I know what I said.' Libby was exasperated. '*You* said you wanted to live here on your own, and look where you are now? Married to Guy, with all that means.'

Fran pursed her lips. 'At least I was honest enough to admit I'd changed my mind. Love does that, doesn't it?'

'Yes, but I've admitted I love Ben. Ever since we came together over that girl's murder three years ago. We've got a lot in common – we're both divorced, we both love the theatre and we have the same social circle. His cousin Peter is one of my best friends.'

Fran looked doubtful. 'That's not love.'

Libby looked up quickly. 'I didn't say it was. I still fancy him.'

'You were the one who lectured me when I was dithering about Guy. I thought you had it sorted.'

'I did.' Libby sighed. 'Sort of.'

'And Steeple Farm's complicated matters?'

'Definitely. You remember why Ben's taken it on?'

'Of course. It belongs to Peter's mum Millie and while she's in care he won't sell it.'

'That's right. As all this happened just before your wedding, I wasn't sure how much you'd taken in. So Ben's going to do it up and live in it, and if Millie dies he'll buy it as a sitting tenant.'

'And the original idea was that you'd both live in it, wasn't it?'

'Yes.' Libby bit her lip. 'It is a lovely house – or it will be, but I love my cottage.'

'There would be much more room at Steeple Farm.'

'I know, I know.' Libby sighed. 'And Adam loves it. Lewis has promised to keep a watching brief over the renovations, and we've got that builder who's a qualified lime plasterer doing the work.'

'And?' prompted Fran after a minute.

'It still gives me a funny feeling when I go in.'

Fran gave a sharp little nod. 'In that case, don't go and live there,' she said. 'You know as well as I do, the atmosphere is paramount, and I know what I'm talking about.'

'I know.' Libby nodded. Fran had been a consultant to the Mayfair estate agents, Goodall and Smythe, who sent her into properties to divine whether there was anything in the atmosphere which would preclude clients from having a positive living experience, as they put it. Put another way, to find out if anything nasty had happened in the woodshed, the cellars or the attic which might make very rich clients very uncomfortable.

'You said you couldn't see me living there,' said Libby slowly. 'Remember?'

'Yes. I also said I could have been wrong. You know how often I'm wrong.'

'I think you were right.' Libby twirled her wine glass. 'I won't live there.'

'What about Ben?'

'He was very understanding last time we spoke about it.' Libby stood up. 'Can I go outside for a fag?'

'You can have one in here, if you like,' said Fran.

'No.' Libby shook her head. 'It's bad enough me still smoking without contaminating everywhere else. I'll go into the yard. Perhaps Balzac will keep me company.'

'He'll be sleeping in the big flowerpot,' said Fran, also getting to her feet. 'Come on, I'll come with you. I want to know what you're going to do about Ben.'

Libby went through the kitchen and out into Fran's little courtyard. 'So do I,' she muttered.